WAR IN LINCOLN COUNTY

W

WAR IN LINCOLN COUNTY
A WESTERN STORY

DANE COOLIDGE

FIVE STAR
A part of Gale, Cengage Learning

GALE
CENGAGE Learning®

Detroit • New York • San Francisco • New Haven, Conn • Waterville, Maine • London

GALE
CENGAGE Learning®

Copyright © 2013 by Golden West Literary Agency.
Five Star™ Publishing, a part of Gale, Cengage Learning.

LIBRARY OF CONGRESS CATALOGING-IN-PUBLICATION DATA

Coolidge, Dane, 1873–1940.
  WAR IN LINCOLN COUNTY : a Western Story / by DANE COOLIDGE. — First Edition.
    pages cm
    "'War in Lincoln County' first appeared under the title 'War Paint' as a five-part serial in The Popular Magazine (5/12/28-6/9/28)"—T.p. verso.
    "A FIVE STAR WESTERN"—T.p. verso.
    ISBN 978-1-4328-2706-9 (hardcover) — ISBN 1-4328-2706-5 (hardcover)
    I. Title.
PS3505.O5697W37 2013
813'.52—dc23   2013019121

First Edition. First Printing: October 2013.
Published in conjunction with Golden West Literary Agency.
Find us on Facebook– https://www.facebook.com/FiveStarCengage
Visit our website– http://www.gale.cengage.com/fivestar/
Contact Five Star™ Publishing at FiveStar@cengage.com

Printed in Mexico
1 2 3 4 5 6 7 17 16 15 14 13

ADDITIONAL COPYRIGHT INFORMATION

CHAPTER ONE

A cold, high wind from the bare plains west of the Pecos swept in on Ganado Crossing, snatching up clouds of sand from the horse-trampled flats and driving them against Johnson's Store. A thousand cattle dotted the landscape—the cows and calves in friendly bunches, the steers and morose old bulls by themselves—while on the salt meadows below a herd of cow ponies grazed, watched over by a huddled wrangler. Against the closed door of the barroom a Mexican dog crouched, shivering, his ear cocked to catch the voices inside. Then suddenly he leaped up and ran cringing around the corner and the Rafter J cowboys surged out.

In the lead came Tuffy Malone, showing his shining buckteeth as he burst into a high-voiced laugh, and with a swift grab at a tin can he chucked it into the air and whipped out his heavy .45.

"How's that?" he challenged as they watched the smashing shots, and the tall riders laughed indulgently.

"Pretty good . . . for a kid," responded one at last, and Tuffy snatched up another can. He let it sail on the wind, then with three lightning shots he knocked it down the breeze into the river.

"Beat that," he said, "and I'll show you some real shooting. Come on, Harry . . . I'll match you for the drinks."

Handsome Harry was the boss, as far as any man could be boss, of Hard Winter Johnson's warriors, but he did not rule by the gun. There was an urbane intelligence in his smiling black eyes, a deep line of thought between his brows, and as he looked down at Tuffy, swaggering about with his big pistol, he shook his head and shrugged.

"No," he decided, "I've tried that before, and so has the rest of the gang. But I tell you what I will do . . . I'll bet you the drinks you can't bunghole this whiskey keg five times."

"Aw!" protested Tuffy. "Somebody come and shoot against me. I'm tired of practicing alone."

"Thar's an *hombre* that will shoot with ye!" shouted a long-legged Texan, suddenly pointing across the river, and on the edge of the high bluff, gazing down at them warily, a lone horseman stood outlined against the sky. On the right side of his saddle the butt of a rifle stuck up, ready to hand if he dropped off his horse. Two pistols hung at his hips. And his head as he leaned forward against the wind had an angry, fighting pose. But more than the man, the cowboys noticed his horse, one of the much-prized Appaloosas or strawberry roans brought by the Spaniards from far Andalusia.

It loomed clean cut and agile against the dusty eastern sky, a young horse, full of power, and on the white of its right hip there was stamped, like a Comanche war sign, the mark of a bloody hand.

"Hel-lo!" exclaimed Tuffy, after a long look at the stranger whose curly hair was blowing in the wind. "Who's this wild, woolly wolf? He's shore got his war paint on!"

"Fine hawse he's got, too," observed the gangling Texan. "Must've stole him to outrun the sheriff. See him looking back over his shoulder?"

At this well-worn jest a roar of laughter went up from the renegade Texas cowboys and the wind bore their words to the stranger.

"Bunch of horse thieves yourselves!" he shouted back

defiantly, and spurred impulsively down to the ford.

"Go easy, boys," warned Handsome Harry anxiously. "That *hombre* has got hell in his neck."

"I'll tame him," Tuffy Malone promised, rolling his eyes at the gang. "But we'll string him along first and git him to betting . . . because I've shore got to have that horse."

He strode back and forth impatiently, his keen, amber-colored eyes lighting up with the joy of battle. And across the river the stranger spurred recklessly as he came clattering down over the rocks. He was a big man, but gaunt, with a month's growth of beard, and, after giving his mount one kick, he splashed into the turbid water, drawing his boots up under him as they slumped. The next minute the river lapped his saddle skirts and he jerked his rifle up out of the wet. Then, catching his stirrups, he charged up the bank at them, and all but Tuffy Malone gave back.

"Hello, Curly," Tuffy mocked, facing the drawn rifle fearlessly, "you came away without yore hat. What's the matter . . . somebody shoot it off?"

"No," responded the stranger, "but some low-down whelp just sent three bullets mighty close."

"Heh-heh!" laughed Tuffy. "Don't get riled up over that. I was shooting a tin can in the air."

"Oh, you was, eh?" Curly returned, still regarding him balefully as he thrust his gun back into its scabbard. "Well, maybe you're the smart aleck that called me a horse thief when I rode up onto the bluff?"

"Nope," replied Tuffy. "That was Hank, over there, but he didn't mean no offense. You see," he went on, showing his teeth in a horse-like grin, "Hank is kinder under a cloud himself. He was walking along the road, back in Texas, when he seen a nice, new rope. 'I better take that along,' he says, 'before some feller comes along and *steals* it.' But when he got home, by grab, there was a *horse* tied to the other end of it!"

His high, teasing laugh rose up again as Hank Swope hung his head, and the cowboys joined in the shout.

"Of course," explained Tuffy, "Hank knew that his neighbors wouldn't listen to no story like that. So he stepped up on that horse and came out here on the Pecos, where horse thieves and such are common."

"Shore . . . 'and sech,' " Hank jeered back. "Lemme tell you something, stranger, about how Tuffy Malone come to be here. He was walking along a road up in Colorado when the stagecoach came galloping by. The black flies was mighty bad and Tuffy had took a handkerchief and tied it over his face, and when he held up his hand for the stage to stop, the driver misunderstood. So he throwed off the express box and drove away down the cañon, leaving Tuffy about forty thousand dollars. Well, he knowed them detectives wouldn't believe no story like that, so he took the money and came out here on the Pecos, where he found another 'and sech' . . . Handsome Harry."

He grinned maliciously at Handsome Harry Vail, and, as Curly joined in on the laugh, Hank finished his slurring remarks.

"Harry," he said, "was riding on a train when he heard a lot of shooting up ahead. So of course, he went forward to investigate. When he opened the door, there was a big, tall man, collecting the purses and watches from the passengers. And he was looking the other way. Well, Harry had lost his watch in a poker game and he seen one there that he liked, so he slammed that man over the head with his six-shooter and come out here on the Pecos for his health."

The cowboys rocked with laughter at this slam at their chief, and, to put an end to their merriment, Handsome Harry stepped inside and came out with an empty keg.

"Stranger," he began, "when you came in sight we were engaged in a little friendly contest. Are you pretty good with a six-shooter?"

"Well . . . fair," admitted Curly as all eyes were fixed upon him.

Handsome Harry nodded. "All right," he went on. "Just the man we've been looking for. I'll match you for the drinks against Tuffy Malone, shooting this bunghole while it rolls downhill."

The stranger's smile disappeared and he glanced about grimly at the crowd of hard-faced men. "Nope," he said. "I'm not shooting or drinking. All I want is some corn for my horse."

"Shore! Shore!" Tuffy Malone spoke up cordially. "Hey, Juan, bring the gentleman some corn! That's a mighty nice horse you're riding, pardner. Would you mind if I look at his teeth?"

"No . . . you leave him alone," Curly Wells answered shortly, and Tuffy raised his eyebrows. But the time had not come for his taming act and he picked up the empty keg.

"So you're a good shot, eh?" he taunted, starting the barrel down the hill. Then, whipping out his pistol, he shot from the hip, making three bull's-eyes as the bunghole came up. But the last two shots, purposely fired to one side, splintered the oak near the edge of the hole. "Beat that," he challenged, "and I'll buy you the drinks. That's shooting, now, ain't it, boys?"

"It shore is!" chorused the well-coached cowboys.

Curly smiled at them wisely as he looked up from feeding his horse. "All right," he said. "Just to pass away the time I'll give it a whirl myself."

He set himself and rolled the barrel and as the bunghole came up he bored it five times in succession. Every shot had been timed, and so accurately were they placed that not a splinter flew.

"Pretty good," he observed as nobody spoke, and then Tuffy gave a laugh.

"Aw, hell!" he scoffed, "you can't shoot for sour apples. I'll tell you what I'll do. I'll bet you my roll against that horse you're riding I can beat you, shooting both guns at once. Two guns . . . two barrels. Roll 'em both down at once. Come on, if you ain't afraid."

Once more the shaggy stranger scratched his head and considered, squinting shrewdly at the men behind, and something in their pose suggested the beginning of a play, well-rehearsed and drawing toward its close. Yet his pokerface did not change.

"Haven't spent much time shooting at whiskey barrels," he said. "How much have you got in that roll?"

"Four hundred and eighty dollars!" Tuffy cried, flaunting the notes. "That's a whole lot of money for one horse."

"Nope. Don't need it," Curly grunted, and Tuffy Malone turned pale as someone in the crowd guffawed.

"Seems to me, my friend," he said, "you're taking a heap for granted. You ain't won this money yet."

"No, and I don't intend to try, kid," Curly answered briefly. "So run along and roll your hoop."

"Say," spoke up Tuffy after a moment of ominous silence, "I reckon you think I'm some boy. Well, I'll bet you my roll against whatever you've got, I can beat you, shooting two barrels at once."

His little eyes were gleaming and there was death in his steady gaze, but Curly still kept his slow smile.

"And I reckon," he retorted, "you think I'm some kid that never heard of the Rafter J. But I'll tell you right now, you boys have got a name, over in Texas. You're known, in fact, for a bunch of damned cow thieves. And I sure would be a sucker to empty both my guns."

"Hey!" Tuffy challenged, stepping from the crowd and facing him with one hand above his belt. "Are you looking for trouble, Mister Man?"

"No," answered Curly, "I'm looking for a horse."

And Handsome Harry laughed, long and loud.

"Oho," Tuffy said, suddenly taking his cue. "So that's what's biting you, eh?" And he in turn gave a short, cackling laugh.

"Well, by grab," drawled Hank Swope, "he shore come to the right place, then. What say if we all have that drink?"

"The drinks are on the house, gents," Handsome Harry announced suavely, but, as he turned, he gave Tuffy the wink.

CHAPTER TWO

"So you've heard of the Rafter J and Hard Winter Johnson, eh?" Harry Vail inquired as they lined up at the bar. "Well, I'm sorry the old rascal isn't here, so he could hear what you had to say. But he's down at Deep Springs, getting religion at the camp meeting." And he grinned as he tossed off his drink.

"That's good," observed Curly, tasting his liquor and setting it down. "Religion is something like whiskey . . . a little of it don't hurt anybody."

"Well, Uncle Henry is sure getting lots of it," Handsome Harry went on unctuously. "Wearing the knees out of his pants at the mourners' bench. . . ."

"Yup, and tomorrow," cut in Hank with a Texas drawl, "he'll be back here wearing the *seat* out . . . backsliding!"

"You bet ye!" yelled the cowboys, slapping Hank on the back, and, as their whoops of delight showed no signs of abating, Handsome Harry beckoned Curly aside.

"That's a good one," he laughed. "Wait till old Hard Winter comes back. The boys will sure hoorah him scandalous."

"He's learned to take a joke, eh?" Curly said, grinning dubiously.

"He has to"—Harry nodded—"with this bunch around. How'd you like a little something to eat?"

"Sure appreciate it," responded Curly. "I slept out last night . . . haven't had a square meal since yesterday."

"I'll get Tula to fix you up . . . guess she'll do it for me,"

14

Harry said. And with a swift glance at Tuffy and a jerk of the head he led the way into the patio.

The stone house at Ganado Crossing was built around a courtyard, for purposes both of convenience and defense, and as they passed in through the gateway, Curly glimpsed a flying skirt and the scared face of a woman as she fled.

"These Mexicans are kind of shy," Handsome Harry explained affably, "but Tula will wait on you . . . for me. She's old Hard Winter's daughter and the belle of the *rancho* . . . only don't you try to cut me out."

He laughed and gave Curly a dig in the ribs, as if that was highly improbable, and, at the sound of his voice, a woman stepped out quickly from a darkened door ahead. For a moment she stood, staring, a pretty girl in blue, but at a word in Spanish from Harry her dark eyes softened and her full lips parted in a smile.

"W'y, yess," she said with a faint, Spanish lisp. "Of course, if this gentleman iss your friend." And her eyes, which before had been blue-black, like polished agate, suddenly took on a velvety glow.

"That's mighty nice of you, Tula," replied Harry, his voice caressingly sweet, and, as she hurried into the kitchen, he turned to Curly, meanwhile thrusting a black pipe between his teeth. "How's that for a girl?" he inquired triumphantly, and Curly saw he was dealing with a lady-killer.

"She's sure a peach," he admitted. "And I can see," he went on, "you've got her nicely trained, so she'll eat out of your hand, like a horse."

"Women and horses," observed Harry portentously. "I've never seen one yet that I couldn't tame, if I wanted to."

"You're quite a winner, eh?" Curly suggested, leading him on. "Didn't you ever have one turn you down? You know . . . 'There ain't no horse that can't be rode . . . and there ain't no man that can't be throwed.' "

"Not me." Handsome Harry smiled, unconscious of the rail-lery. "But you've got to keep 'em guessing. Never let 'em know for sure whether they've got you or not."

"It's a gift, eh?" Curly nodded. "But say, tell me something . . . who is that little straddle bug, Malone?"

"My Lord, man!" exclaimed Harry. "You've been monkeying with dynamite. Never heard of Tuffy Malone? He's killed thirteen men, not counting Mexicans and Indians. Sure death . . . quick as lightning . . . either hand!"

"Tuffy Malone?" Curly repeated. "Seems to me I've heard the name somewhere. But say, now, if he's so bad, how come he never drew? You can't say I didn't give him a chance."

"A chance?" echoed Harry. "Man, you've been so close to heaven you must've heard the angels' wings rustle. If I hadn't laughed, and announced the drinks on the house, you'd be wrapped up in a blanket, right now."

"Think so?" inquired Curly. "You might be planting him. I don't like the little wart, at all."

"Well, now listen," Harry confided with a quick look behind him, "that's what I brought you out here for. Tuffy Malone is all right, unless you beat him at shooting. I just thought I'd warn you in time."

"Huh, much obliged," Curly grunted contemptuously as Tula came hurrying in with the food. "But you tell him," he ended, "to leave my horse alone, all the same. By Joe, that beef sure looks good."

"You are welcome," Tula said with a curtsy and a smile, but the smile was for Handsome Harry.

"Well, treat him right," spoke up Harry abruptly, and, clamping his teeth down on his pipe, he was gone.

The girl gazed after him curiously, then glanced at her guest, who was helping himself to the beef.

"Are you a new man?" she asked, "to work for my father?"

Curly shook his head. "Just stopped," he explained, "to feed my horse some corn." And once more he returned to his food.

Tula went to the kitchen for a second cup of coffee, then regarded him with a shrewd, coquettish smile. "I was watching you," she said, "when you called Tuffy a 'kid'. That makes him very mad."

"I'll call him worse than that," Curly promised, "if he goes to chawing my name."

"He killed a man one time," she observed reminiscently. "Right out in front of the store."

"Kind of putting on a show for the ladies, eh?" he said.

Tula smiled briefly at the jest. Then she turned with a start toward an inner door, where a Mexican woman had suddenly appeared. "This is my mother," she murmured, moving away apologetically, and Curly rose to his feet.

"Good evening," he greeted with a deferential bow, but at his words she threw up her hands.

"Another Texan!" she exclaimed in Spanish, angrily motioning her daughter to be gone.

Curly gazed at her curiously. "How do you know?" he demanded bluntly.

"They are all the same," she replied in English. "They call the afternoon the evening. But sit down and eat. What difference what you call it, so long as this wind will never stop?"

She sank wearily down on a bench and gazed out into the patio, where the dust eddied in from outside. And after a long look at his hostess, Curly did as he was bidden, although he did not like her remarks.

"You are hungry," she observed at last as he filled his dish again. "All the Texans, when they come, are hungry. But when they have filled their bellies, they begin to gamble, and drink, and shoot. What a place to live!"

Curly glanced at her again, then went on with his eating, for he was gaunt from long days on the trail.

"But you," she went on, with a swift, approving smile, "are different from some who are here. When a lady comes in, you rise to your feet. You are a gentleman . . . *muy caballero.*"

"Yes, ma'am," he responded, rising and bowing at the compliment. "You haven't got much use for Texans."

"Oh, well," she sighed, "nothing is gained by complaint. But when they come into my house and make love to my daughter that is something I cannot endure. And when my hosband is away, as he is most of the time, my maids are afraid to work."

"I see." Curly nodded, tending strictly to his eating, but the settled discontent that had marred her handsome face drove her on, in the end, to talk.

"First he goes away to Sumner," she continued drearily, "to sell some herds of cattle at the fort. And then to Fort Stanton . . . to Camp Apache . . . to Arizona. And always he leaves me alone, with these devils carousing in the bar."

"Kind of a tough bunch, eh?" suggested Curly noncommittally, and her mournful eyes flashed fire.

"They do nothing," she declared, "but drink and gamble and eat. Yes, and shoot all our cartridges away. My poor dogs are always frightened . . . they come creeping back to hide. And then I hear a gun go . . . *bong!* But work? They do nothing, not even to brand the calves. And my hosband only laughs at me . . . *bah!*"

She stamped her foot impatiently, and Curly pushed back his chair, though he could still have eaten more. But there was an atmosphere of tragedy, of apprehension and discontent, in these shut-in walls of stone that made him long for the light. It was as if a darkened pall had settled over the house, like a thundercloud before a storm. There was something in the air, something tense and electric, like the silence before the first crash. And this woman, shrouded in black after the custom of her people, sitting and watching him with her melancholy eyes, conveyed to his sharpened senses the last touch of presentiment, a foreboding of some gathering storm.

"Got to go," he spoke up hastily, "and look after my horse." But she stopped him as he strode to the door.

"Are you looking for a job . . . a position as cowboy?" she demanded with nervous insistence. "Then please stop and work for my hosband. He has many, many cattle and no one to brand them. He could hire a hundred men. But these creatures are not cowboys. They call themselves warriors and do all their work with the gun."

"Nope, nope," replied Curly, "I'm not looking for a job. Much obliged for the meal. Good day."

"But, my friend," she said. "You are a gentleman, no? You onderstand to be polite to women? Then stay a little while till my hosband comes back. I am afraid to be alone with these men."

"What's the matter?" he inquired, glancing uneasily out the gateway to catch a glimpse of his horse. "But say, I can't stop . . . I've got business down the line. Why don't you talk to Handsome Harry?"

"Handsome Harry . . . ," she began, her eyes beginning to smolder, and then she waved it aside. "No matter," she went on. "He is afraid of Tuffy. But you are more quick with the gun."

She smiled, and behind her he saw Tula nodding assent, but, as he hesitated, he heard the sound of running horses. He whipped out the door and was gone. A flock of chickens in the courtyard scattered and ran before his rush, and at their sudden, frightened squawk a group of men outside the gateway looked up with a guilty start. They were gathered in a circle about the regal Appaloosa, and while it held its head high, emitting loud, defiant snorts, Tuffy Malone was examining its teeth. One hand still gripped its jaw, but, as Curly Wells appeared, Tuffy let the paint horse go.

"Heh-heh!" he laughed, with a shame-faced shrug. "Jest looking at his teeth."

"You let that horse alone," Curly ordered after a silence, and Tuffy backed meekly away.

"No use getting riled up," he said at last. "I want to *buy* him, maybe."

"You can't do it," answered Curly. "He isn't for sale." And, snatching the bridle from the horn of his saddle, he slipped the bit into Paint's willing mouth. Then with a single, swift movement he swung up on his back and turned to ride away.

"What's your hurry?" called Handsome Harry, emerging from the gateway and motioning Curly to wait. But the thunder of the horse herd, coming in from the flats to drink, had already brought him to a halt. They came on the run, heads up and tails like banners, their long manes floating in the wind. And behind them, popping his rope, the Negro wrangler raced and shouted after sitting his horse all day. It was a glorious sight, but the trained eye of the cowboy was scanning every horse as it passed.

"I say, Curly," Harry urged, "don't go off mad over nothing. That's just the kid's way . . . he's always getting stuck on some horse, or maybe some other fellow's girl. But he's a good-hearted boy. How'd you like to take a job here? Stick around till old Hard Winter gets back."

"Nope. Better be on my way, before we tangle," responded Curly. "And, besides that, I haven't lost any job."

"What have you lost, then?" Harry jested, and Curly's blue eyes gleamed dangerously.

"I've lost a horse," he said. "The pardner of this one here . . . the finest trail and cutting horse in Texas. And if I find him in that remuda, I'm going to take him, savvy? I don't give a damn who claims him."

"Oh, certainly, certainly," Harry assented lamely, and as he spoke, Curly pointed into the herd.

"There he is, then," he said. "Over next to that little gray. Now watch!" And he gave a shrill whistle.

A tiger-striped dun threw up his head and rolled his eyes. Then with a neigh like a trumpet call he quit the galloping herd and came cantering over toward Paint.

"What'd I tell you?" Curly laughed as the two horses touched noses and whickered in recognition. "Here, Tige!" he called, holding a loop in his rope, and the dun put his head in it obediently. "Anybody claim this horse?" inquired Curly of the cowboys. But something in his voice had tamed their boisterous spirits and no one made reply. "Who owns that herd?" he asked the sweating wrangler, and the Negro touched his hat before he spoke.

"W'y, w'y . . . some of 'em, sah, belong to these gentlemen heah, sah. But mostly, you might say, they belongs to Mistah Johnson. Do you reckon this heah is yore hawse?"

"He sure is," responded Curly, "and I'd like to see the man that will try to tell me different. I've trailed old Tige close to four hundred miles, and, if no one objects, I'll just take him."

"The horse is yours." Handsome Harry nodded. "I see he's got the same brand. He must have got mixed in the herd."

"Yeah . . . I reckon so," Curly observed dryly. "Only there were eighteen others took with him."

He touched Paint with the spurs and rode off toward the south. But as he left, a gray cayuse that had been running with Tige came galloping after them and joined his partner.

"You done stole a horse yourself!" Tuffy Malone yelled mockingly as Curly tried in vain to cut it back. "And you'll ketch hell for it, too!" Tuffy added.

"He shore will!" echoed the cowboys, and, as Curly rode off, they gave way to uproarious laughter.

CHAPTER THREE

The keen wind, which at Ganado Crossing had kept the dirt flying, lost its edge as Curly Wells rode south, and, reaching back of his cantle, he untied a crushed sombrero and pulled it down over his curls. Then he unbuttoned his leather coat and rolled a cigarette, and, as Paint jogged along at his tireless Spanish trot, Curly turned and gazed reproachfully at Tige.

"Well, Tige, you old rascal," he said, "you wasn't looking to see Paint again, eh? Went and took up with an Injun cayuse, like Johnson getting married to a Mexican."

He waved his hat threateningly at the pot-bellied gray pony that had never left Tige's side, but, after trying again and again to turn him back, Curly grunted and slumped down in disgust.

"You knot-headed little runt," he grumbled, "ain't worth any man's stealing, nohow! But them Rafter J boys laughed like hell over something . . . might follow me up and shoot me for a horse thief."

He dropped down by a pile of clods on the edge of a cutbank and pelted the cayuse out of range, but no sooner had Curly mounted and ridden out on the open prairie than the pony came nickering up to Tige.

"Yes, and you, you old scoundrel," Curly railed as Tige turned to answer his new mate, "you've got so low-down, associating with these Mexican plugs, you think that ornery skate is some good. If it wasn't he's so gentle, like some kid's pet pony, I'd sure put a bullet between his eyes."

He flipped the rope at Tige and rode on down the trail, which followed the winding river on the west, and far ahead in the dusty haze he could make out a grove of cottonwoods, like an island in a sea of grass. At his feet the rich, black gramma curled up in dry bunches in whose heart there still lived a core of green. The broad bench land and distant ridges were dotted with grazing cattle, whose winding paths led down to the stream. But as he worked over to the west, Curly fell into a broad highway, tramped deep by thousands of feet.

It was the old Goodnight Trail, where every spring thousands of steers passed through on their way to the north—steers from the Brazos and San Angelo and the rolling plains of western Texas, following the Pecos through the desert for its water. Twenty cow paths, side by side, writhing and turning over hill and swale, until far to the north the trail circled the Raton Mountains and struck back toward Denver and the mining camps.

But now the grass was sprouting on the edge of the trampled ruts, for the drive had not begun. There was good feed everywhere, and in the west, behind long ridges, the high peak of El Capitán notched the sky.

"By Joe, boys," exclaimed Curly, "this is a cow country, all right! Might as well look it over, eh?"

Paint turned one ear back, Tige jerked his head and sighed, but the pony, mugging behind, whinnied eagerly and ran up closer until he trotted neck and neck with Tige.

"Aw, shut up, you inbred runt . . . I wasn't talking to you!" burst out Curly. "And by grab, there's a dust cloud, coming this way from Ganado Crossing. I'd sure hate . . . ," he ended, spurring savagely up a rise, where he could look out the country behind, "like a dog to get hung for a horse thief on account of stealing *you*."

He slapped a rope at him insultingly, but the gray ran close to heel, and, as he topped the ridge, Curly beheld a rich valley spread out before his eyes like a fairyland. By a lake that gleamed like silver in the light of the setting sun there was a grove of stately cottonwoods. A broad stream led away from it toward the salt meadows below, its banks lined with hackberries and willows, and on the plains beyond the lake, strung out like a necklace of pearls, there was parked a huge circle of covered wagons. Herds of horses in little bunches were being brought in to drink, men and children carried water from the lake, and from within the enclosure of wagons the smoke of many campfires told of women preparing the evening meal.

Curly glanced back for the last time at the dust point that followed after him and jumped his horse down the slope.

Here were people, a train of emigrants on their way into the West, and among them he could find someone to keep the little gray horse that followed him like a nemesis. For the times were rough in frontier New Mexico. The Pecos country was swarming with horse thieves. And to be caught leading off even a pony like this might be fraught with unpleasant consequences.

The broad trail swung down past a spring of clear water that gushed up at the foot of the hill, and as Curly stood, bridle in hand, watching Paint as he drank his fill, the gray cayuse nosed in with the rest. He was gentle as a dog, evidently somebody's spoiled pet, and while he drank Curly built a quick loop. Then as the pony raised its head, he flipped the noose over it and swung up into the saddle.

"Come on, here, Mister Cayuse," he said. "I'll just put you in that corral where the emigrants are camped and tell them to keep you two days. And meanwhile," he went on as he jerked the rope taut, "I'll take old Tige away."

He rode off laughing, but as he glanced back up the trail, the grin was wiped off his face. Over the ridge behind, a single horseman came charging down at him, brandishing a shotgun

25

and yelling shrilly, and like one not unaccustomed to attacks and defense Curly swung off behind his horse. Yet as he fell, he did not fail to snatch the rifle from its scabbard and the next moment he thrust it quickly out over the saddle.

"Halt!" screamed the rider. "You give me back my pony!" And as Curly's eyes became clear, he saw that it was only a woman. She was a girl, hardly come to her full growth and stature, but her blue eyes were like firebrands, and the huge work horse that she rode fairly made the earth tremble as he charged.

"You blamed horse thief!" she cried, reining up and towering over him as she swung the heavy shotgun to the front. "You let that pony go or I'll fill you so full of buckshot. . . ."

"Sure!" Curly assented, ducking his head down lower. "But for heaven's sake, lady, turn that gun the other way. It's liable to go off and hurt somebody!"

"Well, that's just what it's going to do," she shrilled vindictively, "unless you turn my pony loose, right now. I saw you sneaking off, but I'll tell you right now, you'd better look out what you do. Because I told Jack Moore . . . and he used to be a Ranger . . . and he's out looking for Croppy, this minute!"

"Well, turn that gun away!" Curly bellowed impatiently. "Who wants your little old plug? He's been following me all the way from Ganado Crossing, and danged if I could turn him back."

"You don't need to swear," she warned. "I'm a lady, and I can shoot. Now you march right out there and turn that pony loose . . . and you put your gun up, too."

"Huh," Curly grunted, shoving his carbine into its scabbard. "You must think you've got me scared."

"Never mind what I think. You Rafter J toughs had better leave my father alone. Because Jack Moore promised, unless you brought back our work horses, he'd come up and get them, personally."

"Who's Jack Moore?" demanded Curly as he flipped off the rope and pushed the mild-eyed pony away.

She glared at him, smiling contemptuously. "You'll find out," she said, "if he ever starts after you. Where'd you get that other horse?"

"None of your business," he answered evenly. "You must take me for a horse thief."

She gazed at his uncut hair, his month's growth of curly beard, and his sunburned, wind-sharpened face, and held out her hand to her pony.

"Come on, Croppy," she said, reining her clumsy mount away. "Yes, I do," she answered over her shoulder. "You don't look too good to do anything."

"Have it your own way," Curly retorted. "But if you think I'd steal that plug, you certainly don't know much about horses."

"You hush up," she shot back. "He's the best horse in this country. Here, Croppy!" But the pony stopped short.

"He's took up with Tige," Curly said, laughing as Croppy followed after him. "Go back, there, you little devil." He waved his hat at him menacingly, but Croppy ran up close and nudged his nose against Tige.

"He-ere, Croppy!" the girl called, and then with a jerk she wheeled her lumbering work horse about. "Oh, come, Croppy!" she pleaded, riding up and catching his foretop.

Curly saw that the little hand that grasped the hair was all a-tremble with eagerness. The blue eyes that had blazed at him had suddenly turned soft and appealing, but Croppy, with brutish obstinacy, set back and pulled away, and Curly saw her wipe away a furtive tear.

"Here," he offered, suddenly forgetting his resentment, "let me lend you this rope to lead him."

"No," she answered angrily. "Oh, come on, Croppy, darling! Don't you want to go home and have some honey?" She twined her fingers in his mane and laid her face against his cheek, but Croppy had forgotten his mistress. He pulled away again when she tried to lead him off, and Curly shook out a loop in his reata.

"There's no use monkeying with that *caballo*," he said. "I've been trying to turn him back all day. But he's been running with Tige in the Rafter J remuda and. . . ."

"Don't you dare to rope that horse!" she cried accusingly. "So you're one of those Rafter J Heel Flies? I just hate the whole bunch of you! And that Tuffy Malone . . . if he ever comes near me, I'll kill him!"

"Suits me." Curly grinned. "He's no friend of mine. But what're you going to do about this horse?"

"Well . . . ," she began, gazing helplessly about. "Oh, Croppy!" she burst out reproachfully. "Have you forgotten all the nice things I've done for you?" She put her arm about his neck and tried to lead him away, but a new love had found its way into Croppy's fickle heart, and he turned and came running after Tige.

"I'd better rope the little skate and lead him home for you," proposed Curly. "Or I'll leave him in that pole corral."

For a moment she sat half sobbing on the slow-footed work horse, then she turned and lashed at Croppy with her quirt. "Oh, *take* him, then!" she cried. "I . . . I hate him, the ungrateful thing. But don't you dare to steal him."

"No, ma'am," he replied soberly, but with a twinkle in his eye. "I'll put him in that big corral." He dropped the loop over Croppy's head with a deft turn of the wrist and started toward the distant corral, but suddenly her heart misgave her.

"You'd better," she called after him, "or I'll tell Uncle Jack, and he just hates a horse thief!"

Curly glanced back over his shoulder, a wry smile on his rugged countenance. "Don't let that prey on your mind," he answered. "Because when I turn horse thief, I'll steal a real horse, and not some little, grass-bellied cayuse that. . . ."

"You hush up!" she shouted, raising her shotgun threateningly.

But Curly had swung down behind the shoulder of Paint, and, as he galloped off, he looked back and laughed.

CHAPTER FOUR

There was a merry grin on Curly's wind-burned face as he loped down the trail toward the lake, and, as he rode, he kept an eye on the girl who had held him up at the spring. Here was one little lady who had her opinions of horse thieves and was not afraid to tell them to the world, but his closing remarks about her pony had evidently given her pause. For a long time she sat watching him, astride her slow-footed mount, and then suddenly she turned and rode east across the plains toward a wagon that was parked under the trees.

"Throw up your hands!" mimicked Curly. "Don't you *dare* to steal my horse! I'll make you hard to ketch!" Then he laughed and slapped his leg, towing Croppy at a run in the wake of fast-loping Paint, but, as he drew near the lake, he was aware of a single horseman, riding out to intercept him. Appearing first from a bunch of hackberries, he had started quartering across his course as if heading for a herd on the plain, but, as Curly slowed down and turned aside toward the wagons, the stranger cut across and confronted him. He was a big man with a black beard, trimmed to a brush on the chin like the whiskers of a buffalo bull, and something in the set of his massive head and shoulders made the resemblance even more pronounced.

"Good evening, young man," he said with asperity. "Where you going with that little horse?"

There was something about his tone that Curly did not like and he answered with equal brevity.

"Over to that corral," he said, "if it's any of your business."

"I'm going to make it my business," returned the stranger with heat. "You Rafter J boys are carrying things too far when you rob old Honey McCoy of his work horses. You've been maltreating these poor Mexicans and holding up trail herds until it makes my Texas blood boil. But I'll give you to understand Honey McCoy is my friend, and I won't have him abused, not by anybody."

"Ain't you taking a good deal for granted?" Curly inquired defiantly. "What makes you think I'm a Rafter J hand?"

"Because you're leading that horse . . . and the Rafter Js stole him. He belongs to Melissa McCoy."

"Yes, and I'm leading another horse . . . and the Rafter Js stole *him*. But that don't make me out a Heel Fly."

"Well, how did you get him, then?" demanded the horseman, somewhat mollified. "I'll give you a chance to explain."

"Took him away from 'em," responded Curly. "And this little runt followed me. Say, you think a man would steal that horse?"

He pointed derisively at the puffing pony, but the stranger did not crack a smile.

"All the same," he said, "the horse has been stolen, and you've been found with him in your possession. Now speak up, my boy, and tell me the truth, because I'm not a man to be trifled with. Of course it's all spite work, but Tuffy Malone and his gang. . . ."

"I don't know a thing about them," Curly broke in impatiently. "Never saw 'em in my life until this morning. But if you'll examine the brands, you'll see that both my horses are marked with a Flying W. I'm Curly Wells, of War Bonnet, Texas, and that's my registered iron."

"I've seen the brands already, and I don't doubt they're in the book. But the question is, Mister Wells, how do you happen to be over here, leading another man's horse on a rope?"

"That's easy." Curly smiled. "My zebra dun was stole, and I trailed him to Ganado Crossing. But when I rode away, this Croppy horse followed us . . . and he's been a danged nuisance, ever since."

"You know his name, eh?" queried the stranger, a dark suspicion in his eyes.

Curly threw up his hands. "Oh," he said, "I'll have to tell the whole story. Up here at the spring a girl came riding in on me and accused me of stealing her pony. Well, she finally spared my life, provided I'd take him right down here and leave him in this pole corral. While she was talking, she called the cayuse Croppy . . . if you want him you're more than welcome."

He held out the rope end, but the rider shook his head.

"I'm afraid I've misjudged you, young man," he confessed. "No offense, you understand . . . you can go on about your business. I'm Colonel Jack Moore . . . that's my ranch." He nodded toward a ranch house, half hidden beneath the cotton-woods, and thrust out his hand impulsively. "Glad to meet you, Mister Wells," he said. "Come on home with me and have some supper. Mighty sorry all this has occurred."

"Oh, that's all right," Curly said, and grinned. "Reckon I do look pretty rough. . . . been sleeping on my hat for a month."

"You look rough," admitted the colonel after a final apprais-ing glance, "but you look honest, Mister Wells, and that's what counts with me. I used to be a Ranger . . . four years in Company D . . . and we learned to read men's faces pretty well. But supper is almost ready and Julia hates to be kept waiting, so we'll put Melissa's horse in the pen back of the house and send him over to her later."

"But she told me pointedly," objected Curly, "to put her horse in this big corral."

"That's all right," sputtered Moore. "Melissa and her father are our neighbors . . . she comes over to the house every night.

My wife is a good cook . . . finest cook in the country . . . but she won't stand it to have the food get cold."

"I don't know," Curly grumbled as he followed along behind, still towing the reluctant Croppy. "She's liable to go out there and find her horse gone and. . . ."

"Leave it to me," the colonel promised. "I can square myself with Melissa, but Missus Moore likes folks prompt at their meals."

He proceeded at a lope past the bottomless lake, the famous Deep Springs of the Pecos, and, still at a lope, he crossed the big stream that ran out of it and watered his fields.

"Porfilio!" he shouted as they clattered into the horse yard and threw their reins on the ground. And as a Mexican came running to care for the stock, Jack Moore took his guest by the arm.

"My boy," he said, "I've got the finest wife that a man ever had. She's a treasure, and I want you to meet her. But you'll be marrying someday, and while we're on the subject I want to offer you a few words of advice. Never keep a woman waiting with the meals."

"No, and I won't," agreed Curly. "To say nothing of the fact that I've only et twice in three days. Hard pickings, across those Staked Plains."

"I've been all over them," enthused the colonel, "chasing Comanches and killing buffalo. . . ."

"Jack!" called a silvery voice, and he cut his talk short as he hurried in to wash for supper.

"We've got company, Julia," he announced. "Mister Wells, from War Bonnet, Texas. I've been right to your place, my boy, on War Bonnet Creek and. . . ."

"Now you hurry," chided the voice, "or the biscuits will fall. What *have* you been doing, Jack?"

"Hunting horses," he answered hastily, combing his iron-gray hair. "Mister Wells picked up Croppy and brought him back."

"He did!" she cried, and, as Curly was led in, Mrs. Moore came hurrying to meet him. "Oh, I'm so glad," she said, shaking hands with him warmly. "Melissa has been hunting for him everywhere for days. But sit right down, Mister Wells, before the food gets cold." And she took her place at the table, beaming.

She was a young woman, dark and vital, with shining black hair and brown eyes that fairly danced with delight.

"Oh, how glad she will be," she cooed. "The poor little thing. She just thinks the world and all of that horse."

"The Heel Flies stole him," spoke up the colonel bluntly. "Mister Wells found him running in their herd. But when he came away, Croppy followed his dun horse . . . seems the Heel Flies stole him, too."

"That's right," spoke up Curly, "but I trailed him, close to four hundred miles. He's a horse that people always notice."

"Yes, he is," agreed the colonel. "But that strawberry roan you ride is one in a hundred thousand."

"One in a million," boasted Curly. "I have to watch him night and day or some Indian or white renegade will steal him. And that reminds me," he went on. "Tuffy Malone got so stuck on him he even offered to buy him."

"Tuffy Malone, eh?" repeated Moore, gnashing angrily at his food. "You refused to sell, of course?"

"Well, it wasn't exactly a sale," Curly qualified. "He offered to bet his roll, four hundred and eighty dollars, against Paint in a shooting contest. Roll two whiskey kegs downhill and shoot the bungholes with both hands, but I didn't like the looks of the crowd."

"Perhaps you were afraid," suggested the colonel, "that after you'd emptied both pistols they'd throw down on you and take your horse anyhow."

"That's about it." Curly grinned. "And when they crowded

me to it, I told them what their name was, back in Texas, the worst gang of cow thieves in the country."

"You did?" exulted Moore. "And what did Tuffy say?"

"He wasn't talking much," Curly replied evasively. "Yes, I will take another biscuit, Missus Moore. Lightest biscuits I ever ate."

"Julia's a wonderful cook," praised the colonel. "But I'd like to know how Tuffy took it."

"Well, he stepped out from the bunch and kinda patted his pistol and said . . . 'Are you looking for trouble, Mister Man?' But I thought at the time he was nothing but some kid, come out West and trying to be tough.

" 'No,' I said, 'I'm looking for a horse.' And passed it off with a laugh. But Handsome Harry warned me later the kid was bad medicine, especially if you happened to beat him shooting."

"Did you beat him?" Moore inquired, looking up. "He's considered the best pistol shot in the country."

"Yes, I beat him," admitted Curly, "but I could see he was throwing off on me. Trying to cap me into a contest and win my horse."

"Well, well," observed the colonel, "so you refused to shoot against him? But you'll hear from him, mark my word. There is one of the worst characters on the whole frontier . . . a city tough gone wild in the West. Quick as lightning with a gun and absolutely fearless . . . he's got the whole country terrorized. But here's one man, Mister Wells, that he's never dared to monkey with. I have been a Texas Ranger, and we're trained in the service to handle just such characters as him."

"Now, Jack," Mrs. Moore said as she filled up his cup again, "you remember what you promised me, out under the cottonwoods, that night I said that I'd marry you."

"Yes, yes," her husband responded impatiently. "But I can only be crowded so far. And when they rob Honey McCoy, the most inoffensive old man in the country, they've got to answer to me . . . that's all."

"No, it isn't all," she said. "Because Honey can get more horses, but I can't get another husband like you."

She patted his hand affectionately and his stern eyes softened.

"Well, all right," he sighed. "You seem to take it for granted that the Rafter Js will get the better of me. But I'll tell you, Mister Wells . . . if they ever burn my brand, I'll drive the last Heel Fly out of the country."

"But they won't do that," chimed in his wife, beaming proudly. "Because Jack used to be a Ranger, and he never failed to bring in his man. They leave our cattle alone . . . and perhaps after all, dear, Mister McCoy's horses just strayed away."

"Well, perhaps." The colonel shrugged. "But Mister Wells here found Croppy, right there in the Rafter J horse herd."

"Oh, yes," said Mrs. Moore. "Do tell us, Mister Wells, how you came to get him back. And here's some of the honey that Mister McCoy gives us . . . he keeps bees, you know, right on his wagons."

"Don't they sting him?" Curly asked incredulously. "That's one thing I'm afraid of . . . bees."

"Yes, that's it. But Honey knows how to handle them. He says their sense of smell is very, very sensitive, and at the first sign of fear the human body gives off an unpleasant odor. But if you go among them fearlessly, you can brush them up by the handful. Now do tell us about getting Croppy."

"Nothing to tell, much," stated Curly. "When I took my dun away this little gray pony followed. And when I rode off, I remember now Tuffy Malone hollered after me . . . 'You're stealing a horse yourself. And you'll ketch hell for it, too!' And then all them Heel Flies laughed.

"That made me uneasy, because I'd had a little trouble with them, and I thought, by Joe, they might follow along after me and try to have me hung for a horse thief. So I kept a close watch, and sure enough I saw a dust cloud following right along behind me from the store. But when I got to this spring up here, I gave up the notion, because it was only a little ways to that corral. So I put a rope on Croppy and started to lead him off, and right there I sure did ketch hell."

Curly's eyes lit up as he remembered his fright and he showed all his teeth in a grin.

"Just as I rode away the ground began to tremble. I heard a noise like thunder and looked behind. And there was a big woman, about ten feet tall, on a horse about twenty feet tall, riding down on me like a windstorm. She had a shotgun in one hand and a six-shooter in the other, and when she seen me, she screamed like an eagle." He threw back his head and laughed consumedly, but as his eyes strayed to the door he saw the girl herself, looking in at him.

"What's the matter?" asked Mrs. Moore. And as she caught sight of Melissa her laughter, too, suddenly ceased. "Why . . . Melissa!" she exclaimed. "Why, what is it, darling? We didn't know you were here."

The girl rocked to and fro, her angry eyes blazing, her slim hands still gripping the old shotgun, and for a minute she could not speak.

"I came over," she said slowly, "to get my horse. And, mister, I want him, too."

"Oh, my Lord!" Curly ejaculated, rising up in a panic. "I . . . I put him in Mister Moore's horse yard."

"Yes, and you promised me," she stated, "to put him in the corral. Some people would call that plain lying."

"Now, Melissa," the colonel broke in, "I want you to blame that all on me, because Mister Wells insisted upon stopping at the corral, but I made him come on to the house."

"You can talk all you want to," answered Melissa vindictively.

"But I heard you all laughing, and I know he just did it to tease me. Now I want . . . my . . . horse. Understand?"

"By grab, yes," Curly said, jumping contritely toward the door. "I wouldn't have had this happen for the world. But Mister Moore was late for supper and he. . . ."

"Well, Mister Moore can come then and help me catch my horse. I don't want anything more to do with *you*."

She gave Curly such a look that he stopped dead in his tracks and the colonel leaped into the breach.

"Yes, yes," he soothed, "I'll ketch him for you, Melissa, and get all your others, to boot. No, I mean it now, child. You've been pestered enough."

"You leave it to me, Colonel," Curly said impulsively. "I'll find those horses if it's. . . ."

"You leave them alone . . . and keep out of this!" Melissa blazed back. "I guess my Uncle Jack can take care of me."

"Well, I ought to," answered the colonel. "Texas Ranger for four years and never got turned back yet. I'll get 'em, Melissa, so you run along home. And we'll stop and pick up Croppy."

He put his arm about her shoulder and led her gently out, but as she passed into the darkness, Curly saw her head droop, her twisted face suddenly buried against his coat.

"By Joe," he said, "I feel like a whipped hound. I'll get them other horses myself."

CHAPTER FIVE

"That's a pitiful case," declared Colonel Jack Moore as he came stamping back into the house. "Poor little Melissa . . . she broke down on the way home and told me all about it."

"About what?" his wife asked anxiously.

"About Tuffy Malone," the colonel gritted. "He's been sneaking around trying to make love to her."

"Why, the idea!" exclaimed Julia. "Make love to Melissa? I thought he had a Mexican girl."

"He's got forty," grumbled Moore. "And when Melissa turned him down, he stole their horses, just to spite them. That's why she's been crying all the time."

"Oh, the poor little girl," said Mrs. Moore. "But, Jack, what are you going to do?"

"I'm going to hunt up Henry Johnson," the colonel stated firmly, "and tell him this persecution must stop. And then if he doesn't stop it . . . and get back those horses for Honey . . . I'll go up and do it myself."

"No, you leave that to me," Curly Wells broke in eagerly. "I feel so dog mean, making fun of her pony, I've just got to do something to square myself. So you give me the brands and a description of the horses and I'll guarantee to bring them back."

"That can wait," decided Moore, "until I've seen Henry Johnson. He's over at this emigrant camp, confessing his sins and getting religion, and right back at his store is the worst gang of outlaws that ever infested the country. They make a

39

business of stealing stock, yet he shelters them and pays them wages. And in return they go out and cut down these Texas trail herds to everything except their straight brand. No matter if they've got the best title in the world, Johnson's cowboys will claim every steer in forty brands . . . brands he had when he came into the country. Then they'll run a big Rafter on every brute they steal and turn them out on the range."

"Yes, but, Jack," appealed his wife, "they never touch your cows. Mister Johnson has given them orders to respect the Heart Cross and I don't think you ought to interfere."

"Now, listen, Julia," he said. "I've known Henry Johnson since he couldn't climb up the saddle strings onto a horse. And when he came out here, he was honest. But since that Harry Vail took charge of his affairs, the Rafter Js have gone to the dogs. They don't even brand their calves . . . the range is full of *orejanos* . . . and yet they'll steal every cow they can find. I tell you, Henry Johnson is riding to a fall. Those men will turn around and rob *him*. And when they do, I'm going to tell him it's all his own fault . . . he's a bigger thief than they are."

"No, now Jack," she protested. "You know very well that Mister Johnson has always been our friend. It's all right to warn him what his cowboys are doing, but don't call him a thief."

"I've told him that a hundred times," the colonel said hotly, "but he always laughs it off. He's a man you can't quarrel with, because he'll get you to laughing and. . . ."

"And then, you knew his mother," she reminded him fondly. "Didn't she take care of you when you were young?"

"Yes, and that's the only reason I've ever put up with it, the way he's been robbing these Mexicans. Henry's mother was a woman of the finest Christian character, and she thought to her dying day that Henry was honest. I used to lie to her about it myself. And the last thing she said when I came to this country was . . . 'Now you'll always be a friend to Henry, won't you?'

"Well, I promised her, and I'll do it. But it's time Henry Johnson found out just exactly where he stands. This praying and singing will never get him anywhere until he sets his own house in order."

"All right, Jack." Mrs. Moore smiled. "I know you'll be nice to him. And tell him we'll expect him for breakfast."

"Yes, there you go," he snorted. "You'll undo all I've done, but I'll ask him, all the same."

"And take Mister Wells along, to show there's no hard feeling. And, Jack dear . . . don't interrupt the meeting."

"I'll ketch him before it starts, then," declared the colonel, stumping out of the room.

They went out on the gallery of the spacious adobe house, and in the night the covered wagons stood out on the plains like the lights of some populous city. Against the canvas of the tops, the glow of candle and lantern threw ghostly, distorted shadows on the walls—shadows of women bedding down their children, girls combing out their hair, bearded men peacefully smoking their pipes. But in the center of the great circle, with two flares at its front, there stood a long tent propped open at the sides like the skin shelters of Abraham and Isaac. And toward this, muttering angrily, Colonel Moore made his way, for the services had already begun.

For three days and three nights—morning, afternoon, and evening—the white-haired parson had been exhorting the sinners, until excitement was at a fever pitch. Some were weighed down with their iniquities and with convictions of sin, others were shouting as they felt the glory, while others, already saved, wrestled powerfully with their neighbors or chanted endlessly the old revival song.

Oh, hallelujah, hallelujah, I am glad to say-ee,
Hallelujah, hallelujah, I am saved today!

"There he is," said Moore, peering under the upraised canvas. "That big man, dressed like a tramp. Richest man in this country . . . got eighty thousand cows . . . and look at him, up in front there."

He pointed the finger of scorn at a huge, hulking figure sitting close to the mourners' bench. His shaggy head was thrown back, he patted his knees in a joyous ecstasy, keeping time to the hallelujahs, and, as the preacher paused and asked the brethren to testify, he was first of all to his feet.

"Brothers and sisters," he began, "I have lived in iniquity, but the love of a sainted mother has brought me back to confess all my sins and be saved."

"Hallelujah!" cried the parson as he closed his long testimony. "The Lord is able to save."

But in the darkness outside, Moore muttered in his beard and turned away with a grunt. "No use waiting," he said. "They'll keep that up all night. And old Henry will be right there, confessing his sins at the mourners' bench and calling on the brethren for their prayers. When they pass the hat around, he'll give his last dollar. And yet he makes his wife and daughter work like a couple of Mexican peons . . . won't even buy himself a new hat. Well, that's Henry Johnson, the cattle king. Dresses and looks like a regular tramp, but when you meet him tomorrow you'll think he's the finest gentleman in the country. He's a man you can't stay mad at, but I'm going to cuss him out, all the same. Things are going to hell in this country, Mister Wells. And unless all signs fail we're due to have a big cattle war."

"Wouldn't doubt it," Curly agreed, as they started back toward the house. "Say, I'll sleep out in the corral, tonight."

"No, you'll sleep in a bed," declared the colonel warmly, "and get a shave and maybe a haircut, to boot. Your horses are just as safe in Jack Moore's corral as they would be inside a fort."

"There's something wrong, though," persisted Curly. "I can feel it in the air . . . and those Rafter J boys were following me. They gave me back old Tige, but I'll bet you the drinks they figure on stealing Paint."

"Not from my ranch," Moore stated. "Did you notice that Mexican that I called to unsaddle our horses? That's Porfilio Goya, the best trailer in this country . . . at one time the greatest horse thief. I'll tell him to keep watch, and I'll stake my life on it, no man will touch your horse."

"Yes, but how about Mister Goya?" Curly inquired shrewdly. "Sometimes these ex-horse thieves relapse."

"No, you can set your mind at rest there, and I'll tell you the reason. When I first came into this country, I brought some very fine horses . . . blooded stock from Louisiana . . . and among others who tried to steal them was this same Porfilio that I'd trust now with anything I've got. He knew every trick of a mighty tricky trade, but I hadn't been a Ranger for nothing and at last I ran him down. Of course, you know what generally happens in a case like that. But he swore that if I'd only spare his life, he'd never steal a horse again. Well, I spared it on one condition . . . if I ever caught him stealing, I'd shoot him down like a dog. That was twelve years ago and to my certain knowledge he's never made a crooked move."

"Yes, but he's only a Mexican," protested Curly, "and Tuffy Malone is just crazy about that horse. Suppose he'd come in the night. The Mex wouldn't stand up to him. You know . . . they won't fight a Texan."

"Maybe not," admitted Moore. "But I will, Mister Wells. You're my guest, understand? And any man that steals your horse will have to answer personally, to me."

"Well, all right," grumbled Curly, "if that's the way you feel about it."

But in the morning Paint was gone.

CHAPTER SIX

It was dawn when a growing apprehension of danger routed Curly Wells out of his bed. Not in many a moon had he slept in one so soft, yet all night he had tossed and dreamed. And as he belted on his pistols and stepped out into the cold, he felt the chill hand of fear. Then at the gate of the corral he found Tige whickering, anxious. And Paint, his pet, was gone.

"Where's that dad-burned Mexican?" Curly burst out in a fury as he searched through the stalls for his horse. As his curses drew louder, a form rose from the hay and slipped out as softly as a cat.

"What's the matter?" demanded Moore, looking in through the corral bars. "What's all this excitement about?"

"My horse is gone," yelled Curly, "and that danged horse thief of a Mexican is headed for the line, I'll bet. But you wait till I ketch him and he can pray all he wants to, I'll. . . ."

"Porfilio!" shouted the colonel, and in the silence that followed Curly gave vent to a heartfelt curse. "Yes, you and your prize Mexican! I knowed all the time that goat herder would steal old Paint. But no, I had to sleep inside there, in the house. You sure have played hell with things now."

"Porfilio!" Moore bellowed, with an outburst of Mexican profanity. And at last from around the corner a frightened voice answered: *"Señor."*

"Ven acá, mal nacimiento," rapped out the colonel, striding toward him, and, like a dog that senses a whipping, the Mexican

crept toward him until he fell on his face at his feet.

"Ah, *Don* Jack," he pleaded, "spare my life! I am innocent!" And he rose up, kissing his thumb laid across his forefinger in the form of an improvised crucifix. *"Por esta Cruz,"* he said, trembling, "I swear I did not steal him."

"But where is he?" thundered his master. "Did I not put him in your care? Did I not say to watch him well, since he belonged to my guest? Where were you all night?"

"I slept in the hay," Porfilio quavered abjectly, "and no one came. I swear it."

"Yes, the scoundrel will swear to anything," Curly spoke up cynically. "We'll just take a look in that hay." He led the way to the hollow where Porfilio had made his bed and felt about in the straw. "I thought so," he said, holding up an empty bottle.

The colonel smelled the cork and drew his gun. "Porfilio . . . ," he began, and with an agonizing cry the Mexican threw himself at his feet.

"Ah, no, no!" he begged. "Think of my woman, *Don* Jack. Have pity on my wife and little ones. I was out by the gate and Tomás Saucedo came by. It was he who gave me the drink."

"But it was you who took it," answered the colonel sternly. "And you have made me out a traitor to my guest. Twice he begged for the privilege of sleeping near his horse, but I forced him to come into the house."

"I will get the horse back," Porfilio promised, the tears dripping down his gray beard. "Wherever he is gone, I will follow and steal him back. Did I ever fail to get one, *señor?*"

"You have failed to guard this one," Moore replied. "And now I am dishonored before my guest."

"But I will ketch heem . . . in one day!" Porfilio cried in halting English as he spied a white form coming toward them.

The next minute Mrs. Moore slipped in through the bars and came hurrying across the corral. "Why, Jack!" she exclaimed. "What are you cursing and shouting about? I thought someone certainly had been killed."

"Never mind, dear," responded the colonel. "You go back to the house. Porfilio has let someone steal the paint horse."

"Ah, Mees Hoolia," wept Porfilio, "save my life thees one time. I will never go to sleep again. But that bad mans, Tomás Saucedo, gimme wheesky on purpose. Theenk of my wife and all my leetle ones!"

"Well, all right then . . . *busca!*" Jack Moore burst out savagely. "Hunt, you *pelado,* and bring me back that horse or I'll kill every Mexican in the country."

"Why, Jack, how you talk," his wife said reproachfully, but he cut her short with a look.

"You go back to the house, where you belong," he ordered. "I'll handle this *hombre* myself."

She looked at him again, then turned away obediently, and Moore watched her until she passed through the door.

"Mister Wells," he said, "I'm sorry this has happened. But under the circumstances the only thing to do is to get your paint horse back."

"Yeah," assented Curly, gazing dourly at Porfilio. "Either that or I kill me a Mexican."

"Oh, he can find him," promised Moore. "Never knew him to fail. Oyez, Porfilio, *busca por el caballo.*"

"*¡Ah, sí! Sí, señor,*" responded the Mexican eagerly. He took up the trail like a hunting dog. Leaning close to the ground, one extended forefinger pointing automatically to every track he saw, he scouted along the fence and then up to the gate, where he stiffened and stood gazing at a footprint.

"What is it?" the colonel demanded, hurrying over to look.

The Mexican pointed to a boot track. It was small as a woman's, but without that slender delicacy that marks even the savage woman's foot, and Moore stared at it long, as if he knew it.

"Whose track is that?" he asked, but Porfilio shrugged his shoulders.

"*Quién sabe* . . . who knows?" he evaded.

"Now here," began the colonel, laying a heavy hand upon him. "You're lucky to be alive . . . understand? Now tell me, straight out, whose track you think that is, and don't you make any mistake."

"It is the footprint of Tuffee," answered the Mexican reluctantly.

And Curly stooped closer to study it.

"That is the truth," responded Moore. "I knew it all the time. If you had lied to me, it would have been necessary to shoot you."

"It sure is," agreed Curly. "Happened to notice it, up at the crossing. But I knew that it was him all the time, Colonel."

"*H-m-m,*" meditated the colonel. "He'll hide that horse somewhere and wait till the search is over. My guess is he's taken him to Mike Broiles's place, the other side of those mountains. But don't you try to follow him, Mister Wells, because those outlaws will ambush you, sure. Porfilio, you go right now before the people get up and follow that horse track . . . understand? And if you find him in Mike Broiles's pasture, you come back and tell me. Don't you touch him . . . I'll get him myself."

"You will not," Curly spoke up. "I can get back my own horses. And if Tuffy Malone tries to keep me from doing it. . . ."

"No, no," warned the colonel. "He's as dangerous as a rattlesnake, and he knows those White Mountains like a book. Probably stole your horse on purpose, to get an excuse to kill you, but I'll settle with the little rat. Right here and now I'll have a showdown with Henry Johnson. And either he fires Tuffy

Malone or we split the blankets for good. I'll not consort with a thief."

He motioned the Mexican on his way and strode off to the house. And after a long look at Porfilio, who shrank before his gaze, Curly turned and clumped gloomily after him. The gay vistas that had opened before him when he had won back his Tige horse had turned to a deeper gloom, now that Paint had fallen victim to the thieves. For where other men, with lesser love, cherished their women and children, all Curly's thoughts revolved about Paint and Tige, for whose sakes he would gladly have died. They were his own, raised like children, and trained to do his will, yet left free to gambol and play, and as he gazed at the distant mountains a tear ran down his cheek, but all he could do was wait.

There was silence at the table as the colonel gulped his coffee and wolfed down a few morsels of food. Then he rose up, scowling, and fell to pacing the broad gallery that shaded the front of the house.

"There's nothing I hate like a thief," he spat as Curly came out. "And especially a damned cow thief. Henry Johnson will be here soon to get his cup of coffee . . . he sleeps out, the old fox, every night . . . and if I don't flay him good . . . there's the old scoundrel now, stopping to talk with those children. But I'll skin him alive . . . I will."

He paced back and forth faster, watching Tuffy's indulgent boss, but, when Hard Winter Johnson finally ambled over toward him, Moore slowed down and tugged at his beard. In the cold light of morning the cattle king looked old and shabby, having slept in his clothes on the ground, but his corncob pipe was held at a rakish angle and he greeted his old friend with a smile.

" 'Morning, Jack," he hailed as he came through the gate. " 'Morning, stranger. What's the good word?"

"They ain't none!" exploded Moore. "Henry, this is Mister

Wells. Your cowboys done stole his best horse."

"Oh, sho, sho," protested Johnson. "As bad as all that? I can remember one night, right here where this house stands, when I lost two hundred and fourteen head."

"Yes, and all through your own carelessness," the colonel retorted bitterly. "If you'd had your guards set and brought your herd in at dawn, the Apaches would never have jumped you."

"You lost some yourself," Hard Winter reminded mildly. "Life ain't all peaches and honey in a country like this . . . but I'll try to get Mister Wells's horse back."

"Yes, you'd better," raged Moore, "or I'll step in and do it for you! First they come to his ranch, 'way over in the Panhandle, and steal his zebra dun horse, Tige. And then, last night, after he's got his dun back, they come in and steal his strawberry roan. A very valuable animal . . . and out of my corral. After I'd told him it was perfectly safe."

"Too bad. I'm mighty sorry," replied the cattle king, unruffled. "Ah, good morning, Missus Moore, good morning."

"Good morning, Uncle Henry," she responded sweetly. "Your coffee is still hot on the stove. But you'll have to hurry in, because I've got to tend my milk. Going back to the ranch today?"

"Well, I was," he chuckled heartily, "except for one thing. Can't get no coffee like you make, up there, Missus Moore."

He bowed perfunctorily to the men and passed in to the dining room, and Colonel Moore ground his teeth in exasperation.

"Damn it, Wells," he complained, "you can't make a mark on him. Nothing you say gets under his skin. And Julia was just waiting to horn in and stop the play. But you wait . . . I'll ketch him off by himself."

He resumed his restless pacing, and, when Johnson at last came out, he fell in beside him silently.

"Come out to the corral," he said under his breath. "I want to show you a track."

"Oh, never mind the track," answered the cattle king jovially. "If you say Tuffy stole the horse, I'm taking your word for it, because I know you've been a Ranger, Jack. And that's a weakness of Tuffy's, I'll have to admit it. Every time some new woman or some horse ketches his eye, he. . . ."

"Lookee here, Henry Johnson!" burst out the colonel hoarsely. "This ain't no jesting matter. Do you know what that low-flung renegade has been doing? He's been trying to lead Melissa McCoy astray."

"What . . . Tuffy?" Johnson said. "I knowed he was coming down here mighty regular, but I thought it was that gal of Tomás Saucedo's. . . ."

"It was her, too," broke in Moore. "But I want you to understand that Melissa is just like my daughter. Her old father, Honey, is kind of touched in the head and not competent to protect her, nohow, but I'll kill the dirty dog that takes advantage of Melissa the same as I would a snake. I just found out last night that Tuffy Malone has been annoying her. And when she told him to go away, he turned around and got ugly and threatened to put them afoot. The next night her riding pony and all their work horses but one were run off by parties unknown. Mister Wells here found her pony in your horse herd, so I'll give you one guess who did it."

"I reckon it was Tuffy," Hard Winter observed philosophically. "He's been getting a mite unruly lately. But he's a good-hearted boy . . . ain't a mean hair on him."

"Yes, and that's most of the time," retorted Moore. "Because all those boys do, instead of branding up your calves, is drink and carouse around at the store."

"Well, now, Jack," defended Johnson, "you know yourself you can't hire a working cowboy no more. They've all turned warrior, packing two guns and riding by night, and my boys are jest like the rest. But I've got to have 'em, see, to protect me from these trail herders that come driving up the river from Texas. They'd grab every maverick and slick-ear they could find, and, if it wasn't for Tuffy and them gunmen I've got, I wouldn't have a single cow on my range. It's nothing to me if those boys don't brand my stuff. I don't care who owns the cow, as long as I get the calf. And I don't care who owns the horse as long as I get to ride it. But when everybody's stealing, I'm going to get my share . . . they ain't no two ways about that."

"Well and good," Curly spoke up, laying a hand on his shoulder and looking him squarely in the eye. "You can steal all you want to, Mister Johnson, but don't you steal from me. I'm a lover of peace, but the man that steals my horse has got me to whip, right now."

"Yes, and he's got me to whip, too," Moore chimed in belligerently. "Because I'll give you to understand, Mister Wells was my guest, and the man that steals from him steals from me."

"Oh, sho, sho, now," protested Hard Winter with a benevolent smile. "You gentlemen are getting excited. But I'm a man of peace, myself . . . I never go armed, Mister Wells . . . and I'm always glad to do what seems right. What price do you put on this horse?"

"Price!" Curly scoffed. "You think you could buy that horse? I wouldn't trade Paint for your whole outfit, so you can put your pocketbook away."

"All right," responded Johnson mildly, folding up his long, limp wallet. "Mighty sorry this incident occurred. I'll jest look at that track, so there won't be any question about it, and talk the matter over with Tuffy."

He shambled out to the gate where the boot mark, carefully covered, remained to prove the guilt of the horse thief.

"That's his, all right," he said, after a long look at the track. "Got a foot like a woman's . . . and mighty proud of it, too. I'd know that boot in a thousand. But, Jack, I'm telling you there's no harm in that boy . . . he's nothing, you might say, but a kid. Only you've got to approach him in a reasonable way, and that's what I'll try to do. But if he won't give up the horse, I'll pay you for him well. . . ."

"You will not," cut in Curly. "I'll come up there and take him and run your damned Heel Flies out of the country. I'm burned out on this thieving and foolishness."

"And so am I," added Jack Moore. "I'm giving you notice, Henry Johnson, to go back and set your house in order. Fire those drunken, cow-stealing outlaws and hire some honest men. And if you can't do it, Henry, the Texas Cattlemen's Association has authorized me to do it for you."

He paused, and for the first time the sunny smile left Johnson's eyes and a startled, uneasy stare took its place.

"So that's it," he said. "Is Mister Wells their representative?"

"Not so far as I know," answered the colonel. "But they said they'd send a man over."

"Now, listen," Hard Winter began, throwing his hands out appealingly. "You gentlemen know, if you know anything at all, that I'm a decent citizen. The man that's doing this stealing, and corrupting all my cowboys, is Mike Broiles, over at Alamosa. How can I hire honest men to handle my cattle when Mike Broiles, over the mountains, will buy all they can steal and pay them five dollars a head? If I speak to my boys, they'll jest up and leave me . . . and then, Jack Moore, look out. They're peaceable now. They respect your brand and mine. But the minute they quit me the fat's in the fire. They'll steal every cow we've got."

"The first man that steals a cow of mine," gritted Moore, "had better look for trouble. I don't care if it's Tuffy or Broiles or some Mexican . . . I'll fight to protect my brand. Now, listen to me, Henry, because this is the last time I'll speak to you. I want you to go back and get this gentleman's horse that was stole, as you can see, by Tuffy Malone. And I want you to clean out that nest of thieves at the crossing or I'll come up and do it for you. Enough said . . . if that horse isn't here in three days I'll report it to the Texas Association."

"And I'll do more than that," Curly promised. "I'll come up and get him. Savvy?"

CHAPTER SEVEN

His head on his breast, Hard Winter Johnson rode away toward the house he ruled only in name, and for three days, fretting and fuming, Curly Wells paced the gallery and watched for some sign of his pet. Every night, with his guns beside him, he slept in the hay where he could hear the watchful Tige's least snort, and in the morning at dawn he circled the fence for tracks, then mounted and rode restlessly forth.

Something told him that, not far away, Paint waited for his coming, watching the hilltops and neighing for Tige. A thousand times he saw a vision of his gorgeously painted form, hidden away in some mountain pasture sniffing the wind for his partner and his own beloved master, then snorting at the taint of Malone. Curses rose unbidden to his lips as he loped, scanning the trails that led down from the west, and then, just at dusk, he spied the furtive form of Porfilio, emerging from a narrow ravine.

"I have found him," announced the Mexican as Curly spurred toward him. "In the pasture of Mike Broiles, over the mountain. And the work horses of McCoy are there, also."

"Good." Curly grinned. "Take me over there, savvy? I want to talk to Mister Broiles."

"*Pero no*," objected Porfilio. "The *Tejanos* do not like Mexicans. When they kill one of my people, they laugh."

"And so do I," Curly responded with frank brutality, "if I think he has stolen my horse. But if he takes me to where he is hidden, that is all I require . . . and I will give you twenty dollars, in gold."

"Then I will go," Porfilio decided, after thinking the matter over. "But first I must report to *el patrón*, because he told me to return in three days."

"Correct," Curly agreed, and, falling in beside him, he rode back to the big house, where Moore was awaiting their coming.

"I knew it," declared the colonel. "Porfilio, you did well. Did any of Mike's men see you come?"

"No, nor go," responded the Mexican. "I looked down from thee heights. But, *Don* Jack, there were many *Tejanos.*"

"Any cattle?" demanded the colonel.

And Porfilio threw up his hands. *"¡Muchos!"* he shrilled. "Many horses . . . many cattle!"

"The damned thieves!" exclaimed Moore impatiently. "I'll attend to Mike Broiles myself. He's a man I've avoided, although everybody knows his ranch is a hold-out for rustlers. But I'm responsible for that horse and I'll ride over in the morning. . . ."

"No, you won't, Jack dear," spoke up a voice from behind them, and the colonel smothered an oath in his beard.

"Now, Julia," he complained, "why can't you keep out of this? I'm obligated on my honor to return Mister Wells his horse. . . ."

"That's all right," cut in Curly. "I can skin my own skunks. You lend me this Mexican, to show me where they are, and I'll undertake to bring back all four of 'em."

"Yes, now, honey, please do," Julia murmured caressingly. "Don't you remember what you said to me, out under . . . ?"

"Can't help it!" burst out Moore. "You throw it up to me every day. But do you think it's very honorable, after losing his horse for him, to let Wells go over there alone? And especially when Mike Broiles has the name of a murderer, and a cold-blooded one, at that. But if I go there with him, Mike will know I mean business. . . ."

"No, now, Jack. No fighting . . . you promised me. I'm sorry for Mister Wells, but I don't want you killed."

"Well"—the colonel shrugged—"you see how I'm fixed, my boy. And I'd like to say right now, when you propose to your wife, weigh carefully every word that you say. But I've given my promise and I'll have to live up to it, if it makes me out a coward and no gentleman."

"Oh, no," Curly said blithely, "that's all right with me, Colonel. You just give me a letter, saying you want the four horses, and I'll guarantee to bring them back."

"I believe you can do it," Moore stated judiciously. "But look out for Mike . . . he's treacherous. Don't linger around his ranch. Get your horses and come away. And I'll warn Mister Broiles you're my friend."

He went in to write the letter—and the next morning before daylight Curly had gone. Dawn found them in a cañon where the river, flowing east, suddenly lost itself in an echoing abyss—hence its name, Río Hondo, the deep. To Porfilio it was a place of nameless horrors and fears, a hole where defenseless men, the enemies of those in power, had been cast to a frightful death. Only the thunder of distant waters told Curly of its existence, this chasm that swallowed up men. But as the Mexican babbled on, scanning the valley for lurking foes, he caught the sinister aspect of the land.

The mountains that rose before them were not jagged or too steep. A good man, well mounted, could ride over them anywhere, but they sheltered a war-like brood. Since time began, the mountains have bred robbers, to prey on the plodders of the plains, but here, according to Porfilio, the men were not *ladrónes*— only fighting men, armed against their foes. They rode out in bands, like the war parties of the Apaches who dwelt on the heights behind, and descended upon some luckless enemy. And then, once dispersed, they too suffered a raid from the adherents of the rival band.

"You see thees place?" Porfilio inquired mysteriously, pointing down into the open valley. And where the cañon forked, against the wedge of a high ridge, Curly saw a house and store and two saloons. "Thees San Marcial . . . ver' bad town," went on the Mexican. "Bad mens leeve there . . . all thee time watch thee trail. Tha's why I come on reedge. San Marcial ees great place for cowboys to fight. Geet dronk first, then shoot up town."

Curly gazed down curiously on the collection of mud houses, placed strategically where the two trails from the mountains met and merged into the road to the Pecos.

"Op that cañon," explained Porfilio, indicating the northern fork, "es Leencoln, one ver' beeg town. Two beeg store, one *fonda*. Many saloons there, too. But ba-ad place for Mexican to go. Lots of soldiers from fort come down and geet dronk. Lots of cowboys geet dronk there, too. But that sheriff no good . . . no like Mexican people. We go thees way, you bet."

He pointed approvingly to the broad, wooded valley that broke off to the southwest, winding up between high ridges to the pine-clad peaks beyond, where the Mescalero Apaches pitched their teepees. "Ruidoso men good folks." Porfilio nodded. "Good friends to Mexican people. Beeg trail go t'rough here, for drive cattle to Arizona. Sometimes wagon train go t'rough to California. But all thee time thees Ruidoso boys they fight them ba-ad mens op in Leencoln. Shoot . . . keel! Me no like!"

He shrugged his shoulders and swung off on a long detour, to avoid even the friendly Ruidoso, but as the cedars gave way to piñons and black pines he ventured down into the trail. It swung smoothly on across meadows of tender green where the snow had hardly melted in the sun, until at last, imperceptibly, it crossed the high divide and pitched down through narrow cañons to the west.

A dry, parched wind, with the tang of alkali on it, sucked up into their faces as they rode; the heat of summer seemed to have come before its time. From the shoulder of a point Curly beheld far below him a landscape blighted and accursed. From the foot of the verdant hills it stretched away, gray and forbidding, ninety miles of waterless desert where every puff of wind whirled its spiral of dust into the air. And in its center, a gleaming jewel set in a matrix of blue horizon, White Sands like arabesques thrust long arms across the way, arms that glistened like bleached bones in the sun.

"Ba-ad country . . . ba-ad peoples," observed Porfilio, and pointed up the valley to the north. The gray desert swept on, walled in by jigsaw peaks and mountains of tender blue. But where the white of the sands disappeared at last, a black shadow lay athwart the land. It was lava, the titan flow of some extinct volcano, lost to sight in the vastness of the landscape. Yet where the *malpais* blocked the way even the Indians turned back, or circled to cross through the sands. Here was the end of the rich grassland that spread west like a mat from the far plains of Texas and the Panhandle. Beyond lay sand and desert, jagged mountains that touched the sky, then more desert, more sand, more distant peaks.

"Eet ees ba-ad country," Porfilio croaked in Curly's ear, and turned north along the base of the mountain. "I show you them horses, hey?" he asked over his shoulder.

"And I pay you twenty dollars," responded Curly.

"*¡Bueno!*" And Porfilio nodded, his eyes gleaming avariciously as he worked his way through a labyrinth of trails. He was traveling by landmarks, keeping always to well-used paths where his tracks would be covered over by the cattle. At every turn and tree he craned his neck watchfully, lest he find himself caught in some trap. Then at last, tying his horse, he crept out to a rim of sandstone and beckoned Curly to look.

Where a brawling mountain stream cut its way down through the country rock a huge natural pasture had been formed by the walls, a grassy park where horses fed and drowsed.

"You see?" whispered Porfilio, pointing his finger like a gun barrel. And there in the shade of a broad cottonwood, half concealed by the mottled sun spots, stood Paint, fighting the flies. "Thees beeg bay," went on the Mexican, pointing down at a heavy draft horse, "he belong to Honey McCoy. Over there, them matched grays . . . McCoy's horses, too. All thee others stolen, too, I theenk."

"I bet," Curly muttered, nodding and handing Porfilio a gold piece, and for a long time he studied the pasture.

"Where is the gate?" he asked in Spanish, and the Mexican grinned at him slyly.

"Where you theenk?" he said at last.

"Right down by his house," ventured Curly, "if I'm any judge of horse thieves."

"Ye-es," agreed Porfilio, and waited expectantly.

"You know any other?" demanded Curly roughly, but the Mexican only shrugged his shoulders. "Well . . . oh, hell," Curly grumbled, digging down into his pocket. "Here, I'll tell you what you do. You show me that upper gate and I'll give you ten dollars. But that ain't all, *hombre*. Don't think for a minute I'm a Christmas tree that you can shake and bring down the gold. I'll need another hand, to help drive home these horses. . . ."

"No, *señor*," insisted Porfilio, backing swiftly away. "Me . . . I don't need that ten dollars."

"Well, twenty, then," offered Curly. "And don't forget, Mister Mex, you got me into this jackpot. Drinking Tomás Saucedo's whiskey and going to sleep on your job. I ought to kill you."

"Well, all right," agreed the Mexican, glancing up at him doubtfully. "Twenty dollars . . . what you want me to do?"

"I want you to stay right here," Curly ordered. "Stay good

and hid, understand? And when I drive down those horses and go out the front gate, you watch where I go . . . and follow. I can handle them *hombres* myself, down there, but out on the trail I want both hands to shoot with."

"You want me to drive horse while you watch for Texans, eh?" Porfilio queried with a sickly smile. "But Meester Well-ess, thees Mike Broiles he has keel lots of Mexicans. If he sees me, he keel me, sure."

"Aw, keel nothing!" scoffed Curly. "Ain't you got a six-shooter? And ain't you got me to protect you? Now you show me that gate and skip out up on the mountain. And when you see me going by, you come down and haze the horses, while I keep a look-out behind."

"We-ell, all right." Porfilio shrugged. "But you look out, Meester Well-ess. Because Mike Broiles ees . . . what you call 'im? . . . one assassin."

"So'm I!" laughed Curly recklessly. "Now show me that up-per gate."

CHAPTER EIGHT

Through a gap, cunningly fenced by barbed wires twisted through willows, Curly slipped down into the rustler king's domain. Then, oblivious of his minions wherever they might be, he rode in a straight line to Paint. From the shade of the flaunting cottonwood there came a shrill whinny of welcome, a snort, and an answer from Tige, and then into the sunlight, his dappled coat gleaming, the Appaloosa came like a shot. He touched nose affectionately with his horse partner, Tige, and the next moment Curly had his arms around his neck and was choking out endearing words.

"Nice horse, eh?" observed a voice.

When Curly looked up, he saw a tall cowboy, riding toward him. "Finest horse in the world," he answered amiably. And then he wheeled Tige until the Flying W on his hip came full in the stranger's view.

"Yours?" queried the cowboy, darting a quick glance at Paint's brand.

Curly nodded grimly. "That's right," he said. "Unless you've got some objections."

"None at all," the cowboy responded hastily. "But I ain't quite so sure about Mike."

"You working for him?" inquired Curly. "Then we'll go down and see him. I've got a little letter from Colonel Jack Moore that he asked me to be particular and deliver."

"Jack Moore, eh?" the cowboy repeated, and beneath his ten

days' beard there appeared the crooked semblance of a smile.

"Yes," went on Curly. "Your neighbor . . . over the mountain. And while we're about it, perhaps you wouldn't mind helping me to drive those three big work horses down. They belong to Honey McCoy."

The cowboy eyed him curiously, then with a flip of the reins he turned his agile mount around. "No trouble at all," he said. "It's a pleasure, I assure you."

Curly grinned as he met his glance. "Mighty clever of you," he answered. "I'm a stranger in these parts and I don't rightly know my way around."

"I doubt that like hell," responded the cowboy boldly. "But you can talk this over with Mike."

They rode down through connected pastures, where the cañon walls, pinching in, formed a box that was fenced across with wire, and all the time, with a saturnine smile, the cowboy maintained his silence. It was as if he were nursing some joke, too good to be shared. When they came to the long ranch house, backed up against the bluff, he leaned over and rapped loudly on the door.

"Gentleman here to see you, Mister Broiles," he announced, and sat back to enjoy the show.

The door swung open violently and a mountain of flesh emerged—a short, barrel-shaped man with a double-belted stomach that trembled with windy rage. For a moment, while startled faces peered out of other doors, he stood staring at his unwelcome guest. Then the huge, black eyebrows above his walrus mustache lifted up in a sinister leer.

"Well, my young friend," said with a quick glance at Curly and his horses, "who are you and what is your business? I'm Mike Broiles, the boss of this ranch."

"Name's Wells," answered Curly. "I came over to get this horse." And he pointed with his thumb at Paint.

"Well, well," Broiles sneered, his keen, black eyes dancing. "Is there anything else you'd like, now?"

"Yes," Curly said quietly. "I want these three work horses. They belong to Honey McCoy and I'm going to take them back."

A snicker from the cowboys broke in on the startled silence as Mike Broiles stood glaring at his guest. Then his loud, crashing voice burst out in hoarse curses, though he feigned to direct his anger at his men.

"Out of my sight, you!" he ended in a fury. "And you, Jim Knowles, what the devil do you mean bringing this madman to break up me sleep?"

"Well, you see," the cowboy explained innocently, "I met Mister Wells up there in the far pasture, and he seemed to think this horse was his. So, to avoid any trouble, and possible misunderstanding, I brought him down to you. Got a letter from Jack Moore," he added, *sotto voce.*

And suddenly the immense anger was gone. "From Jack Moore, eh?" Broiles purred as Curly handed over the letter. "Pray excuse me, Mister Wells, while I read what he has to say. He's a good man . . . Jack Moore . . . a good man."

He opened up the letter with ponderous, ape-like hands, knitting his brows as he read it, word by word, and, as the import of the message was borne in upon his mind, he stopped short and glanced up at his guest.

"So you're Mister Wells, eh . . . from Texas?" He bowed. "Glad to meet you, Mister Wells, I'm sure. Is that your brand, Flying W? Well, well, then it's all a mistake. You see, Mister Wells, there's a man over by Deming that uses this same iron for his horse brand. And quite naturally, you understand, when we found him in our pasture, we thought he was Mister Upham's. So I wrote the owner we would hold the horse for him, never thinking that it might come from Texas. Some enemy of mine must have put him in me pasture, because we found him there, three mornings past."

"That's all right, Mister Broiles," Curly responded politely. "I'll explain to the colonel how it happened. You see, I was his guest, and, when someone stole my horse, he thought they were whacking at him."

"Some devilish horse thief," spat the rustler king vehemently, "has done this out of petty spite. And please tell the dear colonel I'm most heartily sorry . . . and accept my apologies yourself. Now these horses of Honey McCoy were put in the same way, and every day I've said . . . 'Boys, the first man that goes there must take back poor Honey's horses. He'll be wanting them to move his bees.' But day by day we've put it off. Would it be too much trouble, since you're going back yourself, to return them to McCoy, with my compliments?"

"No trouble at all," Curly answered promptly. But out of the corner of one eye he saw the cowboy, Jim Knowles, turn to wink at a man behind. Then, like the warning crack before a bolt of lightning strikes, he remembered the colonel's advice. Mike Broiles was a murderer, a past master of treachery. Even now while he smiled, displaying his wide horse teeth, he was hatching some plot to betray Curly. Here was a villainy so perfect, if villainy it was, that it had dispelled the last of his doubts. But it was the mention of Jack Moore's name that had brought about the magical change. Broiles had bristled like a boar, gnashing his teeth in a fighting rage as he kicked open his door and strode out. Now he purred like a cat, and his soft Irish brogue made every palavering word ring true. Only behind him, like a satyr, the sardonic cowboy mocked his master with a knowing grin.

"But get down, man, get down," Broiles was saying with a bow, "and we'll sample a bottle that these cowboys of mine have never once sniffed at, the rascals. I'm sorry, indeed, the colonel is not with you."

"Nope," Curly declined, glancing up at the sun. "I'd better be going, Mister Broiles. Some other time, when I ain't in such a hurry." And he turned the willing horses toward the gate.

"Just a moment," Broiles said, "whilst I write a little note to Colonel Moore. And, Andy, me boy, will you go along with him, to open the gates and such."

"Well, make it brief," Curly agreed reluctantly as Broiles darted like a fat spider into his den.

But the minutes passed, while Curly scanned the faces of the cowboys as one by one they peered furtively out at him. Voices rumbled from the darkness, there was a thud of hurrying feet, and from the cottonwood grove behind, where the corrals were built, Curly heard a saddle slapped on a horse. Then from his doorway, still smiling, Mike Broiles hurried out, holding a crumpled letter in his hand.

"There you are, me boy," he said. "And thank you kindly for waiting. You take the first road to the right."

"To the right," repeated Curly. "I'm going to the left. Isn't the road to Mescalero over there?"

"To be sure," agreed Broiles, "and you can go there if you wish. But 'tis a long, long way around, and the Apaches none too friendly, especially when you're driving loose stock. There's one horse in a thousand, if I may say so, Mister Wells . . . that strawberry roan you've got. And Injuns, as you know, have a liking for such animals. They'd take a long chance to get a war pony like that."

"Sure would," Curly agreed, gazing ruefully at Paint. "Which way does this other road go?"

"Right up over the divide, past Fort Stanton and Lincoln. 'Tis a safe road, I know, and I'll send a boy with you over a short cut we use, through the hills. He'll put you on the wagon road . . . and from there you can't miss your way. All right,

Andy . . . open the gate." He motioned to the cowboy, who had gone on ahead. Then with a last, hearty handshake he bade Curly good bye and hurried back into the house.

Curly drove the horses out slowly, scanning the country to right and left, undecided which way to go, but as Paint and the work animals took the turn to the right he settled back and let them go. They were on the home trail, and that is one road that a range horse never forgets.

The way led off down a broad, sandy valley, where the water from neglected ditches kept green the abandoned fields of what had once been an irrigated farm. Now it grew rank with weeds, which the cattle devoured, for just down the cañon the parched desert began, with its greasewood and gray saltbrush and soap-weed. Thorny mesquite trees and gaunt yuccas dotted the immensity of the plain, and beyond, like a snowbank, White Sands gleamed and shimmered, half hidden by the brush at their base.

"Here's the cut off," announced the cowboy, turning up onto the bench, and Curly smiled as his voice quavered and cracked. Here was no low-browed assassin, sent to murder him on the trail. He was a boy in his first boots, without even a six-shooter, and he rode on in front with bowed head. They swung off across wide flats where the dust from desert sandstorms had laid down strange patterns behind each bush, and ahead of them, like a gash, a deep cañon opened up, black and sinister in the glaring light.

Curly glanced up uneasily at the scarred blank of the mountain, where Porfilio had promised to watch for him, and beckoned to the rat-faced boy.

"Say, kid," he said, "you can go on back now. These horses know their own way home."

"It goes right up that big cañon," directed the boy. "Don't turn off, now . . . you follow this trail."

He pointed, and Curly saw that his skinny hand trembled

and his face had gone white beneath its tan.

"What's the matter?" he demanded. But the boy only mumbled, then spurred his drooping mount and was gone.

"What the devil?" Curly said, gazing after him doubtfully, and then his eyes returned to the gap. In places like that a man could be ambushed, but the trail led on and he followed it mechanically until at last he came to the hills. Here in the shelter of friendly cedars he stopped and considered climbing up to look out the country ahead. As he lay there, watching the ridges for men riding to cut him off, he pondered on his reception by Broiles.

That he was a man capable of murder was written plainly in his eyes, his heavy jaw, and black, beetling brows. But the letter from Jack Moore had changed his humor in an instant, and Curly counted himself safe from attack. Not for one horse, or four, would Mike Broiles dare the anger of this Ranger who watched him from afar. He would not kill Moore's friend, nor steal back his horses—yet the kid had been scared, badly scared.

Curly settled down comfortably behind a big tuft of bear grass and smoked a cigarette while he thought. The trail wound up the gulch—no one knew whether he rode or stopped—and when night came he could turn and ride west. He had Paint now, and Tige—all the world lay before him. Only the work horses of Honey McCoy held him back. With slow, searching eyes he scanned the front of the high mountains, the dark pass, the country behind, and then suddenly he grabbed his rifle and shoved it out through the bear grass. He had spied a furtive form, a bobbing hat. For a minute, while his heart thumped, he followed it through his gun sights, then laughed and put up his gun. It was Porfilio, slipping down to cut his trail.

"*¡Aii, amigo!*" called Curly, showing his head for an instant, and the Mexican came spurring toward him.

"Where you going?" he demanded angrily. "You want to geet

keeled? Thees way is thee trail." And he pointed to the south, scowling arrogantly, but Curly only laughed.

"What's biting on you?" he inquired indulgently. "You saw a ghost, or what?"

"No . . . no ghost. I know thees trail . . . called Rustlers' Trail, you savvy? You come back. I show you thee way."

"Well, say," shrilled Curly, "who's running this, anyway? I'm going out this way, my friend."

"Yes?" responded Porfilio, his stubborn eyes glittering, and he shrugged his shoulders defiantly. "Me, I'm goin' thees way," he stated emphatically, and flung his hand out toward the peaks.

"All right," agreed Curly, "the bridle's off, Mister Mex. But I'll tell you what I'll do. You take back these work horses and I'll give you twenty dollars . . . ten now and ten at the ranch."

" *'Sta bueno,*" agreed the Mexican, thrusting his supple hand out eagerly.

Curly laughed as he gave him the gold. "If I don't show up," he said, "you'll know the rustlers have got me. *¡Adiós!*" And he spurred up the trail.

"You look out!" Porfilio called after him. "Tha' ver' bad pass. I tell you now . . . you better come back."

"Aw," scoffed Curly, "I wasn't born yesterday." But up the cañon he turned out of the trail. Some imp of perversity, against his better judgment, had urged him on up this pass.

He knew in his heart that the safe way lay behind him, but he would not yield his judgment to a Mexican. Porfilio was spoiled, perhaps by the hope of gold that made him magnify the dangers of the way, but Curly was not in the habit of letting some *paisano* direct him, and so the die was cast. He was due to go on— and yet the thought of that black cañon brought up visions of sinister doings at the ranch. Broiles had ducked into his long adobe to give orders to his minions—boots had clumped, a saddle had been slapped on a horse. And, across the bench from the ranch, a man could beat him to Rustlers' Pass and be waiting behind some rock. Curly turned off into a side cañon and watched the ridges as he rode, but, as he neared the summit, he stopped.

The sun was sinking low, a strong wind blurred his eyes, and he felt a creeping fear up his spine. He had kept below the skyline, picking his way up a rocky draw, but now his gulch had run out. He paused, and Paint raised his head.

Paint snorted, and Curly ducked, for to his left he saw two men watching the trail, rifles out—their backs to him. They were waiting to pot him, but he had slipped through behind them. He crouched, and plucked out his carbine. Then a blow like a pole-axe knocked his hat from his head, and, as he fell, he heard the whang of a gun. The earth rose up and met him and he landed in the ditch, his ears ringing, his mouth full of dirt. In a clatter of hoofs he heard his horses stampeding, and suddenly the world went out.

He awoke in a hole, his rifle across his body, the noise of approaching horsemen in his ears, and, writhing like a snake, he crept closer to the bank, cursing silently as he watched for the riders. They came racing over the rocks, knocking stones in every direction, bouncing high as they stood up to look, and over the edge of his gulch Curly watched them like a rattlesnake, shaking the dirt out of the muzzle of his gun.

"There's his hat!" whooped the leader, reining over toward the gulch. But as he rode up, laughing, the grin froze on his face—he turned, but he turned too late.

"Take . . . that," spoke up Curly, working the lever at each shot, but the second man had seen him in time. The dust leaped from his coat as Curly's first bullet struck home. The rider lurched heavily and grabbed at the horn. Then he wheeled to the left and went galloping down the cañon and Curly settled down in his hole. There was another man in the hills, the man who had shot him, but one rustler would never laugh again.

CHAPTER NINE

Night came swiftly in the black cañon, where one man lay dead and another watched the skyline to shoot, and as the dusk dimmed the hilltops Curly rose and looked about, then reached out and picked up his hat. The huge slug from a buffalo gun had gone through the front of it, tearing a hole as big as his fist, and with a grunt he flung it to the ground.

"What do you need a hat for?" he grumbled to himself. "You ain't got enough brains to tan a squirrel skin, to say nothing of getting sunstruck. Why the hell didn't you go back with that Mex?"

He felt the bulge on his head, where the wind of the bullet had raised a sizable lump, and shook out his curly mane.

"*Ump-um,* boy," he said. "That's coming too close. I'm leaving here, right now, before something worse happens. . . . By grab, I bet they got Paint!" He thrust two fingers into his mouth and gave a shrill whistle, but only the wind made answer.

"Clean gone," he declared, leaning low to look for tracks, and, walking at a crouch, he hurried on over the pass, then straightened up and whistled again. He was in the pines now, where the noises of the night were not killed by the wind in his ears, and from far down the cañon he heard an answering neigh, a crash, and the thud of feet.

"Here, Paint!" he called, springing forward on the run. Halfway down the trail he met Paint, trotting fast, nickering joyously as he snuffed the wind.

"Where's Tige?" Curly demanded, swinging up on him bareback. "Go git Tige!" he ordered again. And at a quick, confident trot Paint pattered off down the cañon until he halted before a thicket of oaks.

"Aha!" Curly gloated as he spied a dark form entangled in the stubby growth. "Got hung up, eh, Mister Tige, or, by grab, you'd be going yet. That's just why I use those split reins." He dropped down and unfastened the reins, tightened the cinch with a single jerk, and swung up into the saddle as he turned. "Now," he said, "on your way, you old rascal . . . I thought I had you broke to stand."

He spurred recklessly down the cañon, leaving Rustlers' Pass far behind him, spitting back curses at the thought of Mike Broiles. But as he came out into the wagon road, he pulled up and looked around, then reined away into the brush.

"No more roads for me," he muttered under his breath. "That was pretty danged slick, steering me up over their cut off, but right here is where I get slick myself."

He took shelter in a blind cañon, his two horses staked out like watchdogs, but the gnawings of hunger roused him up before day and he saddled and rode east by the stars. Smooth-molded mountain valleys, where wooded creekbeds made dark lines, appeared before him at the peep of dawn, and to the north, near the base of towering Capitán, he saw the wide parade ground of the fort. A cannon boomed out its greeting as the sun topped the ridge and the flag floated up on its pole, but forts are inhospitable to men of common clay, and Curly kept on down the creek. Mexican houses appeared below him, from which odors of fragrant coffee were wafted to his nostrils as he passed. After circling one or two, Curly forgot his lingering fears and stopped to ask for breakfast.

There was a dead man in Rustlers' Pass, and Curly's bullet-torn hat lay waiting to connect him with the deed, but the assassins of Mike Broiles would be in no hurry to report their find, when they mustered up the nerve to go back. Yet as he rode on down the road, gazing off over the wooded valley to the haze where the distant Pecos lay, Curly felt a growing haste to get clear of the hills, whose very beauty hinted at treachery. They were like a coquette's smile, with their soft, smooth grasslands and alluring, cedar-clad slopes, for every curve of the road held the potent spell of death, and men lurked everywhere in ambush.

The highland creekbeds drew together and formed a river, where wild walnuts and cottonwoods grew and every turn of the trail revealed gardens and little fields where Mexicans stared long as he passed. Then at a bend of the cañon, without the least warning, he rode out into the open street of Lincoln. The broad road had become broader, lined with houses like mud cocoons laid down by busy mason wasps, yet this town, so insignificant in its hidden mountain cañon, was the capital of a wide domain.

From the banks of the Río Grande, a hundred miles to the west, it reached to the Pecos and beyond. And for two hundred miles north from the Mexican line it extended almost to Fort Sumner. Like trails to a desert water hole the dusty roads led into this wasps' nest in a crack of the hills, and from its hidden valley Lincoln ruled the country regally, exacting taxes and laying down the law. Behind the Big Store, the only two-story building, there was a mud jail with an iron door. And above the Big Store the sheriff and judge presided over the destinies of an empire.

Before he knew it, Curly had emerged from a grove of oaks into the center of a bustling town, and, as he reined in before the store, he was aware of many eyes, and of men standing mutely still. In front of the saloon, across the street from the store, a dozen cowboys stood at gaze, their guns conspicuously to the front. The courthouse doorway framed a heavy-set, black-haired man with the star of an officer on his vest. Curly nodded as he met his cold, penetrating gaze. Then, with the sensation of treading among eggs, he stepped into the thronging store.

"Gimme a hat, and a good one," he said to the clerk. And behind him he heard the officer, coming closer to inspect him better.

"Excuse me," he began, flashing a sheriff's star, "are you the owner of that strawberry roan? I'd like to know where you got him. Don't you know that's a stolen horse?"

"Sure"—Curly nodded—"he was stolen from me. I'm Curly Wells . . . from War Bonnet, Texas."

"Glad to meet you, Mister Wells," observed the sheriff perfunctorily. "But you haven't told me yet where you got that horse."

"Over at Mike Broiles's ranch," Curly answered boldly. "That's my brand, a Flying Script W."

He tried on a Texas hat and threw down the money.

Already in the street an eager crowd had gathered, their eyes on Paint and Tige.

"I know that horse," asserted a drunken cowboy. "Ain't that the Appaloosa that Tuffy Malone had when he. . . ."

"Shut up!" broke in another, elbowing him violently aside, but Curly had heard his words.

His blue eyes narrowed, he glanced inquiringly at the sheriff, then grunted and swung up on Tige. There was, to say the least, something rotten in Denmark, but he had no idea of starting a reform. If the sheriff of Lincoln chose to let Tuffy ride through, while he held up the legal owner of the horse, it was not the only county in a wide stretch of country where officers stood in with horse thieves.

"Well, so long." He nodded, as the sheriff still studied him, and rode leisurely on out of town. But around the first turn he broke into a lope, and, when Tige was well lathered, he turned down into the creekbed and changed his saddle to Paint. Then while they panted and puffed he peeped up over the bank, for he had heard a distant drumming of hoofs.

"Hell's bells," he whispered, ducking down out of sight and running to lead his horses into the brush. As he crouched among the walnuts a lot of horsemen went galloping past, with the sheriff of Lincoln in the lead. Twenty cowboys followed him, and in the ruck rode Mike Broiles, his teeth skinned in a wide, vengeful grin.

"That's aplenty," muttered Curly. "I know just where I'm at." And after the posse had rounded a point, he took shelter in the creekbed and followed on down the stream. They had jumped his trail, and when they came back to pick it up, he planned to slip quietly past them. The creek, cut deep by the rush of torrential floods, swung along the north bank of the cañon, and where it turned and swung back, cutting across the trampled road, Curly kept in the middle of the stream.

For five miles, for ten, he worked his way down the bottom, raising his head now and then to look, until at last he saw the dust of the straggling line of riders as they returned from their fruitless chase. The sheriff, O'Keefe, was no longer in the lead. A long, lean cowboy searched each side of the road, hanging low to pick up the sign. Curly hid closer than ever and watched them from afar, and, when the last had toiled past, he laughed.

"You're a hell of a sheriff," he scoffed, and rode boldly off down the road.

The cañon walls had pinched in now, cutting off the rugged horse trails that led up over the ridge. But only a few miles below he could see the wide valley where the Bonito and Ruidoso joined. Once out in the open, with two horses like Paint and Tige, he could laugh the posse to scorn. He rode slowly, saving their strength, and, to defeat curious eyes, he flung his slicker across Paint's white rump. Then as the false fronts of two saloons appeared in the distance he stepped down and tightened his cinch. A line of dust behind him revealed the posse, still in pursuit, but he jogged on slowly, the better to escape attention, for there were cow ponies on the street of San Marcial.

Fourteen horses stood drooping in front of the big saloon, the sweat and dust caked on their flanks, and as Curly looked them over, he spied a Rafter J on the hip of the nearest mount. Here was a Heel Fly from Ganado, one of Hard Winter Johnson's men, but Curly did not alter his pace. Slowly, quietly, at a shuffling Spanish trot he ambled through the adobe town. But as he passed the big saloon, glancing in through the open door, he saw Tuffy Malone at the bar.

There were others, too, whose faces seemed familiar, but Curly did not stop. As Tuffy looked out, Curly leaned forward on Paint and jumped him into a lope. Dogs rushed out to meet him and Curly looked back with a grin. Mexicans ran to their doors. But on through the town the two horses raced, and Curly looked back with a grin. The open valley lay before him, and the long road to the Pecos. What to him were the pistol shots behind?

From the first low bench he could see the excited cowboys as they swarmed out to catch their mounts. A rifle bullet struck behind him but he waved his hat and laughed, then lined out for the race he loved. Nowhere, and he knew it, were there two horses like Tige and Paint—so hardy, so willing, so game—and as he looked back through his dust at the outdistanced pursuers, he slowed down to lead them on. If he left them too far behind, they might quit at the start and take the edge off this sport of kings. And when, at the end, he left their wind-broke mounts, the laugh would be on Tuffy Malone. Both the horses that Curly rode had been stolen, and stolen back. The Heel

Flies whipped after him.

A slim arrow of dust led off down the wide valley, shooting up over benches, darting down across arroyos in a flight as exultant as a bird's. And far behind and getting farther, in twos and dragging threes, the pursuers lagged, and stopped. Not far above the hole where the Bonito takes its plunge into the depths of a black abyss, the wagon road turned up a cañon to climb the high mesa, and the horse trail split in twain. One path turned down the valley, dim and uncertain at best, but the main trail kept straight on, zigzagging up to the top, and Curly went up it on the run.

Two men had pushed ahead, hoping to pot him with their rifles as he toiled up the face of the hill, but with a last burst of speed Paint mounted it on the jump and Curly stepped down, untouched.

"Good boy!" He laughed, patting Paint on the neck. Then, swinging up, he took a last look over the rim before he left the Heel Flies behind. They were gathered in an angry group, about half a mile away, and Curly whooped as he waved his hat. But when he had disappeared a single horseman started after him—a small man on a big, rangy gray.

On the tableland above, Curly rode down the long slope until once more he cut the road, but the man who pursued him turned off down the valley, for he knew every short cut and trail. He rode hard, flogging his horse, his red eyes gleaming vengefully, and far below, where the wagon road swung back toward the river, he dropped off and ran up a gulch. Dwarfed mesquites and patches of bear grass gave him shelter as he sped until at last, on the edge of the prairie, he dropped down behind a yucca and thrust his gun out, panting.

Curly rode on blithely, glancing warily behind him, sparing his mounts for another long run, but no bobbing heads appeared on the long trail behind and he jogged as he came out on the plain. He was humming a little song when something slashed across his back with a sting-like cut of a whip. The next instant, faintly, there came a distant pop, and Paint flinched and threw up his head. Curly swung down along his neck, working his spurs at every jump as the Appaloosa scampered off across the plain. But when, far out in the open, he straightened up and looked back not a living thing was in sight.

"What was that?" he complained, feeling absently of his back. His hand came away red with blood. His shirt was stuck fast, there was a raw place above his belt, and as he felt again, he found a groove across his back whose edges burned like salt. Then far, far behind on the edge of the open ground he saw a man rise up to watch him—a little man with a big black hat.

"By grab," Curly declared. "It's Tuffy Malone." And for a long time he eyed him intently. "All right," he said at last as the black hat bobbed away, "there's a hereafter coming for you, Mister Malone. Come on, boys . . . he's going for his horse."

Curly rode off briskly, to give the lie to any suspicion that the bullet might have found its mark. But along toward sundown a feeling of faintness came over him, and a great thirst clutched at his throat. Yet the river was far away, and out on those arid plains even the Bonito had sunk underground. He jumped his horse into a gallop, the quicker to cover the miles, but, as he looked back over his shoulder, he saw a tall, gray horse top the long roll behind him on the run. Tuffy Malone was hot on his trail.

"Hit the road, boy," implored Curly, grabbing the horn with both hands. Down over hill and swale Paint carried him at a gallop, though his breath came in short, laboring gasps. At last the sun sank slowly and on the edge of the broad valley Curly turned off at a venture from the trail. Night had come in time, covering his agony like a shroud, giving him surcease till he could win to the ranch. But the thought of that gray horse, riding so hard on his trail, drove him on and on through the dark.

He was weak now; he could not shoot. He could not even change horses, though Tige was stumbling from weariness. They seemed like ghostly shadows beneath the pale new moon that hung like a sickle in the west. Yet on and on they plodded until suddenly the moon blinked out and he felt himself sliding to the ground. He woke for a moment to find his horses standing over him, but their hot breaths seemed to scorch his cheeks.

"Get away from me," he cursed, and struck out at them blindly, then fell back, sobbing for a drink.

"Get away!" he cried again as he roused up from his delirium to find a soft nose against his face. "Get away! All I want is a drink!"

Paint whickered and nudged him gently, and, on fire with thirst, Curly rose and climbed up on his back.

"Take me in!" he ordered. "Back to the ranch, old boy." And Paint headed east across the flats.

Curly heard the hoofs pound as Tige followed along behind them. Then through a long eternity of waiting he felt the jar of every step, and the blood running afresh from his wound. He reached weakly for Paint's mane and laid hold of it with both hands, for he felt himself tottering toward a fall. Then, from the darkness ahead, a gray horse emerged and Curly reached for his gun. Somehow in the night his enemy had found him, the boy he had laughed to scorn. But as he let go the mane, Paint snorted and flew back and Curly lurched headlong to the ground.

As if from a great distance he heard high, tremulous laughter. Then with a last defiant curse he sprawled on his face and lay still.

CHAPTER TEN

There was a noise like the song of a waterfall in his ears as Curly came back to earth, and a fragrance, honey sweet, in his nostrils, but when he opened his eyes the night had gone and he saw an old man bending over him. With his long, white beard and blue, visionary eyes he seemed like a picture of Moses or one of the prophets—or the angels who carry men's souls to the sky. And leaning forward he muttered with a fixed, seraphic smile words that Curly could not understand. They sounded like poetry, yet of meaning there was none, and Curly blinked and shut his eyes.

"Have a drink of this metheglin, the nectar of the gods," the lilting voice said in his ear. "Distilled from a thousand flowers by the alchemy of the bees, to lighten the heart of man."

"Huh?" Curly grunted, and one strong hand raised him up while the other pressed a cup to his lips. Curly tasted, and drank deeply of the nectar of the gods. It was sweet, with the bouquet of old wine.

"Have another," invited the old man as Curly sighed and sank back, and then from behind there came a voice that Curly knew, yet somehow could not place.

"No, Father," it said, "Mister Wells has had enough."

Curly glanced up quickly. It was Melissa McCoy, whose pet horse he had stolen, but now her eyes were kind. In the early light of dawn her yellow hair was like an aureole, she looked down on him with a proud, possessive smile, and as Curly stirred feebly on his couch of soft buffalo robes, she pushed him firmly back.

"You're all right, now," she soothed. "I found you and brought you in. But you mustn't twist around and hurt your back."

Curly twisted, experimentally, and like a flash it came back to him—the burning agony of that long, endless night. He remembered Tuffy Malone, rising up to gaze after him like a man who has wounded a deer—and the sting of that bullet slash behind. Then the flight through the darkness, his half-crazed seeking for water, the gray horse looming up in his path.

"Where's Tuffy?" he asked at last.

"Tuffy?" she repeated, and her innocent, angel eyes suddenly narrowed to an angry malevolence. "Did he shoot you?" she demanded. "Well, I might have known it. But he isn't here . . . he's gone."

"Where to?" he inquired steadfastly.

"Never mind," she said. "He's back in the mountains. The Heel Flies have quit Mister Johnson."

"Yes," he persisted, "but wasn't that him that rode in on me, out on the flats? I was expecting a bullet, when I landed on my head. . . ."

"That was me," she said. "Now don't talk such foolishness. I found you, and I brought you in."

"Much obliged," Curly said. "But seeing that gray horse. . . ."

"That was Croppy," she returned with asperity.

"Oh, sure, sure," he said. "Tuffy was riding a gray, too. But say, how'd you come to find me?"

"I am a seer," spoke up the old man. "I can look out through the night and all is as clear as day. My daughter was disturbed when the Mexican returned, bringing the horses but leaving you behind. She was afraid that the Heel Flies would kill you.

So as darkness came on, I gazed out o'er the plain, and there in a vision I saw a piebald horse with a bloody hand stamped on his hip. And before him I saw a man, leaning forward in his saddle, sorely wounded and covered with blood."

"So I went out after you," Melissa broke in impatiently. "And we found you and brought you home."

"Good, good," responded Curly. "Many thanks to you both. That bullet wound was just a scratch, but I was sure perishing for water, and Tuffy Malone was after me. How about another drink of that. . . ."

"Metheglin," supplied Honey McCoy, "the mead of the ancients. Honey and water, fermented and flavored. Here it is, a drink for the gods." And as he poured out a brimming cupful, he rattled off a line of gibberish that Curly knew was intended for poetry.

"He just talks that way," Melissa explained hastily, and Curly nodded as he quaffed off the mead.

"I talk as the poets and philosophers talk," declaimed Honey, throwing out his chest. "It is mine to know the thoughts of the greatest and best of men. Every word is a jewel, every line a string of pearls, every poem a thing perfect in itself. I am a man who fears nothing, and for that the Indians loved me when all other whites they killed. Except for fear there would be no death, no suffering . . .

> *"My good blade carves the casques of men,*
> *My tough lance thrusteth sure,*
> *My strength is as the strength of ten,*
> *Because my heart is pure."*

He rattled the lines off rapidly, and Curly smiled absently, for his eyes were beginning to stray.

"Say," he said as the distant song of the waterfall suddenly resolved itself into a hum, "what's that you've got on your wagon?"

"Bees! Bees!" Honey exclaimed rapturously. "Those are my bee gums, rich with sweets.

> *"He is not worthy of the honeycomb,*
> *Who shuns the hives because the bees have stings."*

"They won't hurt you," soothed Melissa, stooping down with a laugh to shoo a bold visitor from his bed. "We keep them on the trail wagon so we can haul them from place to place. Just be quiet . . . he smells the metheglin."

Curly ducked as a worker zoomed around his head, and the old man held out his hands.

"Have no fear," he exhorted. "The bees are our friends. But the man who turns and runs brings mischief upon himself, for they have soldiers, like ourselves.

> *"They have a queen and officers of sorts,*
> *Where some, like magistrates, correct the home.*
> *Others, like soldiers, armed in their stings,*
> *Make boot upon the summer's velvet buds.*
> *The sad-eyed justice, with his surly hum,*
> *Delivers o'er to executors pale*
> *The lazy, yawning drone."*

"Can't you move 'em away from me?" Curly demanded anxiously. "Because the first one that takes after me, I'm going to make a break, and run my fool self to death."

"Then I'll wash your face," volunteered Melissa promptly, "and maybe they'll leave you alone. But it seems strange," she added maliciously, "that a big man like you should be afraid."

"That's all right," answered Curly. "You can laugh all you want to, but there's two things I just can't stand. One is a June bug down my neck and the other is a stinging bee."

"Now you hold still," she commanded, scrubbing his face off like a boy's. "I'm here, and I'll take care of you. But if you want to," she offered, "we'll move you over to the Moore house. Only it's so nice and cool, here, out under the trees."

"Yes, it is," he agreed as her soft hand brushed his cheeks. "Won't they sting me if I hold right still?"

"No," she replied. "Look at Father over there . . . he can scoop them up in his hands."

Curly turned a startled glance to where Honey McCoy was inspecting the nearest swarm. He was smiling benignly, while his lips, as he worked, emitted a buzzing hum.

"That's his bee song," she whispered. "He hums to them when he works and so the bees never sting him. It's because he's not afraid."

"It beats me," Curly declared, after watching him a minute. "He can take the top right off and lift out the comb . . . have to get him to learn me that song."

"Oh, I'll teach you," promised Melissa. "That is, if you'll ever forgive me for scolding you like I did. But I was so mad at Tuffy Malone. . . ."

"Say, you forgive *me*," Curly broke in huskily. "Mighty sorry I talked like I did."

"Well, all right," she agreed after a moment of pensive silence. "Only . . . well, all right, I'll forgive you. Now listen . . . you make a noise like this."

She pursed her lips and a sound like a droning bee made Curly start back nervously.

"No, now listen," reproved Melissa, a sober twinkle in her eyes. "You mustn't jump like that. If you do, the bee will sting you. You must think kind, loving thoughts and move about gently, and kind of hum, like the noise of that hive."

She pointed toward a section of a hollow sycamore tree,

which served Honey McCoy for his hives, and, as Curly listened, he heard the low, singing hum to which the workers attuned their industry.

"You see," she explained, "they've got different kinds of hums . . . one when they are angry, and another when they are loaded, and another when they are flying afield. But the honey makers in the hive, when they are busy about their work, make a sound that's kind of peaceful . . . like this."

She pursed her lips again and Curly watched her admiringly, and now for the first time she seemed more like a woman and less like a mischievous child. The blue eyes turned soft and wistful, her smile was brooding and kind, and as she hummed the vibrant note her gaze was far away as if she were a bee, honey-bound.

"You ought to be a bee yourself," he suggested, and she nodded with a little sigh.

"Sometimes I wish I were," she confessed, "so I could fly away from it all."

"What you want to fly away for?" he asked. "Hasn't your old man been treating you right?"

"He spoils me." She dimpled. "But it's these Heel Flies, and Tuffy Malone. They steal our horses and everything."

"Say, you keep me here a while," Curly spoke up impulsively, "until my back gets well again. I'll take care of you . . . Melissa."

He spoke her name for the first time, caressingly, and she blushed as she met his eyes.

"Well . . . all right," she agreed. "Are you well enough to eat?"

Suddenly Curly Wells was all smiles. "You try me," he chortled. "How about a big steak . . . rare? The fact is, I haven't had a time to eat lately."

"I'll run over to the house and get one from Aunt Julia," she answered, darting off.

As Curly watched her flight down the path beneath the trees, his eyes lit up admiringly. "Like a deer," he commented. "Don't she throw them feet pretty? Reminds me of Paint . . . or Tige. Hey, Mister McCoy," he called, "what did you do with my horses? Put 'em up in the colonel's corral?"

"Yes, indeed." Honey beamed, looking up from his bee work. "And that Mexican kissed his thumb and swore that. . . ."

"Yeah . . . I know *him*," Curly responded grimly. "Well, if they're stole, I'll declare war on Mexico."

He waited expectantly, and, when Melissa came flying back, the question could not wait.

"Did you see my two horses?" he asked.

"You bet," she answered lightly. "Right there in the corral, and Porfilio throwing down hay. Now for a thick steak . . . rare . . . like mother used to cook, eh?" And she winked as she stirred up the fire.

It was made of mesquite roots, dug up in the hills, and soon the big steak began to sputter over a bed of coals while Melissa mixed bread. Curly was watching the meat expectantly when from the wagon cover above him a long, gray head was thrust out. A half-grown, tiger-striped cat emerged swiftly from its hiding place, its amber eyes fixed on the steak. Before Curly could shout, it had darted to the frying pan and reached out a long, hooked paw.

"Look out!" Curly warned as he beheld his precious steak snatched halfway out of the pan.

Melissa sprang to the rescue. "Why, kitty!" she scolded, slapping him violently away. "Don't you know any better than to steal?"

The cat glared at her indignantly, then, with its back up and legs spread, he advanced sideways and leaped at her hand.

"Why . . . Caesar!" she cried, slapping him back again, harder, while she pushed the steak into the pan. But with a hiss of defiance the cat landed and came back at her, all set to leap once more.

"Well, I'll declare!" Curly exclaimed with sudden admiration. "That's the outfightingest cat I ever saw. Here, kitty . . . let's see how he'll fight." And he advanced a clutching hand, menacingly.

The cat eyed him warily, lashing his tail and strutting stiffly. Then with a playful spit he hurled himself forward and stood crouched while he smelled the strange hand.

"By grab, he's going to like me," Curly said in an ecstasy as the kitten rubbed its head against his fingers. "Say, gimme a piece of meat off the end of that steak. He's a first-class fighting cat, eh?" He glanced up at Honey McCoy, who was beaming from a distance, and then at the smiling Melissa.

"That's the way we train him," she said. "He isn't afraid of anything."

"Not afraid of a mountain lion," boasted Honey, coming over while Curly fed the cat. "I take my bees up near Lincoln when the honeydew is in flow, although it doesn't make the best of comb, and while we were camped there, a lion came down to where Caesar was playing in the road. Well, will you believe it, he never gave an inch. Just arched up his back and stood there, nose to nose. The lion saw me, and went away."

"Regular bearcat, eh?" Curly laughed, and Honey stroked its rough back admiringly.

"We don't feed him much meat," he explained, "because I want him to get out and hunt. But we've taught him from the first to be brave and never weaken. The greatest curse in the world is fear. And what said Julius Caesar, after whom our cat is named?

> *"Cowards die many times before their deaths,*
> *The valiant never taste of death but once.*
> *Of all the wonders that I yet have heard,*

It seems to me most strange that men should fear,
Seeing that death, a necessary end,
Will come when it will come."

"Say, that's good poetry," Curly declared approvingly. "Where do you get all these poems . . . make 'em up?"

"I get them from this book," Honey responded pompously, reaching up into the jockey box of his wagon. "There's a book, Mister Wells, that contains the wisdom of the ages . . . the greatest thoughts of all men and all time. Look it over sometime when you're not otherwise occupied and you will find yourself amply repaid."

He laid the volume reverently in Curly's reluctant hands and stepped back to watch the effect, but the odor of fried steak assailed Curly's nostrils and he laid the *Familiar Quotations* down.

"Yeah, much obliged," he said. "I'll sure do it, sometime. But Jack Moore told me, whatever I did, never to keep a woman waiting with meals. . . ."

"Well, here it is, then." Melissa laughed, putting the steak on a broad platter.

Curly sat up painfully in bed. "If I've got to die," he observed, "I'll die happy . . . eating this steak. Only ate once yesterday . . . breakfast."

"Have a little more metheglin," invited Honey solicitously. "It'll help you to make new blood."

"All right," Curly agreed. "And about a quart of coffee. Say, there's Jack Moore coming . . . hear him cuss?" He glanced over his shoulder and began to wolf down the beef as if he feared he would be deprived of his feast, and the colonel stopped short when he saw him.

"Well!" he exclaimed at last. "I heard you'd been shot. Don't look very sick, to me."

"Nope, nope." Curly grinned. "Still able to sit up and take nourishment. But I did get a bullet burn yesterday."

"Did that thieving whelp, Mike Broiles, dare to attack you?" Moore asked. "After I'd sent him the letter and everything?"

"He sure did," stated Curly. "But them fellers never done this . . . just shot out the front of my hat. It was Tuffy Malone that winged me."

"Why damnation!" exploded the colonel. "Did they attempt your life twice, after I'd served notice that you were my friend?"

"Looks that way," admitted Curly. "And then the sheriff, up in Lincoln, took after me with Mike Broiles and a posse."

"The sheriff?" echoed Moore, throwing his hands up in despair. "So he's standing in with that bunch."

"Well . . . maybe," Curly confided. "But I might as well tell you, I had to kill one of Mike Broiles's assassins. They laid for me at Rustlers' Pass and so I. . . ."

"Well, since when," demanded the colonel, "has that been a crime? Can't a citizen protect his own life? But Ed O'Keefe was a professional gambler, and a man like that will naturally throw in with his element."

"He looked me over mighty hard," Curly went on, "when I stopped at the store to buy a hat. And a big bunch of cowboys all gathered around Paint and claimed he was Tuffy's horse. That showed me, right away, which way the wind would blow if O'Keefe ever heard about that killing, so I drifted out of town in a hurry. But I ran into Tuffy at San Marcial."

"This is organized murder," Moore declared in a fury. "And I see right now I've held my hand too long. But Mike Broiles will pay for this, yet."

"Yes, and Tuffy Malone," added Curly. "As soon as I get back my strength."

"No . . . nothing rash, now," warned the colonel. "You've had your life attempted twice. And I've been thinking, Mister Wells, I could use a man like you . . . for the Cattlemen's Association, you know."

"Uhn-uh," Curly grunted without looking up, and Moore stood muttering to himself.

"The Heel Flies have all quit," he stated at last. "That was the gang that you ran into yesterday. And now that they've turned wolf I look to see the fur fly, once they've gone over and thrown in with Broiles. Henry Johnson was down here yesterday, as full of complaints as a dog is of fleas, and he claimed it was all my fault. But anyhow, he's left flat, without a man around the ranch . . . except that sly devil, Handsome Harry. He stayed for reasons of his own, and now Henry is out looking for me."

"Uhn-uh," Curly responded as Moore waited for an answer.

Bluntly the colonel came to the point. "How'd you like to go up there, when you get well," he inquired, "and take charge of the Rafter J outfit?"

"Not me," grumbled Curly. "I won't work for no crook. Don't like that Handsome Harry, nohow."

"Well, neither do I," admitted Moore. "But Henry has shown his good faith. . . ."

"Don't you believe it," Curly broke in cynically. "He didn't fire 'em . . . those Heel Flies quit him. And why the devil didn't he fire Handsome Harry?"

"You're asking a good question," the colonel observed gloomily. "But I can't stop to explain that now. We'd pay you well, Mister Wells . . . you'd draw two salaries at once. Better think that matter over a few days."

"Nope," answered Curly. "I've got business of my own." And he winced as he moved his back.

"Oh." Moore nodded. And without any more words he turned and strode back to the house.

CHAPTER ELEVEN

Whatever the important business was that kept Curly from accepting a job, it was not of such a nature as to demand any haste in his departure from Honey McCoy's camp. The wound across his back healed with magical quickness, thanks perhaps to the metheglin that the old man provided—or perhaps to Melissa's beefsteaks. There was something, in one or the other, that helped make new red blood, but he lingered, and Melissa made much of him.

"You are always in a hurry," she spoke up chidingly, when he mentioned a certain duty that called. "Didn't Uncle Jack ask you to wait around a while? And we're not going now . . . are we, Father?"

"Not until the alfalfa comes into flower," Honey returned, glancing across at the broad, irrigated fields. "There's more nectar in a crop of clover than in all the flowers of Lincoln . . . and it makes the purest honey. We'll take off fifteen pounds a day from every stand we own when the nectar flow begins. And the soldiers up at the fort will buy every pound of it. They don't get such delicacies very often.

"I remember," he went on, stretching out in the shade of the trees, "when we took the first load to Fort Sumner. Melissa's mother was with us then . . . before she passed on to heaven, leaving me and my honey child alone . . . and the Indians were on the warpath. Not a trail herd came through, but the Comanches attacked it, or the Apaches ran off their stock, but the good Lord watched over us and protected us from all harm, and Hannah was never afraid. So we drove across the desert to Devil's River and the Llano Estacado, and there I cut down bee trees and filled up all our cans, and gathered pecan nuts in the fall. The Indians never harmed us, because they knew we were friendly, and I gave them presents of honey. Melissa, precious child, was only a baby then . . . and how they did admire her yellow hair."

He sighed and Melissa looked up proudly, shaking out her curly locks.

"They used to pick me up and pass me about," she said, "those great, big, black Comanches. But Father was never afraid. They always gave me back . . . and they gave us lots of presents, too. That's where we got all these robes." She pointed to the piles of beautifully tanned buffalo skins that served for both lounging place and bed, but Honey had just begun his story.

"Well, we drove into Fort Sumner the night before pay day," he went on, with his visionary smile, "and those soldiers and teamsters went wild. I got fifty cents a pound for all the honey I had and they paid me twenty-five for the pecans. But when I wanted to go back and gather some more, they begged me on my life not to start. The Mescalero Apaches had quit the reservation, on their way for a big raid into Mexico. But I went right down among them. They saw I was not afraid and so they made friends with me . . . and many are my friends to this day. Of course, I always gave them presents . . . and an Indian does love honey. But if I had shown fear, those Apaches would have caught me and perhaps chained me to a wagon wheel and roasted me. That is why I say that fear is our greatest curse. 'That last infirmity of noble minds.' And yet . . . 'True nobility is exempt from fears.' "

He arose and threw out his hand dramatically and Melissa stirred impatiently.

> *"There is no death! The stars go down*
> *To rise upon some other shore.*
> *And bright in heaven's jeweled crown*
> *They shine forevermore."*

"Mighty pretty," Curly praised, reaching threateningly at the cat, and, as Julius Caesar hurled himself valiantly at his hand, the old man's eloquence was checked.

"Bravest cat I ever saw," Curly laughed, trying to hold Caesar flat on his back, and with a chorus of angry spits the kitten writhed and clawed, taking pains not to scratch too hard.

"Kitty'll be lonely when you go," Melissa ventured at last as the old man went back to his bees. "Why don't you stay and help Uncle Jack?"

"He doesn't need any help," Curly answered promptly. "His fighting days are past. Let him cuss the air blue and paw the ground like a bull. About the time he straps on his gun the general manager will veto his plans."

"Well, she doesn't want him to get killed," Melissa defended indignantly. "But I'll give you to understand Uncle Jack was a Texas Ranger and he's killed lots of men. Just lots of them!"

"Yeah, but the boys all know he's got a corral boss now. He'll never take the warpath again."

"He will, too," declared Melissa. "And bet you, they know it. The first time those Heel Flies touch Uncle Jack's cattle, Aunt Julia has told him he can go."

"Maybe so." Curly grinned. "But don't you reckon, when the time comes, it'll turn out he said something that'll kinda apply to such a case?"

"Now you shut up," warned Melissa. "And don't you dare to make fun of them. Because . . . oh, it was so romantic. Aunt Julia was just a girl when the Apaches carried her off . . . and you know how they treat their prisoners. But Uncle Jack took after them and saved her life. So when she grew up they were married."

"By Joe, I wish somebody would pack *you* off," Curly jested. And as their eyes met, she blushed rosy red.

"Maybe they will," she said. "You know, Tuffy Malone. . . ."

"I've heard about it." He nodded gravely.

"And Uncle Jack is afraid, now he's gone off with the Heel Flies. . . ."

"He'll be back, eh?" finished Curly. "Well, now listen, Melissa . . . you just pass the word on to him. Any time he bothers you, he can count me in, too. I could kill him with the greatest pleasure in life. In fact, I've been hoping he'd show up here some night. But I hear he's away down south."

"Yes, and I heard," she added, "that he's stealing Rafter J cattle and taking them over to Broiles."

"Nope . . . he's stealing for himself," Curly opined. "I'm kinda looking for him to come back for Paint."

"For Paint?" she echoed, flaring up. "Well, I must say you're complimentary. I thought all the time you were staying to protect me. . . ."

"Well, I was," he defended stoutly. But as he met her accusing eyes, he looked away with a guilty smile, and Melissa sprang up angrily.

"I might as well tell you, Mister Wells," she said, "I am perfectly able to take care of myself." And she reached inside the wagon for her shotgun.

"By grab, yes," he agreed, backing away from it. "Say, just turn that muzzle the other way. The first time I saw it, it looked like a cannon, or two mining tunnels in the side of a mountain."

"Yes, and I suppose," she said, "I looked ten feet high and . . . and I suppose I screamed like an eagle." Her voice broke at the memory of those once-forgiven words and there were tears of anger in her eyes. "You can go," she said. "And I'm sorry," she added, "I've kept you away from Paint."

"Oh, that's all right," he answered, looking around for his hat. "I don't know what this is all about, but I know how to take a hint. So you can put up that shotgun," he ended. And, snatching up his hat, he was gone.

There was a silence then as she stood gazing after him, but Curly did not look back. A strange anger had come over him, clutching chokingly at his throat, making the world spin and soar before his eyes. But at sight of Paint and Tige looking over the gate the madness that had held him passed.

"On our way, boys," he said, "before she fills me full of buckshot. Back to War Bonnet, where the girls don't pack guns. To hell with this country . . . even the women are on the fight." And he grabbed down his saddle off the rack.

CHAPTER TWELVE

Curly rode off up the trail, talking brokenly to himself, and the more his mind dwelt on Melissa and her shotgun, the more his mad rage grew.

"What . . . in . . . hell?" he complained. "Can't a man open his mouth without getting a gun shoved down it? Can't I pull a little joke about the bore of that shotgun without looking down the muzzle again? And to think," he added bitterly, "a pretty girl like her, and jealous of a horse."

He threw the spurs into Paint and went north at a gallop, but as they came to the spring where he had first met Melissa, he sighed and shook his head. Here for the love of a pony she had threatened to take his life. And yet when he showed a decent solicitude for Paint she had told him that he could go. He gazed back, scowling, while Paint drank through his bridle bit, and at last from the Moore Ranch he saw a horseman riding after him, hitting the trail at a hard, pounding gallop.

"Now what?" he grumbled. "That ain't Jack Moore, I know. This is one hell of a country . . . a man can't go anywhere without either getting ambushed or chased. And poor old Jack, making faces at them renegades when he knows he can't lift a hand. Well, I'll wait . . . he sure has treated me fine."

He slumped down in the saddle and watched the dashing horseman racing along his trail, and something in the pose seemed vaguely familiar. He was a big man, with an old ragged coat.

"It's Hard Winter Johnson," Curly said with a grunt, then sat back and waited in silence.

Johnson rode up, flying like an animated scarecrow, his coat-tails flapping, his trousers half to his knees, his old brogan shoes in iron stirrups. Yet something in the way he sat his big horse wrote him down as an old-time cowman.

"Hey, young man," he called, "that's no way to ride when you might have some danged good company! I'm going to the Crossing and you're the very man I was looking for. Jack said you'd jest hit the road."

"That's right," assented Curly, "but I'm not feeling very sociable. So if you've got anything on your chest, spit it out right now. What can I do for you, Mister Johnson?"

"Oh, shush now," soothed Hard Winter. "Jest because you had a quarrel, don't take out your spite on me. I seen your gal a while ago and she was crying already . . . heard her telling Auntie Julia all about it. I jest know she thinks the world of you and I'll bet you that, if you'd go back, she'd give you a kiss."

"Don't want no kiss," Curly answered doggedly, though his anger had suddenly left him. "When they tell me to go, I'm going . . . that's all."

"Well, in that case," went on Johnson with a placating smile, "mebbe you and me can talk business. I jest got back from my lower range and I find that Tuffy Malone and them no-'count Heel Flies have stole, easy, three thousand head of my steers. No use beating around the bush . . . I want a man like you to go after 'em and bring back them cattle."

"That's quite a large contract," Curly suggested grimly. "And especially since Mike Broiles, and the sheriff and everybody, is probably in on the deal. I got shot twice in two days when I went back into them mountains, so I don't reckon I want any more."

He reined his horse into the trail, but Hard Winter Johnson

stopped him.

"Jest wait a minute," he implored, "till Jack Moore can git here. He had to ketch up a horse. And those boys have left the mountains and took the trail to Arizona, so you don't need to worry about Mike. At the same time, all my troubles have been brought on by that scoundrel, and I aim to take it out of his hide. He done bribed and corrupted me cowboys until finally they up and left me . . . and jest when I needed 'em most. I kept 'em all winter without doing a rap of work . . . and their bar bills runs up into the thousands . . . and now, when the trail herds are due to come through, I haven't got a fighting man left. Of course Harry Vail and my horse wrangler stayed on. But Tuffy and the boys done turned ag'in' old Henry, and robbed him of three thousand fat steers."

"I knew they were renegades," observed Curly, "the minute I laid eyes on them. And I knew when they quit, they'd turn around and rob you, because that's what they always do. You're lucky to get rid of them, and my advice to you. . . ."

"Yes, but three . . . thousand . . . steers!" Hard Winter protested vehemently. "Do you know what that comes to in money? They're right over the mountains here, crossing that ninety-mile desert. Can't you ride on ahead and git some good, reliable men. . . ."

"That's the business of the officers," Curly broke in shortly. "Those Heel Flies stole my horses and I stole 'em back again. I'm satisfied, and I'm going back to Texas."

"Wait till Jack comes," Johnson insisted. "I'll pay you well, Mister Wells. You're the very man I want . . . and here comes Moore now. Are you working for the Cattlemen's Association?"

"That's my business," responded Curly. "But you can bank on this . . . I'll never take on with a cow thief."

"Well"—Hard Winter grinned—"that's pretty straight talk. But I'll have to admit it's part justified. This is a new country,

Mister Wells, and the man that don't steal is under a considerable handicap. At the same time, I can see now where these cowboys of mine are going to deal me a world of misery. They're heading for Arizona with a big herd of my steers. But that ain't the end . . . they'll be back."

"I'll bet you." Curly nodded. "And a thousand more just like 'em. You'll be plucked like a Christmas goose."

"Don't I know it?" Johnson said, breaking out into a sweat. "And there ain't an honest cowboy in the country. Since Tuffy's gang left, I've hired a passel of Mexicans, but they can't ride the horses, at all. They git busted and throwed in every direction . . . sometimes they don't git started till noon. Only hand I've got left is my old black, Beauregard Jones, and I need him to hold the horse herd."

"Well, you sure are short-handed," observed Curly. "But at the same time, Mister Johnson, while it's none of my business, I believe there's one more man you can spare."

"Who's that?" demanded Hard Winter, his eyes flashing resentfully. "You making some crack about Harry?"

"Yes, sir, I am," Curly replied steadfastly. "Because he and Tuffy Malone were *buen' amigos* when I came through here, and the chances are they're pardners yet."

"Harry Vail," pronounced Johnson, "is the soul of honor and integrity. And more than that, Mister Wells, he's got more brains in his little finger than some folks have in their head."

"All right." Curly shrugged. "It's nothing to me, Mister Johnson. We'll see what the colonel has to say."

He settled down for the short wait, meanwhile wondering at the credulity of this man who was called a cattle king. For unless all signs failed, Handsome Harry was a crook, and a dangerous crook to boot. His very intelligence, which Johnson had praised so, made him doubly dangerous to employ, and Curly recalled the rough jest of Hank Swope, about Harry and the hatful of watches. He was the type of man to hit a train robber over the head and relieve him of his stolen hoard, and, given the opportunity, he would rob his trustful boss as quickly as he would Tuffy Malone. Or, preferably, he would rob them both.

"What does he say?" Jack Moore asked as he reined in beside Johnson and glanced at the sullen cowboy.

"Won't do it," Hard Winter answered succinctly.

"Come over here," ordered the colonel, beckoning Curly out of earshot.

After a half hour of talking, he played his last card, drawing a long, official envelope from his pocket. "Mister Wells," he began, "I want to ask you a question. Were you sent over here by the Cattlemen's Association?"

"Nope," answered Curly. "Those rascals stole my horse. But before I left home a lot of my neighbors kinda deputized me to look up their horses, and such."

"I see." Moore nodded. "There's something kind of mysterious, then. Because the secretary writes that they'd sent a good man over, with orders to report to me."

"He might be the man that Tuffy killed in front of the store. I just happened to hear it mentioned."

"Very likely," the colonel agreed, squinting his eyes down shrewdly. "Now listen, my boy, you can do me a favor. We've been trying for some time to slip a man in at the Crossing to check up on Handsome Harry. Uncle Henry thinks the world of him, but, from certain things we know, he's a man that will stand considerable watching."

"He's a damned crook," Curly whispered earnestly. "I just told the old man to fire him."

"He won't do it," answered Moore. "But we've got him this far . . . he's agreed to run his outfit on the square. No more stealing . . . no more holding up trail herds. And he thinks you're an association man. Now what I want you to do is to take this job he's offered you . . . and I'll see you're well paid, by us. You just hold the outfit down and I'll write the association to drift over some good, reliable men. Because when Tuffy comes back, he'll have a gang behind him and he'll steal old Hard Winter blind."

"I told him that, too," Curly affirmed.

"He's scared up," exulted the colonel, "or he'd never consent to it. But since you rode in on Broiles and got back those horses, Uncle Henry has changed his mind. He thinks you're a pretty good man."

"To hell with him," Curly grumbled morosely.

"And there's someone else," added the colonel, "that thinks the same as he does, although, of course, she wouldn't admit it. I believe Melissa would like you to stay."

"Well, in that case"—Curly grinned—"if she'll put up that shotgun. . . ."

"That's the talk," the colonel said, reaching out to grab his hand. "All right, Henry . . . you've hired a man."

CHAPTER THIRTEEN

It was evening at Ganado Crossing and the lonely horse wrangler had corralled his herd for the night. The times were perilous now, for no longer in front of the store gamboled the warriors of Hard Winter Johnson. Where Tuffy Malone and his rollicking fellowship had shot at tin cans for the drinks, one man stood waiting in the doorway of the bar when Curly Wells rode back. Gone forever and turned outlaw were the lanky Texas gunmen who had cut the trail herds of yore. In their place, smiling affably, stood Handsome Harry Vail, a black pipe clenched tightly between his teeth.

"Good evening, Uncle Henry," he greeted politely. "Howdy do, Mister Wells." He shook hands perfunctorily, his pale face strained and set as he sensed some new setback to his schemes, but Johnson did not beat around the bush.

"Mister Wells is our new range boss," he announced, "and he'll take his orders from me."

For a moment the black eyes of Handsome Harry dilated and he bit down hard on his pipe. Then he smiled with a mocking bow. "Fine and dandy," he said. "We sure need some cowboys." But Curly could see he was sore.

"Mister Wells," went on Hard Winter, "will hire and fire his own hands and have full charge of the work on the range. I've got to build up an outfit, Harry, or them boys will steal me blind. Have you heard about Tuffy Malone?"

"No," answered Harry, cocking his head expectantly, and

Curly watched him grimly.

"He stole three thousand steers, right off my lower range. And he's started with the herd for Arizona."

"You don't say," Harry said eagerly. "Is Mister Wells going after 'em?"

"Well, not so you'd notice it," Curly returned. "He's got all those Heel Flies with him."

"Oh, I see." Harry grinned in sudden good humor. "And you don't care, under the circumstances, to buy in on that game? I can't say, Mister Wells, that I blame you."

"Nope," responded Curly. "I'm a man of peace, Mister Vail. I'm not hired for a gunslinger but to brand and work these cattle. That's an officer's job . . . catching cow thieves."

"Well, well," Harry murmured, looking him over appraisingly while his lip curled up in a smile. "Seems to me I heard somewhere you were a stock detective, sent out here by the Panhandle cattlemen."

"Very likely," Curly answered. "You hear all kinds of things. But as long as those rounders leave our outfit alone. . . ."

"I . . . I . . . see"—Vail nodded—"and I reckon you're wise. Come in, and I'll buy you a drink."

"Don't care if I do," Curly assented cheerfully.

But Hard Winter gazed at him dourly. "Don't git started like them others, now," he warned. "I'm beginning all over again and I want to begin right. You're not hired to belly up to that bar."

"Won't you join us, Uncle Henry," Harry begged teasingly. "It's on me and not on the house. You've had a hard ride and you need a little snort, just to cut the alkali dust."

"Nope, nope," declined Hard Winter. "Liquor and idle living has been the ruination of my hands. They hung around the store until their bar bills ate 'em up and then they threw in with the wild bunch. But I never thought those boys would rob me like that." And he reined away with a sigh.

"Old man is feeling bad," Handsome Harry observed lightly, as he led the way into the bar. "But I'll tell you, Mister Wells, I'm sure glad you've come. Kind of lonely, since the bunch is gone."

"Maybe so," acknowledged Curly, "but I can stand it a while. It's better than having a gun play."

"Hah-hah!" Vail laughed. "They sure smoked you up good. But Tuffy was only funning. He told me afterward he just did it to tease you . . . but I thought I'd warn you, anyhow."

"Much obliged." Curly nodded. "Now have one on me. And by the way, when do we eat?"

"*Poco pronto,*" responded Harry. "Soon as the beans are warmed up. What did you think of Tula, the old man's daughter? You know . . . the Mexican girl that waited on you."

"Oh . . . her," replied Curly. "Why, all right, I reckon. Didn't notice much . . . I was thinking about my horse."

"I'll tell her that," exulted Handsome Harry. "You know, with these girls, if you don't look at them every minute and tell them how pretty they are, they'll pretend to have some case with a dashing stranger. And Tula picked out you."

"Oh, she did, hey?" observed Curly. "That's mighty complimentary, but right then I had another hunch. And sure enough, when I came out, here was Tuffy with my paint horse held by the jaw."

"Ho-ho!" shouted Harry. "He just did that to plague you. No, Tuffy ain't a bad kid, at all."

"All the same," responded Curly, "I'm going to write my name on him, the next time we meet in the road. When you steal a man's horse and then shoot him from ambush, that's carrying a joke too far."

"What? Tuffy steal your horse?" Handsome Harry said innocently.

But Curly looked him straight in the eye. "You know it," he said. "And you can tell your little friend to keep plumb away from these parts. Because I'm here . . . and there ain't room for two."

"O-ho," said Harry. "So that's the way you feel. I thought you were a man of peace."

"Peace at any price," stated Curly. "I want peace so bad I'll fight for it."

"Not necessary," returned Vail. "You'll never see Tuffy around here any more."

But Curly knew better—and inside of two weeks he had twenty good men at his back.

They sprang up miraculously, as if the Staked Plains was suddenly producing warriors for his purpose. First a cowboy drifted in, and then two more. And then, dragging in across the Llano Estacado, there came fifteen hunger-bitten buffalo hunters. Always before, though the herds were thinning, they had found hordes of buffalo, drifting north as the grass grew green, but now with a finality that admitted of no doubt they had discovered their occupation gone. Never again on those broad plains would the buffalo mill and bellow, while from his stand in some gulch the hunter shot them down and the skinners came up with their teams. And meanwhile the hunters must eat.

They were men who had braved the wrath of the Comanches when their anger at the spoilers knew no bounds, and, after a short talk with Curly Wells, they hired on as warriors, well content with no work and good pay. And then in twos and threes the top hands from Texas ranches drifted in to join the fray. For a showdown was at hand with the robbers of the mountains. Mike Broiles was hiring more men. But against him Hard Winter Johnson gathered an army of trained fighters, and awaited the Heel Flies' return.

After years of lip service to the goddess with the scales, the cattle king of the Pecos was whole-souled in his devotion to the cause of honesty and justice. For sixty miles, up and down the broad river that gave him control of the range, his cattle now grazed on a thousand hills, at the mercy of the rustlers from the mountains. And at his line camp to the south every cowboy had left him to throw in with the Heel Flies and Mike Broiles. The bridle was off, and men divided into two hostile camps.

In Lincoln, in Alamosa, and White Sands there were few men indeed who did not stand with the rustlers and live on company beef. But from Texas in angry haste came riders from every outfit that had suffered from the Heel Flies' raids, and while scouts sought out news of Tuffy's return, they forgathered at Ganado Crossing. It was Johnson's beef that filled their warrior bellies, and the pay of his gunmen was staggering, but his old feud with Broiles, now bursting into flame, made the tight-fisted cattle king generous. He fed all who came, and grained their gaunted horses, and, when at last the word came that the Heel Flies were returning, he belted on a pistol and rode the line.

For years it had been his boast that, in camp or on the trail, he had never carried a gun. His voice had been for peace and in a hundred tight jams he had escaped without a scratch. But while he himself talked and laughed, there rode at his back—or at night at his command—a band of reckless cowboys whose pride it was that they never swung a rope. They were gunmen, the predecessors of the new tribe of warriors that had sprung up like a brood of dragon's teeth.

Every day, as Curly's men rode the range to keep down stealing, they found the tracks of driven-off steers. And in the warehouse at the fort, where Broiles held the beef contract, there were Rafter J hides by the score. Spies with field glasses watched Broiles's ranch from the heights of the mountains.

There was much saddling and riding to and fro. Then one evening at dusk old Porfilio came in and beckoned his new boss aside.

"You hurry op," he whispered. "There ees beeg herd . . . very beeg. And Mike Broiles has lots of cowboys driving them steers across thee desert. Santa María, I bet you they fight."

"Yes, and I bet you we fight," Curly answered. And with his cowboys he went dashing through the night.

Chapter Fourteen

After years of toil and danger while he built up his mighty holdings, years of tolerant amusement at the industry of petty thieves who stole calves while he appropriated herds, Hard Winter Johnson at last found himself in the saddle, riding to fight if necessary for his own. The time had gone by when the men who raided his cattle were content with a side of beef. Now they stole by the hundred and came back for more, and over the mountains at Alamosa, like a fat spider in his net, Mike Broiles raked in the spoils. He, too, had become a king—the king of rustlers—but now he had gone entirely too far.

Back in the Indian days, when the Apaches watched the crossings and the Comanches followed his trail herds like wolves, the easy-going cattle king had left his gun in the wagon, for he was the leader of desperate men. The danger from their pistols in some drunken affray was greater than the perils of the trail, and he had prospered where sterner men had failed. His good-natured negligence had disarmed his enemies, while all the time, behind his back, his cowboys did the work that kept his range free of competitors.

But now as he took the old rustler's trail at the head of sixty men, a much-worn six-shooter hung at Hard Winter's hip and a rifle bulged under his knee. Beneath his very eyes the king of Alamosa had grown like a monstrous sloth. By handling stolen cattle he had underbid all comers, selling his steers to the government itself. And there were those who hinted darkly at bribery and corruption in the awarding of contracts for beef. But with a laugh and a merry quip Johnson had sought out other markets, for Broiles was a quarrelsome man. But when his huge, hairy hand had reached over the mountains and snatched up this second herd, the man of peace was carrying the war to Mike Broiles—he was riding into the rustler's domain.

Dawn found the weary posse in the gap of the high trail where Curly Wells had nearly been ambushed, and with a grim tightening of the lips Curly muttered a curse—he was coming to avenge that shot. Two men on two days had attempted his life—Mike Broiles and Tuffy Malone—and now for their treachery he was bringing an answer that would not be turned lightly aside. A great herd was at stake, and the lives of many men, but to Curly there was more—his honor as a fighting man—and he rode at the head of his men. A few months had raised him from an unknown Texas cowboy to the leader of Johnson's warriors.

The lowing of the herd came faintly to their ears as they wound down the mountain trail. Far ahead, out on the desert, they saw a long line of dust, where the vanguard led the way. On that ninety-mile drive there was water at one well—near the point of the drifting White Sands—and regardless of other dangers the great herd had been strung out, lest they crowd about the water troughs and die. Now they moved on endlessly across the alkali flats, bawling their protest to the brazen desert sky.

"Turn 'em back!" Johnson, spurring, shouted down across the valley. "Every steer in that herd is mine."

Curly reined in beside him, the grim warriors trooped behind, and, regardless of the rustlers who swarmed out from the Alamosa ranch house, they raced down across the flats. The men at the drag broke and fled when they sighted them, and the flankers, one by one, whipped away, but at the point they encountered Mike Broiles himself, with twenty desperate men. They had rallied behind their leader, and, while he cursed and shouted, they sat their horses in silence.

"And what do you want?" he demanded with angry arrogance as Johnson rode up and confronted him. "Do you think, you old trail cutter, you can trim down me herd, like you do with those drovers from Texas? I've a bunch of boys behind me that will have a word to say before you perpetrate an outrage like that!"

He turned to roll his eyes on his grim-faced warriors and hearten them with a smile, but Hard Winter only laughed.

"All right, boys," he said to the daunted rustlers. "If you've got a *word* to say, spit it out right now, because I'm not going to cut your herd. Every cow brute you've got is wearing my iron. Turn 'em back, boys. I'm going to take 'em all."

"I'll stay right here, with my friend Mister Broiles," Curly announced in the sudden silence. "And the first move he makes, except to shoot off his mouth, I'll drill a hole plumb through him."

He smiled, and down the line of embattled warriors, he caught an answering grin. It was from Jim Knowles, the rustler who had met him in Broiles's pasture and helped him bring out Paint.

"Any of you gentlemen," he went on, "that have got business elsewhere, hang your gun belts on your horns and hit the trail. But this old walloper here"—and he pointed to Broiles—"is going to stay right under my guns."

"Ah, naw, Mister Wells," began the rustler king ingratiatingly, "I can see you're quite a joker yourself. But ain't this going a little far, threatening the life of a citizen and taking possession of his property? I've a bill of sale, I'll have you know, for every steer in that herd. And Henry Johnson, I warn ye, those cattle are under contract for delivery to the United States government. Turn them back if you will, but, by the gods above, I'll sue you for plenary damages. There's still justice, and if I fail in me delivery, I'll report you to the colonel commanding. A hundred thousand dollars ain't a penny too much for the loss I'm sustaining this day."

"I don't know, Curly," observed Hard Winter, cocking his head at his war captain. "He's a worse man shooting his mouth off than he would be shooting bullets." And the cowboys behind him laughed.

"Nope. He's harmless," Curly responded, shifting easily in his saddle to bring his pistol that much nearer his hand. "But I'll tell you, Mister Broiles . . . cut out them graceful gestures. Keep your hands away from that gun."

"I'll have you to know," Broiles blazed indignantly, "I don't need to resort to the gun. We've got justice in this county, and a true and loyal sheriff to see that you get your deserts. I'm a law-abiding citizen, but that old rascal there is the biggest damned cow thief in the country."

"Except you," retorted Johnson. "But, sheriff or no sheriff, I'll take every cow of mine home."

"You'll defy the sheriff?" Mike Broiles screamed accusingly. "You'll take the law into your hands? Then I warn you, Henry Johnson, the people won't stand for it. There's a hereafter coming . . . I'm telling you!"

"Yes, and there's one coming for you," warned Hard Winter, "if you don't leave my cattle alone. I've put up with you for years, rather than have any trouble, but right now I put my foot down."

He rattled his brogan in the old, iron stirrup that had graced his saddle for years, and with a last, hateful look at his ancient enemy he reined out to help turn the herd.

Behind in a long line the cattle paced steadily on, for there was no grass to tempt them to stop and at the point of a low sand hill the cowboys swung them back, turning the leaders toward Alamosa.

Nor were they loath to turn, for before them in the distance they beheld the cool mountains that they knew. There, rushing down from the peaks, were brooks of sparkling water and shade from the burning sun. They raised their heads and lowed, and soon the long herd was heading back across the flats. The swing trailed on behind, urged forward by Rafter J cowboys, and Mike Broiles with an oath gave over all pretense and rode away with his men.

"We'll hear from him," Curly predicted, "before we cross the range."

But Hard Winter only smiled. "He reminds me," he said, "of a blowed-up toad that thinks he's as big as he looks. But most of that, with him, is wind. He's like several bad men that I've met on the trail. They prefer to do their fighting with their mouth."

As the herd neared Alamosa, Curly touched Johnson on the arm and pointed to a sudden cloud of dust.

"There comes Tuffy Malone," he predicted. "But that's all right . . . you leave him to me."

"No . . . no grudge shooting," Hard Winter vetoed. "I don't want any killing. It'll just bring on a war. Here, you take my carbine and six-shooter and I'll go ahead and meet 'em. That's Tuffy . . . I know his horse."

"Your horse," corrected Curly. "Didn't he steal it when he left? Well, what's the use of monkeying? You keep on fooling around with those renegade Heel Flies, and Tuffy or someone will kill you."

"Not me," Johnson declared. "Just let me do the talking. Never seen a killer yet that I couldn't talk him out of it and I've looked down many a gun."

"You're the boss." Curly shrugged. "But I'll tell you one

thing, Mister Johnson. I'm going to be right there . . . understand?"

"Yes, but no gun plays, no gun plays," Johnson interjected,
"or you'll bring on a general killing. At the same time," he
added as the rustler band drew nearer, "it won't hurt to line up
our men."

"No, I'll bet you," agreed Curly, and, when Tuffy and the
Heel Flies rode up, he had eighty men massed behind him.

"No gun plays, boys," he said. "That's the boss' orders. I'll
tend to Tuffy Malone." And with his face grimly set he reined in
beside Johnson as they moved out to meet the outlaws. Every
Heel Fly was there, many riding the same horses that they had
stolen when they quit the store, and behind them were gathered
every rag-tag and bobtail that Broiles could muster at his ranch.
Yet, even with the corral hands, they were only a scant sixty
against over eighty Pecos warriors. But in the lead, beside
Broiles, rode Tuffy Malone, whose ready gun had killed thirteen
men. He was their champion, and they followed him proudly.

"Mister Johnson," Broiles declaimed, holding his hand up
dramatically, "I have come to demand my cattle. I've got a
straight bill of sale for every cow brute in that herd and I'll not
be deprived of my rights." He reined in his horse and rolled his
eyes left and right, where the Heel Flies had lined up behind
him. Then with a nod he rode up closer.

"If they're yours," responded Johnson, "you'll have to prove
it in the courts. I won't give up a steer."

"But I tell ye," Broiles raged, edging in on him again, "I've
got a clean bill of sale for every one of them!"

"That's all right," answered Hard Winter. "I don't doubt your
word. But if you bought those cattle, you got them from some
thief, because every brand there is mine. And as a matter of
principle I never sell a cow on my home range. So your bills of
sale are n.g."

"Oh, a thief, eh," Broiles sneered, turning his sinister eyes on Tuffy. And then with extravagant politeness he bowed and waved his hand. "Then let me introduce you to the gentleman who sold them. Mister Malone." And he drew back, leering.

"You ornery old scoundrel," Tuffy began, spurring forward regardless of danger. And with a quick turn of the wrist he snatched a pistol from under his arm and thrust it in Johnson's face. "Now!" he shouted. "Damn your black, lying heart . . . who's the cow thief, you or me?"

"Why, you are, Tuffy," Hard Winter responded good-naturedly, "but this don't call for no gun play."

"No," spoke up Curly. "And I'd like to say right now that I've got a gun here myself."

"I ain't talking to you," Tuffy flung back over his shoulder. "I'm talking to this old walloper."

The gun in his hand trembled as he thrust it out closer, but Johnson did not flinch.

"Oh, that's all right, Tuffy," he said. "I reckon you can see I'm unarmed."

"Yes, but that don't buy you nothing, with me," insisted Malone.

Something in the high, rasping pitch of his voice made Curly's hand itch for his gun. Here was a murderer, dead set for a killing.

"You're excited," Johnson soothed, gazing calmly down the gun barrel. And suddenly Tuffy's eyeballs dilated. Then slowly, at a slow pressure on the trigger, the double-action hammer drew back. "Now!" he yapped. "You order back your men. You give me back them steers or I'll kill you!"

A tense silence fell, and every man except Hard Winter sat frozen as if under some spell.

"Tuffy," he began, "you damned little rascal. You can't look me in the eye and pull that trigger. We've known each other too long."

"Oh, I can't, eh?" Tuffy sneered with deadly intentness. "I'd kill you, by grab, for a nickel. Didn't I work for you for years at forty dollars per, cutting these Texas brands out of trail herds? There ain't a straight Rafter J in that herd. Then whose cattle are they, hey? Are they yours or are they mine? Speak up now . . . I want them steers back."

"You don't git 'em," Hard Winter answered resolutely. "And if you shoot me, it's cold-blooded murder."

He eyed him calmly as the hammer moved back down, and then Tuffy lowered his gun.

"Well, you old he-goat!" he burst out insultingly, and gave way to a discordant laugh. "You old blackguard," he went on, "you think more of one cow than you do of keeping clear of hell. Put your gun up on purpose, so I wouldn't dare to shoot you. But I ain't got through with you, yet. Now you order these men away, because I'm going to take them steers, I don't give a damn what you say."

He turned and faced the warriors, and, as his eyes met Curly's, the cold, murderous look returned.

"So here you are," he said at last, and Curly nodded grimly. "On the prod, eh?" went on Tuffy. "Swelling around with two guns on. You git!" And his wicked eyes narrowed.

Curly watched him, leaning forward and waiting for the break, but the slayer of thirteen did not start. He glanced behind him, and the Heel Flies stirred anxiously.

"You get," spoke up Curly. "And be quick about it, too. You don't look bad to me."

He was calm and collected now, but poised for the draw, and, as Tuffy reined away, he smiled.

"He's going," Hard Winter whispered incredulously.

"That's right," answered Curly. "And a damned good idea.

This killing bug he's got is just a nervous habit." He added: "And I aim to break him of it," he added.

Chapter Fifteen

Tuffy Malone, the boy leader of the Heel Flies and Mike Broiles's right-hand man, had been hurled from the pinnacle of his fame. He had ridden out all set to kill Hard Winter Johnson and shoot it out if necessary with his men, and the Heel Flies had ridden behind him. But in the scratch the wily Hard Winter had outfaced and defeated him, and Curly had added to his shame. A sudden hunch, some premonition that the luck had turned against him and that death was hovering near, had turned him from his purpose. And while wranglings and recriminations divided the ranks of the rustlers, the Pecos men drove off the herd.

They were laughing and exultant, now that the man who was their leader had proven his mettle in war, but, as they drifted over the mountains and turned the cattle loose on their range, Mike Broiles came whipping after them. At his stirrup rode the sheriff, Ed O'Keefe, hastily summoned from the saloons of Lincoln. And to enforce a due respect for the law of the land he had thirty-five deputies at his back.

"Mister Johnson," O'Keefe began, fetching a paper from his pocket, "I'll have to arrest you on a charge of grand larceny. Mister Broiles here has sworn out a warrant."

"All right," Hard Winter agreed equably. "I'll swear one out for him, and, believe me, I'll make it stick. I'm a law-abiding citizen, but, when they steal a whole herd, I'll get it back first. Understand?"

"If you're addressing your remarks to me," the sheriff responded stiffly, "you'll have a chance to cool off in jail. I'm the duly elected sheriff and I'm here to enforce the law. So you'd better show a little more respect."

"Respect is one thing," retorted Johnson. "But if I'd waited for you to move, my cattle would have been in Las Cruces. Didn't I appeal to you before to get back them steers that Tuffy Malone and his cowboys stole? Didn't I swear out warrants against every one of them, before they'd crossed the Río Grande into Arizona? I saw all fourteen of 'em yesterday, right over at Alamosa. Why the devil don't you go and arrest them?"

"They're gone," the sheriff answered shortly. "Hit the trail for the Mexican line. But you come back with me and explain matters to the judge. I'm placing you under arrest."

He rode forward and laid his hand on Hard Winter's shoulder and the cattle king laughed indulgently.

"Very well, Mister O'Keefe," he said. "I'm unarmed, so you don't need to grab me. And before I get through, I'm going to prove to the world that Mike Broiles is nothing but a cow thief."

"And I'll prove," promised Broiles, "that Hard Winter Johnson is the biggest damned thief in the country. We'll leave it to the judge, and a jury of your peers. All right, Ed, you can let the hired hands go."

He waved insultingly at the band of Pecos warriors, who were lined up with Curly at their head, and Hard Winter nodded his dismissal.

"That's all, boys," he said. "You can wait for me at the Crossing. I'll prove every claim with this." He tapped a section of gutter pipe, tightly plugged at both ends, that he had carried wrapped up in his slicker, and Curly smiled as he turned away.

In that homemade receptacle the cattle king of the Pecos carried papers that he never displayed. But he had hinted to Wells that it contained powers of attorney for over a hundred and fifty

Texas brands.

Under these powers of attorney, which had been given him long before, he was authorized to seize and sell, on behalf of the owners, every cow of their brand in New Mexico. They had been given to him freely when, leaving Texas with his first trail herds, he had taken his neighbors' cattle with his own. It had been necessary, to prove title when the time came for selling. But it had hardly been contemplated that they would serve as a pretext for cutting other Texas herds.

Yet year by year, as the trail herds came through on the long drive to Arizona or Colorado, Johnson's Heel Flies had ridden out and taken by force every steer in a hundred brands. That much the Heel Flies knew—but what they did not know was that Hard Winter was justified by law. He had saved his legal papers for some emergency, such as this, concealed in that section of zinc pipe.

So he rode off confidently in the midst of his enemies—and, when he was arraigned before the judge, he proved title to every brand by an ironclad power of attorney. The case against him was dismissed, perforce, since a man cannot steal his own cows. And, then, turning grimly upon his ancient enemy, he swore out a warrant against Broiles.

Twist and squirm as he would, the crafty king of Alamosa found himself caught in the trap he had set. He had admitted the possession of the cattle, in his testimony against Hard Winter Johnson, and neither judge nor sheriff, or a jury of his partisans, could find a loophole for escape. Hurried conferences were held, a postponement was granted, and then, fresh from Santa Fe, a new lawyer was rushed in to save the fat from the fire. Spartan measures were adopted—a verdict of guilty was handed in. Then with a smirk the judge fined him $500 and Mike Broiles rose up, panting for revenge. His lawyer was smiling now as he faced Hard Winter's wrath, and on behalf of his client he filed suit for $100,000 damages.

It was night when Henry Johnson rode his foaming horse home and summoned Curly and Handsome Harry from their beds. He was excited and his eyes glowed like coals.

"They've jobbed me!" Then he cursed, forgetting his scruples against profanity. "They've jobbed me, the dirty crooks! I knowed there was something wrong when Mike Broiles pleaded guilty and they let him off with a fine. He owns every one of them . . . judge, sheriff, and jury, and the little dog under the wagon. He's greased their paws until they'll do anything he tells 'em. I ain't got a Chinaman's chance. I expect to lose the case, but, so help me, I'll never pay a cent to Mike Broiles!"

"Then they'll throw you into jail," suggested the practical Curly. "You'd better hire a lawyer that's smarter than this Sweitzer and fight the devil with fire."

"No! No lawyers!" Hard Winter raved. "There ain't an honest man in ten thousand. I'm ag'in' 'em, the danged shysters, and I'll fight this out myself. I don't want a lawyer around."

"I know a few tricks of the law myself," observed Vail, after a contemplative silence. "And you're right, Uncle Henry . . . if you ever hire a shyster, he'll grab every cent you've got. There'll be expenses and continuances and appeals to the higher courts, and, first thing you know, you'd've been better off to pay the hundred thousand and be done with it."

"I won't pay it!" yelled Hard Winter. "I won't pay a cent! What? Sue a man for taking back his own cattle? After Broiles has pleaded guilty of stealing them? That bunch has got together to rob me, right or wrong. They're after the hundred thousand dollars."

"A good lawyer," Curly predicted, "would put his finger right through that damage claim. He'd have the case thrown out of court. But if you don't get an attorney. . . ."

"I won't do it," insisted Johnson. "I won't pay a damned

cent. And I won't have a lawyer around. I'll lay in jail and rot before I'll give up a nickel. Now that's settled. There's no use talking."

"Well, let him have his own way," Handsome Harry said at last. "Because when Uncle Henry makes up his mind, you can't turn him back with a club."

"They'll grab every cow and every acre of land he's got, then," Curly returned as he rose to go. "That's the law, and Ed O'Keefe will enforce it. You're playing right into his hands."

"Let him grab," grumbled Hard Winter. "I'll find some way to beat him. It's just a plot to rob me and I'm not going to stand it. Good night, boys . . . I'll see you in the morning."

Curly went back to bed with the stunning realization that their victory had been turned to defeat. After losing in the field, and the courtroom, Broiles had found the weak joint in Johnson's armor—his unreasoning suspicion of lawyers—and he would press his advantage to the full. But in the morning, when Curly tried to point out the danger, he was met with a surly rebuff.

"That's my business," Hard Winter answered, his face bleak and set.

And as Curly went out muttering, he met Mrs. Johnson, waiting anxiously to get the news. "Nothing doing," he reported, stumping glumly away. And for him the matter was closed. But not for Handsome Harry.

He, too, had pondered long on the intricacies of this case, but with an eye on its possibilities for profit, and more and more as Esperanza sought advice he played on her ignorance and fear. When she wept, he comforted her—and once in the dusk he kissed her and hurried away. But on the morrow she was there again, a strange look on her face, a new light in her melancholy eyes, and, when no one was near, she let him kiss her again and murmur words that meant much—to her.

"Ah, my hosband," she sighed. "If he were only like you. But he will not listen when I talk. Is there no way, Harry, that we can save our property? We have worked so hard . . . me and Tula."

"There is a way," Vail answered mysteriously. "I will tell you, some other time. When men lose their reason and try to turn their wives into paupers. . . ."

"We must oppose them!" she responded fiercely.

"No . . . lead them." He nodded, with a meaning smile. "Can you trust me, Esperanza? Then listen." And he whispered in her ear.

Other days came and went, there were kisses when no one looked, secret meetings, and strange, desperate confidences. Then Johnson came riding from Lincoln with the news that he had lost. How could it be otherwise when he had not engaged a lawyer? The judgment was for $100,000.

"I won't pay a cent," Hard Winter declared grimly, and Harry and Esperanza exchanged glances.

"There is a way, Henry," his wife said at last. "I have heard how it was used before. You could transfer all your property to one that you trust, and then the lawyer would get nothing."

"Yes, but who to?" demanded Hard Winter eagerly, and suddenly her eyes lit up.

"There is Harry," she whispered, slipping her arms around his neck.

"I'll do it," Johnson decided.

And before the day was done he had signed all his property away.

Chapter Sixteen

Curly Wells was far to the south with the Rafter J wagon, branding the calves that the roundup had missed, when the news of Broiles's victory reached his ears. Adolph Sweitzer, the lawyer, pleaded his case well, showing the loss to his client in money and prestige from his failure to deliver the cattle. The government, lacking the steers that they had contracted for with Broiles, had been compelled at great loss to buy beef in the open market, thus injuring the good name of the plaintiff and closing the door to future sales.

The judge had listened gravely to Hard Winter Johnson as he delivered his impassioned denunciation, but, deciding the case on the law and the evidence, he had awarded the full damage to Broiles. One hundred thousand dollars. And all for the lack of a lawyer to present Johnson's case in legal form. Curly grunted and said nothing, for a good lawyer could beat it yet, but when a cowboy from the ranch brought the news of the property transfer, he leaped on his horse and rode hard.

A thousand times as he pounded north he cursed himself for a fool for leaving the ignorant Hard Winter to his fate. And not until, in the barroom doorway, he saw Handsome Harry watching, did he rein in his foaming steed. He was in time—the schemer had not fled.

"Where's Johnson?" he demanded as Vail came out to meet him.

Handsome Harry looked him over shrewdly. "He's around

here, somewhere," he answered indifferently. "What's the matter . . . lose some more cows?"

"By grab . . . yes," Curly stated. "We're losing 'em every night. But that ain't a patching to this lawsuit. What's the use of my saving a few steers?"

"They'll all come in handy," Harry returned jauntily, "when we get the old man straightened out. And meanwhile, Mister Wells, you can keep right on working. I'll see that your wages are paid."

"Yes, you'll play hell," Curly retorted indignantly. "I don't need the damned job or the wages, either. So if you're my new boss . . . I quit."

"Well, sorry to lose you," Handsome Harry replied suavely. And then the exultant smile suddenly left his face, for Johnson had stepped out behind him.

"Why, why . . . what you want to quit for?" he demanded of Curly, then beckoned him mysteriously inside. "Come into the office," he said. "I was just about to send for you, anyway. And don't git bowed up, jest because I picked Harry . . . I know you're jest as honest as he is."

He led the way into a darkened room, its one high window barred with steel, its door a solid panel of oak, and Curly followed like a man in a dream. So the old man thought Harry was honest—as honest as he was.

"Mister Johnson," he spoke up, "there's no use talking to me, if you think I'll take orders from Vail. I just came up to warn you to get that property back, before he skips out and leaves you flat."

"Aw, boy," Hard Winter soothed. "Don't be jealous of Harry. I need you mighty bad now, to look after my range stuff while I'm busy here with this lawsuit."

"You haven't got any range stuff," Curly answered hotly. "You made Handsome Harry a present of it. What would you think of a man that would up and blow his head off, to keep from losing his fingernail? That's just what you've done . . . you're so danged mad at Broiles you've gone plumb out of your head. What's to hinder Handsome Harry from opening up that safe and taking every dollar you've got?"

"He don't know the combination," Hard Winter returned shrewdly, and Curly laughed and scratched his jaw.

"No, I'll tell you," went on Johnson, "I wasn't born yesterday. There's no one in this world . . . except my wife, of course . . . that knows the combination of that safe. And the old Salamander has never been cracked yet . . . it's tight, or they'd've blowed it, sure." He laid his hand fondly on the huge steel safe, on the front of which was stamped in brass the figure of a salamander, symbolizing its immunity from fire.

"I see." Curly nodded. "You ain't trusting Harry too far, then."

"No farther than I have to, because I don't trust anybody," returned Hard Winter with engaging frankness. "But when that suit was decided I had to trust somebody . . . they'd get me if I just gave it to my wife."

"Yes . . . and why the hell, then," demanded Curly, "didn't you hire a lawyer, and trust him? He could break this suit. . . ."

"No lawyers," pronounced Johnson. "I'm looking right now for the sheriff and Broiles to come . . . and maybe that shyster, Adolph Sweitzer . . . and I just want you to be here and observe the expression on his face when Broiles sees he's euchred again. I've got this all planned out, down to the finest point, and Mike Broiles will never git a cent."

"He's got a judgment against you for a hundred thousand dollars. That's pretty good, for a start. And meanwhile you're tied up . . . you can neither buy nor sell . . . and Harry is holding the dough. What's to keep him from hitting the trail and hypothecating your property? I can see by his eye that's just what he's counting on. He was sure pleased when I told him I'd quit."

"Now, Curly," Johnson pleaded, "ain't I got troubles enough already without my boss gunfighter quitting me? Tuffy Malone is around here, somewhere, keeping track of all these doings, and the minute you're gone he'll hop in and steal me blind, the same as he did before."

"Nope . . . he's skipped," Curly said. "But I'll tell you what I will do. You revoke that power of attorney that you gave to Handsome Harry. . . ."

"He's a good boy, Curly," Hard Winter broke in persuasively, "and honest as the day is long. I don't know what I'd've done when them Heel Flies was here, without Harry to hold 'em down. He sure had a way with him, when they'd all git drunk at once. . . ."

"Yes, and the reason was," charged Curly, "he was hand and glove with the whole outfit. I believe he's the head of the gang. I could tell when I rode in and Tuffy Malone started to get funny with. . . ."

"He stood in with 'em, sure," conceded Johnson. "But every evening he'd come in and tell me all about it. I know him, and he's smart as a whip."

"Well . . . hell," Curly decided, "I'll stay, just to spite him."

And the next morning, while he lounged in front of the store, he saw Broiles and the sheriff coming. But no posse rode behind them—just a little man wearing glasses, who held fast to the horn as he rode.

"Here's where I git the laugh on that lawyer," Hard Winter chuckled as he came out to gloat at his foes. "But you watch Mike Broiles, and if he starts to pull a gun on me. . . ."

"I'll fix him," Curly promised agreeably. "But don't laugh till you're sure you've won."

Ed O'Keefe rode erect, for he had once been a soldier, his

long mustaches whipping in the wind. Beside him, rolling haughtily in the saddle, Mike Broiles seemed to swell with triumph.

"Good morning to you, gentlemen," he greeted unctuously. "Sure, it's a foine place you have here, Mister Johnson. But it's the order of the court that the sheriff seize and sell it, unless you pay me that hundred thousand dollars."

"Yes, indeed, it's a fine place," Hard Winter replied genially, "and I'm sorry you had your long ride for nothing. But I've deeded all my property to Mister Harry Vail." And he bowed to the smiling Harry.

"At your service, gentlemen," responded Handsome Harry. "I've been thinking for some time of entering the cattle business. So I took the occasion of this . . . er . . . slight misunderstanding . . . to buy Uncle Henry out."

"Lock, stock and barrel," Johnson continued, grinning maliciously at Mike Broiles's chagrin.

But as Broiles exploded in a series of fervid curses, the little lawyer plucked at his sleeve. He was a man so small and stooped he looked almost like a boy, perched up on the back of his horse, but the eyes behind his glasses were keen and aggressive, and his hooked nose was thrust forward like a beak.

"Are you aware, Mister Johnson," he inquired in measured tones, "that the statutes of New Mexico permit imprisonment for debt? That is the law, and Sheriff O'Keefe is here to enforce it, without fear and without favor, as is his duty. May I suggest then, since you say you have sold your place, that you take from the purchase price a sufficient sum to pay my client, and meet the judgment of the court?"

He paused and cleared his throat, and as Mike Broiles heard his words, his huge paunch began to quiver like jelly.

"Aha, my foine fellow," he said, waving a fat, hairy hand at Johnson. "So you thought you'd play me a trick, eh? You may scold about the shysters, but I notice, when you can, you try some of their hocus-pocus yourself."

He laughed heartily, and in his shadow the little lawyer peeped about, his black eyes as sharp as a bird's. But when he saw Curly, with two pistols in his belt, he drew back quickly out of sight.

"Well, gentlemen," spoke up the sheriff, "this has gone far enough. What is your answer, Mister Johnson, to the order of the court that your property be taken and sold?"

"My answer?" Hard Winter stated, rocking drunkenly on his feet as he beheld his fine plans brought to naught. And as he turned, Handsome Harry drew his eyebrows up quizzically and met his stare with a smile.

Curly Wells, looking on, read the answer in Harry's face, in case Johnson asked for his land. It was hidden behind that smile in a leer of studded insolence, but Hard Winter did not ask.

"To hell with the court!" he burst out with savage vehemence. "And to hell with you, Mike Broiles. So help me, I'll never pay a cent. You can put me in jail if you wish."

Broiles pulled down his lip and glanced inquiringly at the lawyer, then turned and nodded to the sheriff. "All right, Ed," he said.

And half an hour later Johnson rode off to Lincoln, a prisoner.

CHAPTER SEVENTEEN

Like the tramp that he looked in his old, shabby clothes and his splay-footed, cow-hide brogans, Henry Johnson, the cattle king of the Pecos, was cast into the Lincoln jail. All the town came to stare at him, like a monkey in a cage, and Mike Broiles shook with laughter, but with cold, vindictive rage Johnson repeated for the thousandth time the phrase that had become like a litany.

"You can keep me in jail till I rot, but I'll never pay Mike Broiles a cent."

Jack Moore rode up to see him and arrange a reasonable compromise, or carry it to a higher court, but, though by either way he could escape from the adobe jail, Johnson doggedly shook his head, He was deaf alike to the appeals of his friends and the loud guffaws of his enemies. It was as if some sudden madness had cast reason from its throne, leaving him sane on all subjects, save one.

Back at the store Curly Wells lingered about from day to day, not unlike a faithful dog whose master has gone—for he expected Henry Johnson to return. A day and a night in the foul Lincoln jail would soon cure him of his stubborn fit. And meanwhile, at Ganado Crossing, there was something in the air that made Curly afraid to go.

Handsome Harry regarded him dourly when he looked at him at all. Mrs. Johnson was malevolently silent. And Tula, when she grudgingly served him his breakfast, wore a fixed and frozen smile. Her blue-black eyes, at once so cold and so fraught with passion, seemed to stab him when he entered the room. And yet for the very reason that he found himself unwelcome, Curly Wells hung around the store. At times the impulse seized him to take his horses and ride home, leaving this ill-omened house to its fate, but Hard Winter had trusted him to look after his cattle—how much more so his wife and daughter.

There was something strange going on—he discovered Tula and Harry with their heads close together in a corner. And then, when he decided that they were planning to elope, he discovered Harry making love to her mother. There were quarrels late at night in which women's voices were suddenly raised and as suddenly drowned in silence, and all the time, with his wise, blasé smile, Handsome Harry strode across the scene, like the villain in a tank-town play. Only this was no make-believe, for Harry Vail took himself seriously. He was the lady-killer.

Curly gazed at him scornfully when they met face to face and his lips curled with grim, unspoken words. But Harry passed him by with a leer and a swagger, his pipe clenched jauntily between his teeth. They did not speak, for each knew what the other thought, and each had his reasons for silence. There was a fortune in the safe, where with miserly thrift Hard Winter had stored away like a pack rat every paper and every dollar that he got.

When he had ridden home from some far journey with his saddlebags full of gold, it had gone into the safe until every corner was crammed, to make room for the currency and deeds. For forty miles, along both sides of the river, he held title to the land that controlled the water of the Pecos. There were huge bundles of quitclaims, deeds for thousands of homesteads. There were mortgages on range land and cattle. And only the combination, and the presence of Curly Wells, prevented Vail from opening the safe.

The property was his—every cow and every acre—until his

power of attorney was revoked, and yet by force of habit he put up with Curly's presence, for his instinct was that of the fox. Where others fought and killed to gain what they desired, he resorted to subterfuge—to persuasion and guile. He had even learned to wait. Curly Wells strode forth restlessly a thousand times a day to look up the road for his boss, but Harry, behind the scenes, bent the women to his will and in the end Mrs. Johnson broke the spell.

"Mister Welless," she said one morning, as he stood outside the door, gazing off up the Lincoln trail. "My hosband will never return. Do not look, and look and look . . . you make me very nervous. But Henry has gone out of his head. He is craze."

"He sure is," agreed Curly, "if he thinks for a minute I'm going to hang round this *rancho* much longer."

"Then why do you stay?" she asked, and Curly glanced at her curiously. She, too, had that look of smoldering, tense agony that comes from long waiting and thinking over haunting thoughts—from loving and hating, at once. Like Tula, her blue-black eyes were bidding him be gone, but Curly had steeled his heart.

"I stay," he said, "because he told me to stay. I know about how welcome I am."

"And how welcome is that?" she inquired, smiling darkly. But Curly only shrugged his shoulders.

"You are foolish," she chided. "Tula and I are perfectly safe. It was different, I admit, when Tuffee was here. But he is gone . . . all them bad men are gone."

"Yes . . . all except Harry," Curly answered grimly, and instantly her anger was aflame.

"Shut your mouth!" she cried in Spanish. "I am tired of your dog's tricks, you yapping cur of a *Tejano*. You are trying to drive out Harry, so you can have a free field with Tula and. . . ."

"Say, you shut your own mouth," Curly replied in rattling

Mexican. "What do I care for your daughter? Have you ever seen me give her a look? The Texans are wolves . . . they do not mix with coyotes. And no one can call me a dog."

"Then I call you that!" she screamed. "Leave my house. And when my hosband comes home, I will tell him what you said . . . that the *Tejanos* do not mate with dogs. He will take his gon and shoot you."

"Yes, and serve me right, too," Curly agreed, "for trying to protect his womenfolk. You can save them Mexican cuss words for some yap that don't speak Spanish. I'm through!"

He flung his saddle on Paint and rode off south without a word. But two days later he rode back at a mad gallop, for Handsome Harry had fled. A Mexican had come spurring to beg him, for the *señora,* to come and come at once. And he had added that Tula was gone.

The sordid play was ended, the base pretense was over. As well as he knew anything, Curly knew the safe was empty—and he knew who had revealed the combination. Only Esperanza Johnson, faithless wife of the cattle king, could betray that secret to Harry.

"Damn a Mexican," he grumbled. "You can't trust none of 'em. And she called me a *Tejano* dog."

But when he reined in before the door and she beckoned him in, he spoke more kindly, for she was weeping bitterly.

"Look! Look!" she cried, wringing her hands in anguish as she showed him the open safe. "All is lost! He has taken everything!"

"That's right," agreed Curly. "Which way did they go? Or don't you want me to kill him?"

"Kill him . . . yes!" she raged. "But before you shoot the dog, give him first the brand of a traitor. Slash a knife across his face, so that all men may know him. He has betrayed me, and stolen my daughter!"

"Of course." Curly nodded. "I knew it all the time. This is going to be bad news for Uncle Henry."

"He must never know," she pleaded. "Do not tell him, Mister Welless. I am very sorry now that I sent you away, but I. . . ."

"I reckon you figured," Curly suggested, "that he'd take *you* with him."

"You have guessed it," she wept, "my terrible secret. But do not inform Henry or he will cast me off. I shall die of the shame and disgrace. And yet, how could I know? Harry was always so kind to me . . . he did not seem that kind of a man. And Henry, my hosband, he never spoke nice to me. He never introduced me to his friends. He was ashamed to have married a Mexican."

"Oh, no," defended Curly. "That's just his way. But don't talk so loud . . . your servants will hear."

"I have sent them all away and barred every door. They do not even know we are robbed. And now, if you ride hard and catch up with Harry, they will think it is all about Tula."

She glanced up at him eagerly, but Curly shrugged his shoulders. "Yes, and then I'd catch hell," he said, "for getting into a fight over a woman."

"Oh, you mean from Meleessa, the honey man's daughter? But I thought you had quarreled and parted."

"Well, I seen her last month and she kinda smiled at me," explained Curly. "So I reckon I'll turn this over to Tula's father."

"But he is shut op . . . in jail!" Esperanza shrilled, her eyes dilating. "And please do not inform him, Mister Welless."

"He'll find out, sooner or later," Curly observed philosophically. "But I'll tell him," he added, "that Harry was a burglar, and he opened the safe himself."

"What you mean?" she demanded. "Oh, you know everything . . . everything. Will you tell Henry that I betrayed his secret? Then on that day he will take my life."

"You can do your own talking," Curly answered shortly.

"Which way did Harry go?"

"He went north, toward Las Vegas," she replied reluctantly. "He took our buggy, and two fast horses."

"They're on the train, by this time," decided Curly.

And he rode hard, changing horses, to Lincoln.

That night when the jailer came to look at his prisoners, the door to the adobe still stood. But the stout iron bars had been torn from the window and Henry Johnson was gone.

CHAPTER EIGHTEEN

It was the joke of Lincoln County that their adobe jail would not hold anybody but a drunk. Once recovered from his cups the prisoner dug out or was rescued by some friend with a crowbar. The sheriff found the tracks of a pair of high-heeled boots outside Henry Johnson's cell, but both Henry and his rescuer were gone.

A long line of dust swept north like a meteor on the trail of Handsome Harry. But Curly Wells rode south, wondering deeply on the perfidy of women with blue-black eyes. There was something in the breed, and no pure-strain Texan would seek his mate in a Mexican *jacal*. Or if he did, he lived to regret it. Fair hair and blue eyes were the signs that Curly banked on, even if she did pack a gun.

There was a familiar covered wagon in the shade of Jack Moore's cottonwoods, on the edge of the irrigated hay fields, and on the trail wagon behind was a tier of sawed-off stumps, the bee gums of Honey McCoy. The old man pottered about among his stands beneath the trees, and by the wagons Curly spied the spritely Julius Caesar, leaping and running in kittenish delight.

"Oh, hell," he sighed, "she sure was like an angel, till she reached up and grabbed out that shotgun. Well, I'll stop in and tell Jack the news."

He reined in before the gate in front of the long, shady gallery where the colonel generally sat when at home, but only an old hound ambled forth to greet him, yawning and stretching as he whined his welcome.

"Well, Rowdy, old boy," Curly said, patting the dog. "How's the coyote business, huh? You been fighting them Mexican dogs again?"

Rowdy flapped his chewed ears and whined again, joyously, and then in the doorway the angel face appeared that had haunted Curly's dreams for months. Fair hair and blue eyes, fairer and bluer than ever, and even the suspicion of a smile, but one glance at his grim face, drawn by day-and-night riding, and Melissa gasped and fled.

"She's going for that gun," Curly predicted to the hound, but he tramped boldly into the house. It was his home, when he came in that way.

"Why, Curly Wells!" exclaimed Mrs. Moore, rising up from her sewing. "And Jack has been looking for you everywhere. Did you know that Tuffy Malone and the Heel Flies are back? They were seen at the lower crossing yesterday."

"Nope," Curly answered. "Where's the vision in blue that I saw just now at the door? Ain't she the prettiest little trick you ever saw? Even the honey bees like her . . . mebby because she's so sweet. . . ."

"You hush up," Mrs. Moore said reproachfully. "She ran away home, of course. Don't you ever take anything seriously?"

"Sure do." Curly grinned. "When she reached for that. . . ."

"Be still," signaled the lady, pointing anxiously at a door.

Curly opened it with ponderous directness. "Well, well," he declared, "if here ain't Melissa, the queen of the honey-making bees." And he threw open the door with a flourish. "I met a bee up in Lincoln . . . a yaller-legged feller . . . and he told me the wagon had moved back."

"Yes, we've moved down again," Melissa responded, stepping shyly into the room. "Only. . . ."

"Oh, that's all right." Curly smiled. "There's plenty of room for both of us, and I ain't going to be here long, nohow. I saw Caesar, out under the trees."

"Yes . . . he's there," she answered, and glanced up at him with scared, appealing eyes.

"Bravest cat I ever saw," praised Curly. "The old man says he stood off a mountain lion. Let's go out and see him after a while."

"I . . . I don't know whether you'd dare to come," she faltered. "After all I said . . . that day."

"Oh, that's all right." Curly nodded. "You stand up for your rights. I've looked down so many guns since you pulled that old slug-thrower, I reckon I've got back my nerve."

"You . . . you're always laughing at me," she said, looking him straight in the eye, "but I'll bet you were scared, at the time."

"Well, I was mad," Curly replied, "if that's what you mean. Came mighty nigh going back to Texas."

"Only you saw that pretty Mexican girl, up at Ganado Crossing, so you decided to stop over a while, eh?"

"Who . . . Tula?" demanded Curly, now suddenly on the defensive, and Melissa nodded mischievously.

"And then," she went on, pursing her lips to show the dimples, "Handsome Harry cut you out, and ran away with her."

"He didn't cut nothing," Curly said indignantly. "Old Hard Winter told me, when they took him off to jail, to stay there and watch that big safe. It was plumb full of money . . . and papers."

"Oh, that's all right," Melissa mimicked sweetly, "you don't need to explain, Mister Wells. Only Manuel Ortiz came down from there last week, and he said. . . ."

"He lies in his throat," Curly interrupted. "And I'll take it out of his hide if I see him. But of course if you want to believe a danged Mexican *pelado*. . . ."

"Now, Melissa," Mrs. Wells chided, "you stop making things up. Manuel said nothing of the kind. Mister Wells might go out and shoot him."

"Nope, nope," broke in Curly, rising up and bowing gallantly. "If he's a friend of Melissa's. . . ."

"He is not," she denied, and then her dimples grew until she burst into a gurgling laugh. "I thought I'd just show you," she said, "that I can lie as well as you can. But now that Tuffy has come back, I expect you to stay right here. Because you know," she ended gravely, "he might come up and try to steal . . . Paint."

"Melissa McCoy!" Mrs. Moore exclaimed reprovingly. And then she, too, burst into laughter. "Well, anyway," she said, "I guess there's no harm done. Now you children run out and pay a visit to Father McCoy . . . and, Mister Wells, we'll expect you for supper."

"I'll be back," Curly promised, but, as he romped out the door, a stern voice called his name.

It was Jack Moore on a ridden-down horse. "Come over here," he ordered. "I want to see you."

"All right," Curly answered without breaking his stride. "Be back in a minute, Mister Moore."

"This is important!" the colonel barked imperatively.

"Sure . . . and so is this," retorted Curly, helping Melissa over an imaginary ditch, but at the gate he paused reluctantly.

"Well, so long, Melissa," he said, offering his hand.

And the queen of the honey bees pouted. "Good bye, Mister Wells," she said, bowing. "I hope you won't kill Manuel."

"Come, come!" spoke up Moore impatiently.

So they shook hands and parted, with a smile.

"What's your dad-burned hurry?" Curly demanded querulously as he turned back to join the colonel. "When you see two young people, holding hands and swapping confidences. . . ."

"Say! Do you know," burst out the colonel, "that Tuffy Malone and his gang are back? They crossed a big herd down the river yesterday."

"It's all right with me," Curly said. "My boss has gone broke and skipped the country between two days. I don't care whether school keeps or not."

"But he left his cattle, didn't he?" snapped Moore. "And I reckon he left them in your care."

"Sure did," agreed Curly. "Only he didn't leave any money. And who's going to pay my men?"

"I will," the colonel answered. "Or, that is, I'll see they're paid. The wages of a cowhand are a first lien on the property, no matter who owns the herd."

"Fine and dandy," Curly retorted. "But did you ever think, Colonel, we ain't got any law in this country? It's all right to talk of liens, but that sheriff up at Lincoln wouldn't give me a dollar on a bet. So I'm on my way south to fire the whole outfit. Have to pay 'em off with horses, at that."

"Now here," Moore yapped. "Will you listen to me a minute? I don't want a single man fired. Things have been kind of quiet, but, with Tuffy Malone back, we'll need every warrior we've got. And I'd like to inform you, young man, that the Texas Cattlemen's Association is ready to back my hand."

"I . . . see." Curly nodded. "Them cattle that Tuffy crossed. . . ."

". . . were stolen in Texas . . . every one of them!"

"Well, if that's the way you put it," observed Curly, "I reckon I'm due to stay."

"You are," rapped out the colonel. "And don't you stop for anything until you take up those outlaws' trail."

"How about a little supper?" Curly inquired. "I've been riding two days and a night."

"No, you want to see that girl," replied the colonel accusingly. "But this is no boy's play."

"Well, gimme a strip of jerked beef to gnaw on when I'm riding." And Curly swung up into the saddle.

The next day, and the next month, he was on the trail of Tuffy Malone. Then he came back, driving the herd.

Slowly, with travel-worn feet and the alkali of distant deserts still crusted on their gaunted sides, the bawling Texas steers moved in to Deep Springs and spread out along the water front to drink. It was like a bovine heaven, but the cowboys lopped wearily in the saddle. Curly Wells stepped down and stripped the bridle off of Tige, who sighed deeply as he drank his fill. Then he raised his head and whinnied to Croppy, who was neighing to him from the wagons.

Curly knelt down stiffly and washed the grime from his bearded cheeks. In the shade of the cottonwoods he saw a little girl in blue, holding a tiger-striped kitten in her arms. But as he stepped up on his horse Jack Moore came riding out, to inspect the captured herd.

"Well," he said. "You've been gone quite a while. I've had a man out looking for you. Bad news."

"I got plenty myself . . . you can keep it," Curly returned, "until the boys and I make up our sleep."

"But this is urgent," insisted the colonel. "Something that's got to be attended to. A big gang of men has entered your upper range and is driving off your cattle by the thousand."

"Too bad." Curly shrugged. "But didn't you hear, Colonel, that General Lee has surrendered? The war's over now and they ain't no slaves, for you slave drivers to pop your whips over. So you and your association can wait."

"Well, get your supper first," Moore conceded. "And I'll give you a change of horses, all around. But I'm satisfied this Texas raid was nothing but a ruse, to draw you and your men out of the country."

"All right," Curly grumbled, "have it your own way, Mister Ranger. But if that was a ruse, excuse me from the real thing. I've been plumb to San Simon, Arizona. There's your steers, all right, but there's nothing much left of 'em but horns, rawhide, and backbone. You can believe it or not, but them steers beat us to the river, and only had a two days' start. They rushed 'em across the desert on a long, high trot and turned 'em loose in the Río Grande *bosques*. Then while we were chasing Tuffy, his side-kickers gathered 'em up again and shot 'em across the country to Stein's Pass. Did I hear you mention supper?"

"Supper's waiting," answered the colonel. "But there's one thing more."

"Never mind it," replied Curly. "Unless my girl has gone back on me. Ain't that Melissa, out under the trees?"

"Missus Johnson sent a man, not an hour ago. . . ."

"All right!" Curly yelled back. "Gimme a horse and I'll go up there. Plenty time for a rest when I'm dead. I take it all back about the war being over." And he spurred poor Tige into a lope.

CHAPTER NINETEEN

A big band of cowboys rode out of the south at dawn, heading in toward Ganado Crossing, and, as they sighted the store, Curly Wells spurred on ahead, to do his duty by Esperanza Johnson. She was a woman that, for some reason, he could not wholly despise, although she had betrayed her husband's secret to her lover. For in his heart he knew that old Hard Winter had neglected her and compelled her to work like a slave.

She stood waiting by the gate, a broken creature in somber black with eyes that were tragic with despair.

"Oh, Mister Welless!" she cried, running out to meet him. "Now what do you think has happened? A man came here yesterday and walked into my house, just as if it belonged to him. He said he had a mortgage, and if my hosband did not pay him, he would turn me out of my home."

"Who from?" Curly demanded. "Who gave him the mortgage? I'll bet this is Mike Broiles's work."

"May the saints protect me . . . I did not think to ask. When he came in so cheeky and looked at all my furniture, I just told him to go away."

"Where is he?" asked Curly. "I'm going up north, where there's a big bunch driving off cattle."

"I do not know," she mourned. "When I thought of my house being taken by some stranger, I almost went out of my head. I was craze . . . and then he was gone."

"Well, you're all right," Curly soothed. "I'll attend to him later. Looks to me like Mike Broiles was trying to collect, now that Hard Winter is out of the country."

"They will leave us nothing . . . nothing," she said disconsolately. "And now they are stealing our cattle. A *vaquero* rode in yesterday and said they were sweeping the range, taking every steer and cow that they found."

"We'll see about that," Curly responded grimly, and spurred out to join his men.

The whole country was at war, men were fighting and stealing everywhere—even Jack Moore was beginning to miss cattle. But never before had the rustlers entered a range and rounded it up by days' work. The tired Pecos warriors scanned the ridges as they advanced until they came out on the broad, rolling plains. There before their eyes they beheld a regular roundup, with two wagons and a big herd of horses.

"Well, well," Curly observed as he saw the wide-flung circle sweeping the prairie clean of cattle. "Right here is where we get to burn a little powder, unless all signs and omens fail."

He reined in on top of a knoll to look out over the country, and behind him, with bloodshot eyes, the desert-weary warriors sized up the opposing band. They had ridden so long on the trail of elusive cow thieves that the sight of this big outfit, calmly gathering in their cattle, almost gave them a thrill of joy. But no scouts rode to meet them; there was no bunching up of warriors. As if nothing had happened the circle of men kept their stations and Curly glanced back at his cowboys.

"Something funny here, fellers," he said. "Let's ride down and eat up the cook's grub."

They let out a yip as they fell in behind him, four abreast and sixty strong, the hardest-looking men that the Pecos country had ever seen, ready at once for a feed or a fight.

" 'Morning, Cusi!" hailed Curly as they rode up to the

wagons where the grizzled old cook eyed him sourly. "What's the chance for a little breakfast for a bunch of poor cowboys that's got lost and been traveling all night?"

"Well, I might be able to feed you . . . but keep your horses out of my camp. I won't have 'em tracking around."

"Sure, sure," agreed Curly. "And thank you kindly, uncle. What outfit are you working for, anyhow?"

"Jackson and Tuttle," announced the cook, turning back to his pots and ovens.

Curly glanced at the wagons. On the side of each was burned the familiar **JT** connected, for Jackson and Tuttle were a big firm of commission men that bought for the St. Louis stockyards.

"Where's the boss?" Curly inquired at length.

The cook pointed briefly with his butcher knife. "That's him with the white hat," he said.

Curly rode out alone. Something told him that the Rafter Js were doomed.

"Good morning." He nodded to a man by the fire, where a big battery of stamp irons was laid out. "I'm Curly Wells of the Rafter J outfit. What's your idea . . . rounding up all our stuff?"

The JT boss looked him over for a moment, then reached into the pocket of his vest. "Your outfit's sold," he answered, "to the Stockyards Bank, Saint Louis. We're gathering the cattle for the bank." He handed over an official paper.

Curly glanced at it briefly. "Happen to remember," he inquired, "the name of the seller?"

"Harry Vail," replied the foreman promptly.

"You win," Curly responded, and turned back to the wagons, where the cook was pouring out coffee.

There would be no more range riding and chasing of cow thieves. Handsome Harry had cashed in on his power of attorney—and Hard Winter's land was gone, too.

"Well, boys," he announced to the expectant cowboys, "Handsome Harry has sold the whole outfit. So here's where we make up our sleep."

"How about our pay?" inquired a warrior suspiciously. "Have we done all this riding for nothing?"

"Your wages are a lien on the cattle," Curly replied. "Jack Moore will see that you're paid."

"Then drink hearty, boys," cheered the warrior, holding up his tin cup. "This will break Tuffy Malone's little heart."

"No more Rafter Js to steal," chanted another. "What will poor old Mike Broiles do?"

"He'll start to work on Jack Moore," predicted Curly. "So don't any of you boys hurry off."

They rode back leisurely to Johnson's Store where they rested for two days and cleaned up.

And then, just at dusk, Hard Winter came in sight on the trail that led down from the north. "Howdy, boys!" he greeted cheerily as he passed the cowboys' camp. "What're you all doing here? I done lost all my cattle. Lost all my land, too . . . so I don't reckon I need you any more."

"Oh, that's all right, uncle," Curly replied for the crowd. "We're waiting to hear from Jack Moore."

"Are they stealing from him?" Hard Winter demanded eagerly, stepping down from his old crow-bait horse. "Well, Jack will need you all if he makes good his word. . . . Have you got any coffee in that pot?"

He poured out a generous cupful, sipping it off little by little as he squatted on his heels by the fire, and the cowboys gazed in awe at his old, ragged clothes and the holes in his worn-out shoes. But as if nothing had happened to mar his fortunes, the cattle king told stories and jokes. Soon he had the boys all laughing, as on many another night he had furnished the entertainment for the crowd. Not until the last of them began to nod by the fire did he rise up and look toward the house.

"Come over a minute," he beckoned to Curly, and led the way into his deserted store. The shelves were half empty now, the floor cluttered with papers and waste where the cowboys had been helping themselves, and Hard Winter heaved a sigh.

"Well, they're all robbing me now, eh?" he said. "What's the news from Tuffy Malone?"

"We gave him a little run into Arizona last week. But he'll be back . . . the pickings are good."

"I reckon so," observed Johnson. "This Jackson and Tuttle outfit seems satisfied to gather as they go."

"The boss was down yesterday trying to hire us boys to protect the lower range. But I told the ornery yap to skin his own skunks . . . he's working for a thief, and he knows it."

"Oh, no," Hard Winter defended, "Jackson and Tuttle are all right. It's Harry Vail that robbed me . . . but by grab, Curly, I couldn't ketch up with him, nowhere."

"Too smart for you." Curly nodded. "That man is a crook."

"Don't I know it?" Johnson sighed. "I'd've saved a million dollars if I'd taken your advice at the start. The low-lived whelp, I'll kill him."

"I'll save you the trouble, if he shows up here," promised Curly. "What did you find out about him, back East?"

"Well, he went to Saint Louis, and the Stockyards Bank bought the cattle for ten dollars, round. Paid him cash for thirty thousand . . . and there's thirty thousand more. But whether they'll ever git 'em is a question."

"Yes, and a big one," agreed Curly. "The rustlers are whirling into 'em. Running 'em off every day by the hundred. And Ed O'Keefe is letting 'em steal the limit while he carries on his own private feud. Seems he's fell out with his posse and they're fighting among themselves. Where did Handsome Harry go from Saint Louis?"

"Oh, back to Kentucky." Johnson shrugged. "That's where he came from, originally. I found out he'd been a train robber in the old Newton gang . . . that's how come he drifted out West. Well, he went to a big banker in Louisville and showed the papers that he'd stole from my safe. And then he gave a blanket mortgage on all the property I've got for two hundred and twenty thousand dollars. They sold it to a big investment company."

"So you're cleaned, eh?" Curly said.

Johnson nodded. "Yes, I'm cleaned," he stated. "It's going to be a long, hard winter for me. But I aim to fool 'em, yet. I'm going to homestead the quarter section on both sides of the crossing, and a homestead is exempt from foreclosure. That'll give me the store and the corrals and my house, and I'll manage to scrape a living, somehow. I can see it all now, and I made a big mistake. But Mike Broiles will never get a red cent."

"You figure you've beat him, anyhow, eh?" Curly grinned.

Hard Winter showed his teeth. "Yes, and I'll kill him," he cursed, "if he ever crosses my path. And I'll get Handsome Harry, too."

"That can wait," observed Curly. "But take a tip from me and file on this land . . . right now. Luck's running against you, uncle, so don't take no chances. Write a notice and stick it on the door."

"Oh, shore," Hard Winter protested, but at last he posted the notice and Curly went off to bed.

In the morning a sheriff's posse was riding through, with Mike Broiles at its head.

CHAPTER TWENTY

Curly Wells and his warriors were sleeping in the open, their tarp-covered beds flung down along the fence to escape the full sweep of the wind. Inside the corral their horses raised their heads, then circled in a flurry of speed. As Curly rose up, he saw a big posse of men riding boldly through their camp. Then on the vest of one of the leaders he caught the flash of a silver star—and Mike Broiles craned his head to look down.

"Well, well." He grinned exultantly as he caught sight of his archenemy in bed. But as dust-covered tarpaulins gave up men in every direction he held up his hand for peace.

"Good morning, boys!" he hailed. "Did I break up your beauty sleep? Har-har! It's only Mike Broiles and Johnny King with his deputies, on our way to the JT wagon."

"All right, then . . . keep a-going," Curly answered shortly.

But the posse had come to a halt.

"Oh, no hurry," replied Broiles. "We might even stop for breakfast if any of you gentlemen insisted. It's been a long ride, and a windy one, since we left Lincoln yesterday evening. What's the news from Henry Johnson?"

"We ain't giving out news," returned Curly. "And next time you fellers ride into my camp, you sing a little song on the way."

"Ah-ha-ha!" laughed Broiles. "We caught you napping that time. But a posse of deputy sheriffs can ride where they will. No offense, of course . . . no offense."

Curly had risen to his feet, buckling his gun belt around his waist, and all along the fence warriors were stamping on their boots and reaching for their pistols and guns. There was something vaguely sinister in this invasion of their camp, but Broiles was still holding up his hand.

"That's all right, boys," he soothed. "We ain't looking for any trouble. But say, by the great horn spoons, who the hell is this now? If it ain't Henry Johnson himself."

He threw up both hands in affected surprise as Hard Winter appeared in the doorway, but the deputies smiled grimly, reining their horses around, the better to keep him in sight.

"Yes, it's Henry Johnson," the old man answered defiantly. "And you git off my land, you dad-burned cow thief. I don't want you around . . . understand?"

"To be sure, I understand," retorted Mike Broiles fiercely. "But since when, Mister Johnson, has this become your land? Didn't you sell it to Handsome Harry Vail?"

He grinned provokingly as he mouthed out that hateful name, and Johnson came down toward him, bristling.

"Since last night," he said, "when I homesteaded the place. It's exempt now from judgment, and the mortgage to boot. And I'm ordering you off my premises."

"Well, order all you want to!" Broiles howled back in a fury. "I'll give you to understand I'm the undersheriff now, and as such I'll go where I please. And another thing, Mister Johnson, you're a fugitive from justice. You broke out of the Lincoln County jail." He pointed a quivering finger at Hard Winter's breast and swelled with avenging wrath. "I have a warrant here for you," he announced. "So keep a civil tongue in your head."

"And you keep your mouth . . . shut," Curly cut in, stepping forward and confronting Broiles. "You and your little tin badge . . . you can't arrest nobody. When a goat herder like you claims to represent the law. . . ."

"I'm a deputy sheriff!" Broiles yelled.

Curly beckoned his men up behind him. "You're a deputy nothing," he answered. "Now shut up and let Uncle Henry talk. You've dealt him enough misery, and me and the boys won't stand for it. He won't leave this ranch unless he wants to."

"Mike Broiles," quavered Hard Winter, "you've ruined me and I'll admit it. But you'll never get my house or my store. I've preëmpted this quarter section and there's the notice, on the door. As for the rest, I haven't got anything. You can go to hell with your judgment."

I'm not talking about me judgment," Broiles rapped out, shifting his ground. "You threw away your fortune, rather than pay me what you owe me, and elected to go to jail. You were legally imprisoned for debt. Now I ask you, Mister Johnson, to do one of two things . . . either pay me one dollar in acknowledgment of your debt, or go back and serve out your sentence. If you refuse to do either, I'll have martial law declared and come down and get you with soldiers."

"I won't pay you a cent," Hard Winter declared grimly. "But, damn you," he burst out, "if it will give you any satisfaction, I'll go back to jail!"

"Suit yourself," purred Broiles. "One or the other . . . I don't care which."

Hard Winter stood gazing at the ground. "I'll go with him," he said at last, turning to Curly. "This place ain't home, any more. I'll go back to jail. But, Mike Broiles, I'll get you yet. And I'll never pay you a cent."

"Very well," agreed Broiles. "And I'll remember that threat. Johnny King, you take him to Lincoln."

"Yes, and the rest of you fellers . . . get!" Curly ordered peremptorily. "Out of camp . . . we don't want you around. Any skunk that will work for Mike Broiles can cook his own grub, out in the brush."

"Very well for you, too." Broiles nodded, reining away. "I'm a man that never forgets."

"Here, too," returned Curly. "I can remember Rustlers' Pass. So you'd better hit the wind, while you're lucky." He laid one hand on the butt of his pistol, and Mike Broiles threw the spurs into his horse.

"The damned murderer!" Curly burst out as he watched Broiles's precipitate departure. "What the devil is this country coming to, when a man like that can hold down a job as deputy? Well, he's downed poor old Hard Winter and now he's riding north to throw a scare into those JT boys."

"Yes, and the next man," predicted a warrior, "will be Colonel Jack Moore. Mike is out to break 'em all."

"We'll go down and see Jack," observed Curly. "It's all right, boys, to be a man of peace . . . but look what happened to Henry."

The cowboys ate and mounted grimly, throwing their beds over the spare horses that were driven along in their wake. Then like mercenaries of old they rode south to Deep Springs to offer their services to another cattle king. When they reined in at the old camping grounds, the colonel came out to meet them, while a Mexican brought a side of beef.

"Good morning, boys," he greeted. "Just make yourselves at home." And he beckoned Curly off to one side. "Have you heard the news from Lincoln?" he asked portentously. "Well, hell has broke loose. The sheriff is killed, and the soldiers have marched down from Fort Stanton."

"Who killed him?" Curly demanded eagerly.

The colonel drew down his brows. "Tuffy Malone," he said. "Laid in wait and ambushed him, right there on the main street of Lincoln. Some grudge they had, over a killing up in the hills. And now Mike Broiles is chief deputy."

"I met the gentleman, up at the Crossing this morning," Curly observed, nodding wisely, "and I thought he was badly swelled over something. Well, the break has come, Jack. Now what are you going to do about it? Lay down, like old Hard Winter, or stand up and fight 'em? I've got the men, right here."

"I'm going to fight 'em," Jack Moore answered harshly. "But not right now, Mister Wells. They're fighting up in Lincoln . . . shooting it out from house to house . . . and already they've looted one store. Tuffy Malone and his Heel Flies have thrown in with one faction, and the rest of them have been appointed deputies mostly. It's going to be mighty unhealthy in that town for some time. Let the murdering rascals kill each other off."

"Suits me," agreed Curly. "But what about my boys, here? If we turn 'em loose now, they'll ride up and join in on it, like an Irishman at the Donnybrook fair. On the other hand, Colonel, it will cost you four dollars a day."

"I'll pay it," rapped out the colonel. "The money's nothing to me, compared to the cattle I'd lose. I'm fighting for a principle . . . and to protect my own property. But, of course, there's my promise to Julia."

"Aha." Curly grinned. "So that's what's eating on you? Well, it won't be long, Colonel, it won't be long. Mike Broiles went up this morning to pick a fight with the JTs . . . or that's the way we figure it out . . . and, after he smokes them out, he'll come down and tackle you . . . unless I'm a danged poor guesser."

"This has got to go beyond guessing," Moore declared. "What I want is some accurate information, and I know how to get it, too. Do you remember that night when Honey McCoy found you, when you were wounded out on the flats? He told you, I suppose, that he's a seer, and all that . . . the Comanches always called him See Far. But as a matter of fact he's got some fine marine glasses . . . that explains how he sees at night."

"You don't say," remarked Curly. "I wondered how he could find me. Say, that old man ain't so crazy, after all. He knows how to keep his mouth shut."

"That's it." The colonel nodded. "He's been of great service to me, both here and up at Lincoln. No, Honey isn't crazy . . . but the time has come, Curly, when I've got to get the goods on Mike Broiles. He's behind this whole business, and now he's in the saddle . . . undersheriff and in control of the government. It'll take more than hearsay to prove he's stealing my cattle. Can I trust you for a little night work?"

"With those glasses?" Curly beamed. "Getting the goods on Mike Broiles? Say, Jack, I'd work for nothing and board myself, to boot. I'll just stop at the wagon and say howdy to Melissa before. . . ."

"The man that gets this job," Moore spoke up implacably, "is going to start . . . right now."

"Well, gimme the glasses, then," Curly decided promptly, and rode off alone, to the north.

CHAPTER TWENTY-ONE

See Far had done well to conceal from savage eyes the glasses that turned night to day. For not only did they see far but they turned moonlight into daylight, and starlight into the gray of dawn. They were without a doubt the only night glasses in New Mexico, and as Curly Wells scouted around on the trail of Mike Broiles, he beheld strange things from afar.

The time had come, after years of waiting, when the king of Alamosa was king indeed, and ruler of Lincoln as well. Ed O'Keefe was dead, shot down in the street by the rifle of Tuffy Malone. But before he died, for some mysterious reason, he had made Broiles his undersheriff. Perhaps it was coincidence, but there was a sinister aspect to his sudden and immediate taking over, and now, in the saddle, Mike Broiles raked in the spoils with no one to say him nay.

With the colonel at the fort he was on terms of such intimacy that the tongue of scandal wagged madly. For both the soldiers and their wards—the Apaches—were fed exclusively on Broiles's MB beef. When Ed O'Keefe had been killed and the nonchalant Tuffy Malone had robbed his body on the street, and when Lincoln had swarmed with contending warriors and looting and arson had begun, then, opportunely, the black troopers from the fort had marched in and the Heel Flies had taken to the hills.

The circuit judge, for reasons of safety, had declined to return and hold court, and the justice of the peace was Broiles's man.

So, with him, he owned them all and there was no man to oppose him—as long as he kept to the hills. In the valley Jack Moore maintained a state of armed neutrality, while Curly Wells scouted for evidence.

In the saturnalia of cattle stealing that had followed Johnson's downfall and the sale of his brand to the bank, there was no one who doubted that Mike Broiles and his hirelings were pulling Rafter steers by the thousand. There they were, as unprotected as a herd of wild buffalo, and free to the first man who came. For who would lift a hand to protect the bankers in St. Louis that had bought the stolen stock from Harry Vail?

But to prove that Broiles's greed had led him on to take gratuitously the cattle of his neighbor, Jack Moore, that was something that called for riding—and time. Curly rode at night, watching the camp of Broiles's rustlers, watching Broiles's own camp when the king was abroad. And first he saw them combing the range for fat steers, then harrying their rivals, Jackson and Tuttle. Under a blanket order, the JT foreman was gathering every Rafter J cow. But he had not been hired to fight, nor could he match the men who swooped down on his herds at night. They dashed in like Indians, under cover of night and storm, and every cow brute that was stampeded was counted his own by the Alamosa king.

He grew greater each day, greater in wealth and cattle and power. But his greed outgrew his wealth, and at last his crafty brain evolved a scheme for the destruction of his enemies. Henry Johnson was in jail. Only two enemies were left—Jackson and Tuttle, and Colonel Moore. They were working closely together on the lower range—the JTs gathering in cattle before they were all stolen, and Jack Moore cutting their herds for Heart Crosses. Yet so far they had avoided war.

It was a cold, blustery night when Curly Wells, through his night glasses, saw Mike Broiles and some of his men round up a bunch of Heart Cross cattle and drive them into a rocky ravine. Then as the glow of a fire was reflected against the clouds, he crept down closer until, from behind a boulder, he saw them heating a big stamp iron. One by one the cows were branded and turned loose down the cañon, to return to their range on the plains. But before their work was finished another gang came in, driving a cut of Rafter J cattle.

Through his glasses Curly could see their earmarks against the firelight—but he could not read the brand that was burned on their hips with another stamp iron that they brought. Nor could he wait to see what disposition was made of this last of a thousand midnight stealings. The evidence that he sought was in his hands at last, and he galloped across the plains to Deep Springs. Jack Moore's brand had been burned, but the cattle had been turned loose to mingle with their fellows on the plains. Curly routed out his warriors, and, with the colonel at their head, they rode back at the first peep of dawn.

On the cold, wind-swept plains hardly a cow was in sight, but as the tardy sun appeared they came stringing out, to bask in its warmth while they fed. Curly spread a great dragnet of hawk-eyed cowboys, on the alert for bloody ears and fresh-burned brands, and they closed in on the rustlers' ravine. But it was the colonel himself who spied the first animal with the mark of an iron on its hip. He jumped his horse into a gallop, shaking out a hasty loop to rope the fleeing steer. When the cowboys rode up, he was standing over its body, where he had thrown it with the slack as he passed. But the freshly made mark was not the MB of Mike Broiles—it was the road brand of the hated JTs.

"Aha!" the colonel yelled, holding the steer down by the tail while he gazed at this new evidence of perfidy. "So those dad-burned JTs are out doing night work, putting hair brands on my Heart Cross steers! Spread out, boys . . . this is beginning to get interesting."

The half circle grew wider, swinging in toward the ravine where the rustlers had had their fire, and soon a dozen animals had been added to the bunch that was driven along in the rear. Beneath their long, shaggy coats the Heart Cross was almost obscured, but, burned into the hair for identification on the trail, the JT stood out, big and plain. And it was made with a company stamp iron, not seared with a red-hot running iron, after the manner of the rustlers from the hills. It was *prima facie* evidence that the cattle had been stolen, but Curly was not convinced.

Jack Moore was cursing mad, and the sight of the JT roundup only drove him to new flights of oratory. "I don't give a damn!" he shouted as Curly attempted to reason with him. "Mike Broiles ain't the only man that can brand a steer . . . and these are right here on my range. There ain't a man, by grab, on the whole Pecos River that isn't pulling and stealing from somebody. But I'm going to tell that JT foreman that this has got to stop. And if he says a damned word, I'll shoot him!"

"Leave the shooting to me," advised Curly. "You know what you promised your wife. And why would the JTs be branding your steers at night when they can't gather their own, working by day?"

"Young man," the colonel reminded, "you're working for me. I'm not taking orders from you. And when I want any advice, I'll ask for it. I'll attend to this foreman, personally."

He spurred ahead of his men, who were bringing up the herd, and Curly tagged discreetly behind. But he was hardly prepared for the whole-hearted cursing with which the JT foreman greeted his enemy. For weeks and months now, from summer till late in the fall, he had seen the Rafter J cattle disappearing day by day even while he was gathering his toll. And when herd after herd that he had saved from the rustlers was started on the long trip north, Jack Moore and his warriors had cut them, willy-nilly, letting pass only animals with straight brands.

There had been wrangling and recriminations, in which the hot-headed colonel had used the words "cow thief" several times. But now as they came together, Mr. Shannon of the JTs was mouthing that same word himself. His wrath was so apparent that it checked Moore at the start—and Shannon, too, had his cowboys behind him.

"Call *me* a thief!" he yelled. "I've got the goods on you this time. I've knowed all along you were stealing my stuff, but now I've got the proof." He waved his hand at a little cut of steers that his cowboys were hazing along, and the colonel sat back, astonished.

"Mister Shannon," he said, "I've lived here sixteen years, ever since there were white people in the country, and you're the first man to accuse me of theft."

"That's all right!" Shannon bawled. "That's just what I accuse you of. I've only been here six months, but, if there's an honest man in the country, it hasn't been my good fortune to meet him. I've taken a whole lot and kept my mouth shut about it, but now I've got the . . . proof!"

He pointed a long, gnarled finger at the freshly branded steers, and Moore passed his hand across his eyes. They were Rafter J cattle, but on the hip of every one there was a deep-burned Heart Cross—stamp branded.

"There's some mistake here," he began weakly. "Some enemy of mine has got possession of one of my stamp irons and done this out of spite."

"Yes, and naming no names, someone has been stealing from me . . . out of spite. You can talk all you want to, but I've got the goods on you, mister . . . and I say that you're a damned cow thief."

The foreman pointed an accusing finger, and with a roar of rage the colonel pointed his own.

"And I say," he returned, "that you know what you are, so there's no use of my trying to tell you. You're gathering the cattle of an old man that was robbed, and sold out at half price to some bank. He never got a dollar, and the bank that took his paper knew all along it was stolen. But you can't steal from me, Mister Shannon, not even if you did take a bunch of Rafter Js and burn 'em with my iron, out of spite."

"Eh, eh . . . ," bleated the foreman, but, as he sought for a word to smite him, Curly Wells stepped boldly between them.

"Now here," he said, "before you leap down each other's throats, I'd like to get a word in edgeways. I saw Mike Broiles, last night, branding that brockle-faced old steer . . . and there's one critter a man would know anywhere."

He pointed to a big red steer with its face plentifully sprinkled with white spots, but Shannon only glared at him balefully.

"That's what *you* say," he sneered. "But you're working for him." And he jerked his thumb insultingly at Moore.

"Sure I am," assented Curly, "or I wouldn't be out here, taking chances on stopping some bullet. But I can take you to the place where all them steers were branded. You gentlemen have been framed by Mike Broiles. I've been watching him, night and day, and I saw him bring in two herds . . . one of Rafters and one Heart Crosses. He had his branding fire going up in yon narrow cañon, and I'll bet you we can trail him to his camp."

"Now, see here, Curly," rebuked the colonel, "why didn't you tell me this before?"

"You wouldn't listen to me," Curly retorted. "Didn't want any advice. When you did you'd danged sure ask for it."

"I'll admit I was a little hasty," Moore conceded after a pause. "And, Mister Shannon, while we've had our troubles, I believe in this case we're both wrong. Let's go over and look at that fire."

"We-ell . . . ," began Shannon. Then, beckoning to his

cowboys, he headed toward the distant ravine.

When his quick eyes caught the tracks of shod horses, superimposed upon those of driven steers, his deep-seated grouch suddenly left him. He spurred up to the front and questioned Curly closely as they entered the rustlers' hold-out, and, when from the deep sand a plunging horse kicked up a stamp iron, he leaped at it with an oath.

"That's my iron!" he exclaimed. "Some danged whelp has stole it. Have you missed any of your irons, Colonel Moore?"

"Not that I know of," replied the colonel. "But I don't doubt they've got one, because both of our brands have been burned. I'm very sorry, Mister Shannon, that I spoke as I did. I hope you won't hold it against me."

"Well . . . no," Shannon returned, after swallowing his gorge. "I spoke a little hasty myself. Let's follow these horse tracks, before the wind blows 'em out, and see who's been doing this work."

"And then what?" Curly inquired as they turned their faces north. "What's the answer, if this takes us to Mike Broiles?"

"I'll kill him!" Shannon spat back vindictively.

Curly glanced at Jack Moore.

"I'll never quit his trail," the colonel stated grimly. "If he's guilty, I'll run him out of the country."

"He's guilty," answered Curly. "I saw him."

"Then we'll fight it out together," spoke up Shannon.

CHAPTER TWENTY-TWO

A small army of cowboys, brought together by converging horse trails, surged up a narrow cañon and into the heart of the rustlers' camp, where Broiles's night riders were sleeping like the dead. Jack Moore's Pecos warriors and the JT cowboys rode in on them, side-by-side, but no cow thief reached for his gun. They rose up meekly, their hands in the air, their eyes still heavy with sleep, and the colonel looked them over sternly.

"Where's Mike Broiles?" he barked.

But no one made answer, and Curly Wells stepped down from his horse.

"Here's your stamp iron, Colonel," he announced, walking over to the fire. And at this last, indisputable evidence that the branding had been phony even Jim Shannon was convinced.

"You damned rascals!" he raved as he whirled on the startled rustlers. "We've followed your tracks in and we know what you've been up to. Now where's that scoundrel, Mike Broiles?"

"He . . . he went back to Lincoln," a boy stammered at last

Shannon reined away. "All right," he challenged. "Let's go up and git him."

The colonel nodded agreement. "I just want to say a few words to these men, first," he said as he confronted the rustlers. "Now, boys, this stealing has been carried too far, and from now on it's liable to be dangerous. My advice to you is to hit the trail, north or south. Don't let me ketch you when I round up Mike's ranch or there'll be trouble."

He looked each man over carefully, to make no mistake, and an old cowhand answered for them all.

"All right, Colonel," he said. "We ain't hunting for trouble. And I can see Mike's finish, right now."

"It's him or me," stated Moore. "I'm out for his hide. So unless you want to figure on the wrong end of a killing, I'd advise you, one and all, to stay away. Don't try to spring some alibi if I ketch you back with Broiles. That's all, boys . . . and remember what I say."

He glanced at Shannon and they rode away like brothers, while their cowboys fell in behind. But that evening, when they filed into Lincoln, Mike Broiles and his satellites had fled. The word had gone before them, and rustler and deputy alike had mounted and taken to the hills. Hardly a man walked the streets that night, and in the morning Moore's warriors were gone.

The next day at noon they rode up to Broiles's ranch, only to find it silent and deserted. A distant cloud of dust across White Sands showed the trail where the rustlers had fled. Arizona lay before them, across the broad Río Grande, and Mike Broiles had led the flight. It was never his way to stand up and fight. For after each storm there always came a lull, when all that was lost could be regained.

After years of petty stealing the king of Alamosa had emerged from the ruck of his kind. He had formed alliances not only with rustlers but with other men, high in power. Army contractors, venal commanders, and officers of greater rank had shared in the profits of his thefts; until at last, swollen with pride, he had dared to lay his hand on the reins of government itself.

The men who should have prosecuted him and punished him for his crimes fell one by one under his spell. And then ruthlessly he crushed them, making them subservient to his will, until at last he had usurped their power. Not satisfied with ruling over judge and sheriff alike, he had intimidated the one and taken the place of the other, until he held the county government in his hands. He was king, and he took with regal greed. And then in a day he fell.

He had branded the forbidden cattle of the ever-watchful Jack Moore, and overnight he found himself ruined. His rustlers scattered to the winds, his deputy sheriffs cast off their stars, his retainers fled to the west. And without firing a shot, Mike Broiles hit the trail, leaving his stealings to be seized by his enemies.

"Curly," remarked the colonel as he surveyed the broad pastures, "if I'd known how easy it was, I'd've done this long ago. All it took was a little nerve . . . but of course I'd promised Julia."

"Uhn-huh," Curly assented. "What you going to do now?" And he jerked his head toward the herds of fat steers.

"I'm going to round up these cattle," declared the colonel with sudden heat, "and put the fear into those rustlers' black hearts. Here's a country without a government, and, while I've got no legal right to, I'm going to give 'em a little law. Ranger law, if you want to call it that . . . and when I get through, Lincoln County will notice a change. Send your men up to gather those cattle and push 'em down to the corrals. We'll cut out everything but straight MBs."

No trail cutter of old, not even Hard Winter Johnson, ever trimmed half as close as Colonel Jack Moore when he worked over Mike Broiles's herd. For a week, while his scouts scoured the country for signs of rustlers, the colonel raked the country from White Sands to the peaks and cut out every outside brand. There were cattle from half the western counties of Texas, and horses from Colorado and Arizona, and when the last waif and stray had been thrown into the town herd, they drifted them over the mountains to Lincoln.

Jim Shannon alone had nearly two thousand Rafter Js to

show for his little fling, and his hard face was wreathed with smiles. But little man or big was free to claim his property, and ranchers flocked in by the hundreds. On the flats below town the herd was cut and cut again, and, Mexican or Indian, no man was denied his rights if he could prove that the animal was his. It was like the millennium to many a humble homesteader, and to put the stamp of official approval upon these extra-legal acts the governor appointed Jack Moore sheriff. He was the man that New Mexico had been looking for.

Not a shot had been fired, not a rustler had been killed, but before his resolute charge every cow thief had fled—and Mike Broiles farthest of all. It was too much like a miracle to give promise of any permanence, in a county so thickly populated with outlaws, but for the moment all was enthusiasm, and the colonel set grimly forth, to carry the law into the hills.

Already the scattered Heel Flies were gathering along the border, carrying on their old traffic in steers under the leadership of Tuffy Malone. Since the murder of Ed O'Keefe he had turned badman and outlaw, riding into frontier towns and holding them for weeks while he laughed at the officers of the law. Nor was he slow to see that, in driving out Mike Broiles, Moore had gained but a semblance of victory. The cow thieves still remained, and the men who would buy from them—the butchers and government contractors. And on the plains of the Pecos, greatest temptation of all, Rafter J steers still ranged by the thousand.

Not in one year, or two, would Jim Shannon and his cowboys complete the final tally of that brand, and in the meanwhile, from Fort Sumner to the Mexican line, the cattle spread and strayed and were stolen. There was no band of gunmen to put the fear into hungry homesteaders and the butchers in the railroad towns, nor could the men be found to gather at one swoop all the cows in this empire of the plains.

Henry Johnson after all had hit upon the only way to keep his vast herds under control. He had let the branding go until, to meet some contract, he rounded up the steers by the thousand. He did not care who owned the cow so long as he got the calf—and he managed to get nearly all. Tuffy Malone and his wild riders had attended to that, but now they were stealing for themselves. And what cowboy would work long for $40 a month, when steers were worth $20 a head?

To protect his own brand Jack Moore retained in his service the pick of Curly Wells's cowboys. But Curly himself became a deputy overnight—chief deputy, in place of Mike Broiles. Forty warriors were sworn in as deputy sheriffs, although the county was almost bankrupt. For the war had just begun, and never would it cease until Tuffy Malone was killed. From the Panhandle there came fresh complaints of his wholesale depredations, and the Texas stock detectives traced their steers clear to Tombstone, the boom silver camp of Arizona. Nothing indeed had been changed—except that Mike Broiles had fled— and the colonel ground his teeth with rage.

"Curly," he complained, late at night in his office, "these rustlers are laughing at us, right now. Can't you find where Tuffy is hiding? He comes and goes as he pleases and no one will inform on him. They don't dare to, for fear of their lives."

"Nope," Curly answered. "They've all got me spotted. But I might go down to Deep Springs and borrow those glasses from Honey. Believe I will, first thing in the morning."

"Now, here," the colonel scolded. "This is no laughing matter . . . and there's no time for sparking Melissa. It's getting so, by grab, I'm afraid to pass that window for fear some rustler will shoot me."

"Here, too." Curly nodded. "Mike Broiles is back in the country . . . I heard yesterday he was over in Mesilla. Let's hang a piece of blanket over the. . . ."

"No, no!" Moore protested. "That's all right, out in some cabin. But I'm the sheriff of Lincoln County and I'd just make myself a laughingstock. What's that noise, down there in the corral?"

He leaped up and looked down into the big adobe enclosure that served as jail yard and corral for their mounts, and the next moment a bullet smashed the window above him and sent him sprawling in a shower of glass.

"Git the damned assassin!" he barked as he scrambled up. "I've expected this, all the time. You ride down the cañon . . . that shot came from the hillside. Head him off . . . I'll attend to the rest."

He ran stamping down the stairway and out into the cold night where the horses were wildly circling the corral, and the deputies came rushing from their quarters.

"Surround that hill over there, boys," he ordered, "and guard the road, both ways! Don't let a single man leave town. This is Mike Broiles's work, so look for some Mexican. What the devil is the matter, Curly? Ride!"

"I can't," Curly said. "Paint has been stole! This ain't Mike Broiles's work . . . it's Tuffy Malone's!" He ran about in a fury, then jumped a bareback horse and rode off down the road at a gallop.

CHAPTER TWENTY-THREE

There was mounting and hot riding until far into the night, and a search of the town by day, but the assassin who had fired at Moore, and the man who had stolen Paint, escaped without leaving a sign. In the corner of the corral, where he had been crowded in the darkness, Curly found old Tige and rode him hard, but after three days of useless search he came back to Lincoln—every man that he questioned was afraid.

"Lost . . . nothing!" he grumbled as he dragged into the office and sank down in a chair. "You can't lose Paint, nowhere. Every place that horse goes the people see him and remember him. But, by grab, they're afraid to talk."

"Well, what you going to do?" Jack Moore demanded impatiently. "There's other horses stole, too."

"I'm going to hunt Tuffy Malone," declared Curly. "When I find him, I'll find my horse."

"Go get him, then." The sheriff nodded encouragingly. "There's one man that's got to be caught. He's got this country buffaloed until half the people in it are scared to speak his name. And by the way, Curly, my boy, Hard Winter Johnson has been asking for you. Something important . . . or that's what he says."

"Yes, the old walloper," Curly growled. "All he does is lay in jail and think up more things for me to do. Why the devil don't you throw him out, and let him tend to his own business? I'm wore out, going to see his old woman."

"Well, he doesn't stay in jail much, except nights," observed the colonel. "The rest of the time he's over playing cards with the jailer . . . but this is something important."

"It always is important," Curly returned ungraciously. "But, all right . . . after I make up my sleep."

He yawned and stumbled out, but at the foot of the twisted stairway he found the one-time cattle king waiting for him. There was a fanatical gleam now in the shrewd blue eyes, and he beckoned Curly aside mysteriously.

"I've been looking for you, everywhere," he said. "Do you want to do something for me?"

"Why, yes, uncle," Curly acceded. "After I ketch up on my sleep. I been riding three days and three nights."

"That's nothing," Hard Winter insisted, "when you know what I know. Do you want to git Handsome Harry?"

"You bet." Curly nodded. "Where is he?"

"I don't know," Johnson confessed, "but Tula. . . ."

"Is she home?" Curly demanded eagerly. "By grab, I'll go right down."

"No, she's in town," confided Hard Winter. "But, poor girl, you'd hardly know her. He treated her shameful, Curly."

"Does she know where he is?" asked Curly.

"He's with Tuffy," Johnson replied, winking wisely.

"That helps me a whole lot, now, don't it?" Wells sneered. "The question is . . . where the hell is Tuffy?"

"She knows," responded Hard Winter. "You ask her."

"All right," Curly agreed. And washing the sleep from his eyes, he set out on his quest. Here was something that could not wait.

But when he saw her, he forgot his errand. She was broken, emaciated, with deep lines in her young face. But the look in her blue-black eyes was like the glint of a dagger as she beckoned him into the house. It was a dirt-floor adobe in the poorer quarter of town, where she was staying with Mexican friends, and Tula herself looked poor.

"You do not know me." She smiled as he stepped back, startled. "But, yes, I am Tula. How are you?"

She offered her hand and Curly took it dumbly, then sat down in a rawhide chair.

"I wish now," she went on, "that I had taken your advice. But, no, we will not talk about that. Yet how can I forget what Harry has done? He has left me with nothing . . . nothing."

"Too bad," Curly mumbled. And he reached down into his pocket.

"Oh, no, no," she protested. "I do not want your money. My friends here have made me welcome. The Mexican people are very kind to each other. I am sorry you have lost your horse."

Curly glanced up at her shrewdly, for something told him that Tula had spoken those words with a purpose.

"Say," he began, reaching once more into his pocket, "will you do me a favor, Tula? You know I think a lot of that horse. More, I reckon, than lots of men think of their womenfolk. Now here's what I want you to do." He drew out a roll of bills and peeled three from the top, and he saw her eyes rest on them avidly. "I know," he went on, "that every Mexican in this town savvies just what has happened to Paint. But they're all afraid to talk. Now you take this twenty dollars and kinda circulate around among 'em and bring me back the news. That is, unless you're afraid, too."

"Ha-ha!" she laughed stridently. "What should I be afraid of?" And she reached out and took the money. "I do not care," she said, "if Tuffy kills me tomorrow. So I will tell you where your horse is . . . now. And then you must do something for me."

"Sure," Curly agreed. "What is it you want?"

"I will tell you first," she said, "about your horse. It fits in so

nice with my plan. I saw Paint only two days ago, up at White
Oaks in the mountains, and Tuffy Malone was riding him. He is
camping, away back in the hills."

"Good enough," Curly said, nodding as she described the
outlaws' camp. "Now don't tell this to the Mexicans or
anybody." And he gave her $10 more.

"Oh, thank you." She smiled. "It is hard to be poor when
your hosband has money to burn. But, of course, it was all stole
from my father."

"That's right," Curly agreed, leading her on. "I reckon you
rolled 'em high, though, back in Saint Louie."

"I was never so poor in my life," she snapped. "Harry Vail
would not give me a cent. Every night we went out and spent
hundreds of dollars. But one evening, when I was mad at him, I
walked all the way home. I did not have a nickel for the
streetcar."

"Well, well," Curly murmured, "that's no way to treat a lady.
What'd he do with all that money he got?"

"He hid it," she said mysteriously. "No, not in the banks. He
made them pay it all in bills. Oh, I did feel so rich when he
showed me all those banknotes. But no, he would not give me
one."

"And then he left you flat, eh?" Curly observed unfeelingly.

"Yes," she hissed. "But I will make him pay for it, yet. He left
me at Saint Louis and went on to Kentucky, and there he sold
all our land. My poor father has nothing . . . he is living in the
jail. But I am not so meek. I am a woman, but I will fight. I will
show him what a gr-greaser can do." She spat the word out
hatefully, and Curly knew that Handsome Harry had applied
the epithet to her. "I will show him," she went on, "that a greaser
girl fears nothing, if only it will give her revenge. Harry Vail is a
train robber. There is a reward for his arrest. And he is up in
that cañon . . . with Tuffy."

"Good again." Curly grinned, handing over his last $10. "I'll attend to Handsome Harry myself."

"You will kill him?" she inquired, smiling archly.

But Curly only shrugged his shoulders. "No-o," he said, "not unless he resists. I'm an officer now and. . . ."

"But I think he will resist," she hinted. "He was recognized in Kentucky and an officer tried to catch him. That is why he came back. He is hiding."

"Nope," dissented Curly. "I've known Harry some time. He'll weaken when he faces a gun."

"But you shoot him, anyway," Tula urged. "Only this would be better, maybe."

She paused in brooding thought, and Curly stirred uneasily. He did not like the look in her eyes.

"There is one thousand dollars reward," she said. "And then all the money he has hid. He did not spend it all, I know. It is better to arrest him, no?"

"You bet . . . and shake him down," Curly agreed heartily. But when he strode away, he shook his head.

"*Hm-m-m,*" he muttered. "There's that Mexican blood again. Gimme fair hair and blue eyes, every time. But here's where I get back Paint."

CHAPTER TWENTY-FOUR

Tuffy Malone and his Heel Flies and all the Lincoln outlaws who had made common cause against Jack Moore, had thrown down the gauntlet to the sheriff. Perhaps merely to intimidate him—but more likely to murder him—they had fired a bullet through his window. And with malevolent derision Tuffy had stolen back Paint from the yard of the jail itself.

It was a challenge, and so taken by every citizen of the county. But not more so than by Colonel Moore himself. He had been a Texas Ranger too long not to understand the bravado of these outlaws. Unless he struck, and struck quickly, the forces of evil would overwhelm him, and Tuffy Malone would laugh in his face.

Without pretense of concealment Tuffy and three of his followers had shot down the previous sheriff, and killed one of his deputies, to boot. And now, as a warning, they had smashed Jack Moore's window and stolen his chief deputy's horse. Moore was pacing the floor when Curly Wells came back with the light of a great discovery in his eyes.

"I've located Tuffy Malone," he whispered, when he had got the colonel off by himself. "He's up in that big cañon that comes down east of White Oaks . . . the right-hand fork as you go up. He and his whole gang are up there, and have been for a month. The saloonkeepers are coining money and the rest are afraid to talk. Tula Johnson saw Tuffy on my horse."

"In White Oaks," Moore said in disgust. "I was over there

myself not ten days ago, and the people all reported the town quiet. That's the curse of this country . . . there's too much money in dishonesty. There's nobody wants this outlawry to stop. These cow thieves will ride in and ring their money on the bar and spend a thousand dollars in one night. And the merchants will hush it up, every time. Do you remember, two weeks ago, when somebody shot up White Oaks? That was Tuffy Malone and his gang, for a certainty."

"Yes, and say, Jack," Curly said, "they'll be coming to town again. Christmas night . . . for their annual drunk."

He nodded his head confidently, and the sheriff drew down his bushy eyebrows.

"Curly," he said, "don't mention this to anyone. Not a soul . . . and I'll do the same. You make up your sleep while I send for Honey's glasses, and we'll scout their camp by night. And the day before Christmas we'll lay for 'em, up that cañon. They started this shooting from ambush."

"I'm with you," answered Curly. "Only what about Paint? Tuffy Malone will be riding him, sure."

"Well, we'll have to take a chance on not hitting him," replied Moore. "I'll tell all the boys to hold high."

"Yes, and some crazy fool will get to pumping his Winchester and fill old Paint full of lead. You lend me Porfilio, to steal my horse back. . . ."

"No," the colonel rapped out. "The minute that horse is stole, you've tipped our hand to Malone. There isn't a man in this county that dares to touch a horse of his, let alone that Appaloosa. Hasn't he stolen it from you twice? Then you let him have it, until we get Mister Malone himself."

"He might sneak him out of the country . . . it's five days yet till Christmas. And when the shooting begins, they'll all pull down on Tuffy. What chance has poor old Paint got?"

"The same chance as any horse," contended the colonel.

"The boys will all be warned not to hit him. And I'll tell you how I'll arrange it . . . I'll just turn Tuffy over to you. Only don't you shoot high and miss him."

"I'll bore him plumb through, right where his suspenders cross," Curly promised, and went off to sleep the clock around.

Then, riding by night, he entered the high, wooded mountains, where the gold of Baxter Mountain had lured hundreds of miners, before the mills at White Oaks Spring had made the town. Now the high ridges were deserted, except for Mexican woodchoppers, and chance prospectors still seeking rich ore. And Curly, to look the part, laid off his high sombrero and hung a pick and shovel on his pack.

For three nights, hiding by day, he watched the rustlers' camp at an abandoned cattle ranch in the mountains. Through the magic of his night glasses he traced their comings and goings, saw the horse herd brought into the big rock corral, and spotted their stolen cattle, up a cañon. But not until the third night did he catch a glimpse of Paint, so closely did Tuffy Malone keep him hidden. Then, stalking out sedately, Paint appeared from a stone house, and Curly saw that the colonel was right. The man who stole back Paint would have a war on his hands—a score of vengeful Heel Flies, skilled at trailing by day or night, would follow on his tracks like the wind. For Tuffy kept his war pony in a house like a human, and slept behind the same walls himself.

The day before Christmas was clear and cold, with patches of snow on the ground. Jack Moore and his deputies appeared on the streets of Lincoln as if nothing unusual was planned. Only the sheriff himself and Curly Wells knew of their rendezvous with death, of the twenty desperate outlaws, not thirty miles away, who were due to ride into their trap. Curly had scouted the mountains for miles, locating every spring and cabin, every sheep camp and woodchopper's *jacal,* and now in his darkened room he was sleeping all day, the better to lead the posse by night.

The sheriff was in his office when a messenger from the Pecos came riding through the spy-infested town. It was Porfilio Goya, his well-coached Mexican servant, and he leaped down and ran up the steps. Then the colonel came rushing out, summoning his posse in all haste, and, while the populace looked on, they rode away down the cañon, their guns gleaming beneath their coats. But when darkness came on and they had cleared the encircling hills, the posse swung north around the flank of Capitán Mountain and headed for White Oaks on the trot.

It was 10:00 p.m. beneath an overcast sky when they came at last to the mouth of White Oaks cañon and looked for signs of horse tracks in the snow. But the outlaws, wary as wolves, had not yet descended upon the town. The posse took shelter in an abandoned stone house that stood at the entrance to the pass. Then while some watched the road, Porfilio was sent ahead to see if the Heel Flies were in White Oaks.

A fire was kindled in the fireplace of the old road house, coffee was boiled, and blankets thrown down, but hardly had the warriors stretched out on the hard floor when a sentry came rushing in.

"They're coming," he announced, and, each snatching up his gun, the posse crowded out the door. Across the open door yard a stone wall flanked the road, where freighters had been accustomed to camp, and as they dropped down behind it, a high yell came to their ears and the distant pop of a pistol. From the right-hand cañon a dark mass emerged, seen dimly against the white of the snow, and Curly whipped up his night glasses.

"That's them," he reported to Moore. "I can see Paint, up in the lead. And behind, on that black, is Handsome Harry."

"Now, listen, boys," spoke up the sheriff. "I don't want any careless shooting. Let Curly take the man on his paint horse. And don't any man fire until I summon them to. That's the law, and I intend to live up to it. I'll attend to Handsome Harry myself."

He passed swiftly down the line, warning the men to keep cover. Then as the clatter of hoofs came nearer, he peered over the wall, his rifle held ready to shoot. They were coming at a gallop, Tuffy Malone in the lead, Handsome Harry on his black close behind.

"Halt! Throw up your hands!" the colonel shouted, rising up.

And both horses shied clear across the road. There was an instant of wild confusion, of whirling horsemen and plunging mounts, then two tongues of spitting red fire.

"Fire!" ordered Moore, pulling trigger as he spoke.

Handsome Harry tumbled from his saddle. There was a volley from along the wall as Curly pulled down on Malone, but as he aimed at the agile form on Paint, Tuffy swung down behind his shoulder. Paint swerved at a sudden jerk on the reins, the rake of a roweling spur. The next moment he had whirled in behind the mass of frenzied riders. There was the flash of a painted hip and he was gone.

Three men lay in the snow. A horse tottered and fell. Then the night swallowed up the fleeing forms of the Heel Flies and Curly ran for Tige.

With half the posse at his back he rode into the bitter wind that was sweeping down from the heights, but their mounts were worn out from the long ride from Lincoln and, one by one, they lagged and fell behind. At a turn of the cañon only three men remained with him, and the storm was closing down.

"We'd better wait, boys," he decided, "until Jack Moore comes up. It isn't far now to Tuffy's camp."

He stepped down to breathe his horse and peer ahead

through his glasses, but not an outlaw was in sight and the storm was increasing in violence. It was a wild night to be abroad, but when the sheriff rode up, he bowed his head and bored into the blast.

"We got three of 'em," he gritted, "and Handsome Harry took prisoner. The rest of 'em will scatter. You lead the way."

Curly spurred out in front, bending low to escape the wind that was spitting sleet and snow in their faces. And when he sighted the low, stone buildings of the rustlers' camp, he headed straight for Paint's place of hiding. He had failed in his trust and allowed Tuffy to escape, although the colonel as yet had not mentioned it. But for the fraction of a second, perhaps, Curly's finger had hesitated on the trigger. And at the roar of Jack Moore's rifle, Tuffy had swung down out of sight. But he had not escaped—not yet.

Dropping down before the door, Curly kicked it open violently, then stepped aside and stood waiting to shoot. But Tuffy had come and gone, leaving a trail of corn behind him where he had run out with a full *morral*. Even now in the fresh snow Curly could see Paint's hoof prints where he had headed up the cañon on the lope, and, while the others searched the houses, he followed the prints swiftly, lest the deputies should trample them out. Three other horses had fallen in behind, superimposing their tracks on Paint's, and the outlaw took a trail that Curly knew.

"Colonel," he panted as he whipped back from his scouting, "I've found where Tuffy Malone and three others rode away. Gimme three men to match them and I'll get him."

"Take your pick," responded the sheriff. "We'll wait for you here." And Curly looked over the men.

"I'll take Lee Pope . . . and Vosberg . . . and Emmett," he said. They were Panhandle men like himself, and Pope was a cattle detective. All three were dead shots, to boot.

"Good luck, Curly!" called the colonel as they headed off into the storm. "And never mind that horse . . . get Tuffy!"

"I'll git 'im!" promised Curly, almost crying with chagrin, and at the head of the three warriors he took the long trail that brought them, at dawn, to a house.

It was a house fort, of solid stone, with no opening but the doorway and a rock fireplace set at one end. And standing outside, with their ropes running in, were three gaunted ponies. But Paint was not with the rest.

"Tuffy has skipped out and left 'em," growled the high-strung Lee Pope as they jerked their horses down out of sight. "He's outfoxed us, the little rat."

"Nope," Curly responded, plucking his rifle out of the scabbard. "He's there . . . he's got Paint inside."

"There's one horse I know," spoke up Vosberg as they crept back to watch the house. "That big bay is Indian Charley's. Let's slip up and get 'em in the door."

"Tie the horses first," Curly ordered. "They might get scared and run. Then we'll sneak up the bottom of this gulch."

Rubbing their hands to limber their fingers and with rifles under their arms, they crept swiftly up the wash and gathered silently behind the cutbank, not forty feet from the door. A horse raised its head and snorted as four rifles were thrust out, four battered hats tipped to the wind. But when no one came out, he slouched back apathetically and wearily awaited the dawn.

It came slowly, but at last the dim cañon grew light and there was a noise of thumping boots inside the house. The horses whinnied eagerly, every eye on the door as the chain that held it shut was unbound. Then it swung quickly open and Indian Charley stepped out, a *morral* full of corn on his arm. For a moment he stood still, searching the cañon with keen, black eyes, and Curly spoke to him softly.

"Come out here . . . we've got you," he said.

But Charley's hand leaped to his pistol. Then Lee Pope shot twice and Charley dropped his nose bag. He staggered drunkenly and turned toward the door.

"I'm killed!" he called, and fell forward in the snow, while the door was slammed shut from behind.

"Come out, boys!" Curly summoned. "We've got you surrounded. Sheriff's posse . . . you haven't got a chance."

"Go to hell!" came the answer in a high, boyish voice, and Curly knew that Tuffy was there. After leading the chase for nearly a year, the fox was brought to den. But he was far from being caught.

There was the sound of heavy blows as the outlaws, shouting threats, began to punch a row of loopholes through the walls. Outside, the four deputies lay watching expectantly, each man with rifle trained on a hole. It was going to be a battle, after all. The mud plaster began to yield and they smashed slugs against it. Then a rifle rang out in a fierce staccato of rapid fire and the deputies ducked down, just in time. A patter of bullets swept the spot where their rifles had been thrust out—plunging shots from the broad throat of the fireplace—and when it ceased abruptly and they peered over the edge, one of the horses had been pulled in the door.

It was Vosberg, a former soldier, who detected the trick first, and with two lightning shots he dispatched the remaining horses, just as their owners were dragging them inside.

"They're going to make a break, boys," he warned, and from the stone house Tuffy Malone laughed recklessly.

"Yes, and we're going to come a-shooting," he answered. And once more his rifle hurled a stream of lead.

Curly ducked until it passed, but he rose up promptly, stripping the glove from his pistol hand. Through the doorway like a shot there came a horse, carrying double, spurred and lashed into a frenzy to escape. But behind through the smoke he saw Paint, and Tuffy mounting, and suddenly his heart went cold. There was the whang of ready rifles as the deputies, taking the leaders, shot their horse down and sent them sprawling. Then Paint charged out the doorway and headed straight for him, with Tuffy hugging his neck like a bat.

Once before Curly had hesitated and let his enemy escape. Now he fired two shots, quick as light and yet aimed, and the hand on Paint's neck lost its hold. With a grunt and a plunge Paint gathered himself and leaped clean over the wide gulch and away. But Tuffy Malone went tumbling, one arm suddenly limp, a bloody smear along the side of his face.

"Don't shoot me!" he shrilled, rolling over to stick up his hands.

And Curly laughed, for Paint was not scratched.

CHAPTER TWENTY-FIVE

With a bullet through his shoulder and a nick in his left ear, Tuffy Malone scrambled up to hold his hands for the handcuffs, for Curly was taking no chances. One outlaw lay dead, the two others were bruised and hurt. Only Paint, of all the outlaw horses, had come through the battle alive.

Curly walked out to him tremulously, holding a fistful of corn from Indian Charley's *morral,* and Paint, snorting loudly, circled again and again before he came to his master's side. He had seen the pistol flash, felt the wind as the bullets sped past, and read the hate in Curly's blue eyes.

From his place with the other prisoners Tuffy Malone laughed mockingly, while he wiped away the blood from his ear. "He don't know you!" he hollered. "That's my horse, now! Here, Paint!"

"You shut up!" Curly shouted back savagely, and Tuffy laughed again.

He was shot through the shoulder, but no bones had been struck and his arm would heal quickly. It was the wound in his ear, where half the lobe had been shot away, that seemed to concern him most.

"I put my mark on you," Curly taunted as he looked him over grimly. "Underbit the left . . . that's my regular earmark. Next time I'll put a swallow fork in the right."

"Yes, and the next time I draw down on you," bantered Tuffy, "there won't be any next time . . . understand? I'll beef you . . .

right there in the pen."

"Done tried that, already." Curly shrugged. "Have you fellers got any grub?"

"There's some coffee," Tuffy responded, "on the back of my saddle. Just unlock these handcuffs and I'll go and git it for you. Don't want to? You must be scairt."

"Sure am," Curly agreed. "So you mind your Ps and Qs. Keep an eye on him, boys . . . he's dangerous."

They searched the three prisoners and made them sit against the wall while they breakfasted on coffee and horse meat. Then, mounting two of them double, they tied Tuffy's hands to the saddle horn and began the long, tiresome return.

The snow lay deep on the trail and the horses toiled and stumbled. A cold wind drew the water from their eyes, but never for an instant did the deputies relax their vigilance, though Tuffy treated his plight as a joke.

He had shot down Sheriff O'Keefe and sixteen other men who had dared to challenge his power. He was guilty of murder, and, rather than die on the gallows, he would take any risk to escape. Two deputies rode behind him, their rifles deep in the scabbards to keep them from being snatched away, their iron faces unchanged by his raillery. For while he laughed so recklessly, his little eyes danced like pin points from one armed guard to another, on the watch for any desperate chance.

In the rear rode Curly Wells, ready to whip off his glove and shoot at the first crooked move. And while he bestrode Paint, the fastest of all their horses, Tuffy Malone was mounted on the slowest. Down the long, tortuous trail they plodded in surly silence after Tuffy had given over his jokes. But when they came in sight of the ranch where the posse was camped a joyous procession spurred out to meet them.

"Good for you, Curly, my boy!" the colonel cried ecstatically, when he dashed up and saw the prisoners. "And I'm glad to see," he added, "that you're taking no chances. That man Malone will strike like a rattlesnake."

"Oh, hello, Colonel," Tuffy hailed, his amber eyes laughing. "You don't need to worry about me. I'm shot in two places and my hands are tied to the horn. Did you bring any leg irons along?"

"Yes, and I'll use 'em," the sheriff promised, "the minute you dismount. I know you, young man, so there's no use trying to fool me. I've got you and I intend to keep you."

"All right," agreed Tuffy, "as long as you feed me. These raw-hiding deputies of yours gimme a breakfast of horse meat . . . and Indian Charley's horse, at that."

"We killed Charley, up at the house," Curly explained. "But Tuffy seems to think it's a joke."

"Well, he's dead, ain't he?" defended Tuffy. "And I owed him forty dollars that he'll damn' sure never collect."

"Now, boys," the colonel protested as his deputies chuckled grimly, "I want to warn you . . . don't laugh at his jokes. He'll toll you along, making you think he's harmless, and you'll wake up looking down a gun."

"Yes, and you'll see a bullet coming out of it," Tuffy added, making a face.

The sheriff confronted him sternly. "Mister Malone," he said, "you're in a serious position. You're charged with the murder of Ed O'Keefe . . . a cold-blooded, brutal crime . . . and if the courts give you justice, you'll hang. Now keep your mouth shut. Understand?"

The reckless, boyish laughter died away in Tuffy's eyes as he met the sheriff's gaze, and he turned his face away sullenly. "Gimme a smoke," he demanded of a deputy that he knew.

But the colonel shook his head. "Keep away from him," he warned. "He'll grab your gun and shoot you. I've seen men like him before, and I know what I'm talking about. Mister Wells,

I'll place him in your care."

"All right," Curly agreed. "And you picked the right man. Because if Tuffy ever gets loose, I know danged well what he'll do. He'll kill me . . . and then he'll steal Paint."

"Heh-heh!" Tuffy laughed as their level eyes met. "You're dead right about Paint. Ain't he, baby?" And he thrust his smiling face out coaxingly.

"Damn your heart!" Curly snarled. "You leave that horse alone."

But Tuffy only leered at him impudently. "Never mind," he said. "I haven't kicked the bucket, yet. There's many a slip between the cup and the lip. Say, gimme a smoke . . . I'm perishing."

"Yes, and a danged good thing for you," Curly answered shortly. "What's next on the program, Colonel?"

"Put your prisoner in that stone house and guard him," ordered Moore. "When we've rounded up their cattle and that bunch of stolen horses, we'll return at once to Lincoln."

The next morning, like Indians returning from the warpath, the warriors of Colonel Moore rode out across the plain, driving their cattle and horses before them. They had struck swiftly, and struck again, ambushing their outlaw enemies and running down their leader overnight. Four Heel Flies had been killed, four more were led back prisoners, and the remnants were scattered through the hills. The forces of law and order had triumphed again, but they were still outnumbered a hundred to one.

In every cañon of the mountains there was some family of whites or Mexicans that had known the Heel Flies' bounty, or received a yearling from Tuffy Malone. He had given with prodigal hands, since what he gave was stolen, and those who he helped had helped him in return while they fattened on company beef.

In the saloons of Fort Sumner and White Oaks he had spent money like water over the bar. All the Mexicans were his *cuñados*, or *compadres* at the least, and the *señoritas* listened for his footsteps. Yet he was an outlaw, a murderer, and according to the law he should die.

Jack Moore rode back grimly down the silent, empty street where the people peeped out from their houses, for he knew that the battle was not won. Where in Lincoln would he find twelve good men and true to condemn Tuffy Malone to death? Where was the judge who would try the case, unless with military protection? Where was the attorney who would prosecute the murderer? He left his prisoners in chains on the second floor of the Big Store, where their partisans could not release them by night, and two days later he laid his case before the governor, who had been appointed by the President himself.

A week later a column of cavalry entered Lincoln from the west and lined up in front of the store. A circuit judge, who in his day had been a soldier of note, stepped down from his carriage and entered. And from Las Cruces there came a prosecuting attorney who wore a six-shooter under his coat. Then in the heavily guarded courtroom Tuffy Malone was tried and convicted and given a sentence of death. But as he walked out with his jailer, he stepped off jauntily, and Curly Wells set a double guard.

The old element was drifting back into Lincoln's crowded streets—the gamblers, the gunmen, the rustlers—and in the saloons that night rebellion was preached openly. But already the jail was full. Henry Johnson had been ousted from his airy cell to make room for cow thieves and murderers. He slept with the old jailer in his shack behind the courthouse, and half the deputies had given up their rooms. Prisoners were chained, hand and foot, and guarded day and night, and still the mill of justice ground on.

It was said of Judge Milligan that he had sworn an oath to send up every cow thief in the county. That he was a stern man was evident by the batches of sullen prisoners who were sent off under guard to the penitentiary. Angry mutterings were heard and threats against his life, the atmosphere in Lincoln was tense, and over the mountains there came the news that Mike Broiles was back at his Alamosa ranch. But through it all Jack Moore never deviated from his purpose, which was to hang Tuffy Malone.

He was the leader of them all, the perfect embodiment of that youthful deviltry that led on from cattle stealing to worse crimes. And, though his youth had its appeal, there was an innate depravity in his make-up that helped the colonel to harden his heart. He held his grizzled head lower now, glaring up from under his eyebrows like a buffalo bull on the prod, and as the day approached for the execution to take place he took charge of the prisoner himself. A special set of shackles was fitted to Tuffy's feet and welded by the local blacksmith. And with Handsome Harry, who was being held for extradition, he was moved to the second-story courtroom.

Every force of good and evil was being mustered for the struggle, to say whether Tuffy should die. Texas Rangers came drifting in—unofficially as stock detectives—and were sworn in as special deputies. The governor of the territory visited the town in person and exhorted the citizens to obey the law. But across the street, in Mike Broiles's old saloon and the *cantinas* and deadfalls of the Mexicans, there was much said of a conspiracy on the part of the cattlemen to send poor Tuffy to his grave.

He was sobered at last now, lynx-eyed and malevolent, refusing food like a caged mountain lion. And every night in the silent guard room as Curly took his turn at guard, he could feel the killing hate of his glare. It was more to divert Tuffy than to guard Harry Vail that he was moved from the cells to keep him company. After the battle below White Oaks it was discovered that Handsome Harry had come down like Davy Crockett's raccoon. He had tumbled from his horse a scant second before the colonel had unhooked with his big buffalo gun. The bullet had passed over him but Harry had surrendered anyway, thus proving himself far from a warrior.

As they sat together, hour by hour, playing cards for matches, it fell in well with Tuffy's mood to twit Handsome Harry on his discretion in that moment of peril. But, still smiling and imperturbable, Vail smoked his pipe in silence, meanwhile studying on some scheme of his own. He was wanted for train robbery, and a reward of $1,000 was offered for his arrest and conviction. But on the other hand he was reputed to have several hundred thousand dollars safely hidden somewhere in the hills.

It was the chance of recovering this that had tempted Tula Johnson to reveal his place of hiding to the officers. And, although Tuffy did not know it, the girl who brought in their supper had put him on the road to death. She came in smiling now, a tray piled high with delicacies for Harry and his prison companion. And each evening, by arrangement, she and Harry sat alone, for she was determined to get possession of his secret. Jack Moore could do no less than grant her this privilege, since her treachery had betrayed Tuffy into his hands, but Curly Wells watched them narrowly as they put their heads together.

As for Tula, she stated frankly that all she wanted was the money that Harry had stolen from her father. All the rest was forgiven—or if not forgiven, then forgotten—for she had inherited her father's miser soul. He had lived his life for money, and thrown the money away rather than pay Mike Broiles his judgment. Broiles had even reduced his demands from $1 to 1¢, and still Hard Winter had refused to yield. So he lived on in jail, a pensioner of the county, still nursing his grudge against

Mike Broiles. But the more practical Tula had set her mind on one thing—to wheedle his secret from Harry.

But what was it that Harry, with equal insistence, was attempting to wheedle from Tula? It was that which prompted Curly to watch them when they talked, for there was treachery in the air. To save Tuffy from the gallows a hundred men in Lincoln were ready to put up a fight, but the man to lead them was lacking. Judge Milligan had sentenced half the Heel Flies to prison, and Jack Moore had chased the rest across the line. Only Mike Broiles remained, and he lived in hiding where once he had ruled like a king. Yet even then, for his own revenge, he was laying the plot that should set Vail and Tuffy free.

Judge Milligan had cleared his calendar and declared court adjourned. Then, declining as superfluous the military escort, he had started for Las Cruces alone. Days passed and a telegram had announced his non-arrival. Sheriff Moore had wired back when he had left. A search party had gone out, and the tracks of his buckboard had led to White Sands—and stopped. Blood was found, and starved horses, still dragging their reins many miles from the scene of the crime. Then Jack Moore came rushing in to where Curly stood his guard and ordered him to saddle and ride.

"This is Mike Broiles's work," he declared. "It shows every earmark, and he's known to be back at his ranch. You run down these murderers and bring them in, dead or alive. They've struck at the court itself."

"All right," agreed Curly. "But who's going to guard these prisoners?" He beckoned him off to one side. "You look out," he whispered. "There's something going on. I believe they're planning a break."

"I'll watch 'em myself," the colonel promised. "It's only one week more. Ketch Mike if you can, and next Friday I'll hang Tuffy and get the damned job over with."

"Then keep your eye on Tula," Curly warned, and rode off to White Sands.

The next day a messenger came riding to summon him back. Tuffy Malone and Handsome Harry had killed their guards and escaped. And Tula had smuggled in the pistol.

CHAPTER TWENTY-SIX

Law and order had come to Lincoln—and then in a day it had gone. When his guard was not looking, Handsome Harry, who had seemed so harmless, had fished out a short-nosed pistol from the bottom of a coffee pot, and shot the guard down for his keys. And starving Tuffy Malone, who had not eaten for days, slipped his thin, emaciated wrists out of the handcuffs that held them and grabbed up a double-barreled shotgun. From the window of his prison, as the other guard came running, he had given him both barrels of buckshot, and so intimidated the rest of the townspeople that no man dared venture on the street.

Then for hours, while his friends in the saloons looked on, Tuffy had worked on the shackles on his legs until at last he filed himself free. A horse was brought at his orders and he rode away laughing, loaded down with the weapons of his victims. No one knew how it had happened until a deputy, mounting the stairs, discovered a coffee-soaked pistol. But Handsome Harry had fled, and with him the fickle Tula, persuaded over by his false words of love.

She had had two horses waiting in the jail yard behind—for the sheriff that morning had ridden off with a posse, following a rumor that Mike Broiles had been seen. He came back, breathless with rage, unable to speak for the fury that raged in his breast. Then with curses that made them quail, he ordered the people to their homes and sent his deputies riding the trails.

The man who called back Curly was followed by another

who sent him dashing to bar the way to the border.

Then for a month they combed the back country, searching the mountains and desert valleys, but no trace of Tuffy could be found. He was free, and the terror that his name inspired had been magnified a hundred times. For him to be taken now meant death on Jack Moore's scaffold that stood half erected in the yard. From the window Tuffy had laughed as he had looked down on his guard and given him both barrels of buckshot. And for the man who betrayed his hiding place there would be another shot, unless Tuffy himself was killed.

He had risen up raging against the minions of the law, ordering the jailer about with such menacing looks that the old man could hardly catch a horse. Then he had jogged out of town slowly, his leg irons still dangling where he had filed them off of one foot. But from the time he took the turn past the oak grove no man had seen him, and told. Was he there, hiding close in the wooded mountains, protected by the fear of his guns? Or had he, despite the cordon of officers thrown between, escaped across the Mexican line?

Curly Wells rode back at last from his search along the border. If Tuffy Malone had passed over, he had left no sign, nor was he to be found in old Mexico.

"He's here," Curly declared as he sat late at night in the office of the despondent sheriff. "He's right here in this country, hiding out among these Mexicans. But now there's no Tula to tell on him. He'll show up one of these days when we least expect him . . . and then it'll be him or me. Or maybe him or you."

"He'll find me looking for him," stated the sheriff. "I'll not be surprised like Ed O'Keefe, walking along with my eyes on the ground. And if I see him first, I'll shoot quick and holler afterward. He's dangerous, and I'll take no more chances."

"Well, he's not in Mexico," Curly resumed, "although they're all looking for him to come. Every saloonkeeper in Chihuahua is just hoping and praying to see him, because, if he shows, their fortune is made. Tuffy's a big man with those outlaws, and if he arrives, we'll sure hear about it. I've got look-outs in every big town."

"I'd take my oath," the colonel grumbled, "he isn't within a hundred miles of Lincoln. And yet, you never can tell. These Mexicans don't know yet that they're citizens of the United States. They're opposed to the law, to a man. But if they're hiding him, I'll punish them severely."

"I'll bet you," Curly bantered, "that every Mex in this town knows right where Tuffy is hid out. No use sending me riding all over the country. Poor old Tige and Paint are ridden down to a shadow. What's this wagon I seen down the road?"

"That's Honey McCoy's bee wagon," the sheriff returned stiffly. "He's doing a little night work, with his glasses."

"Aw, that old man," scoffed Curly. "What the devil is he good for? I'm going down and borrow 'em, right now."

"What, at eleven o'clock at night? You'll give the whole snap away, if anybody sees you down there. No, you go west in the morning and try to locate Mike Broiles, the murdering hound. He killed Judge Milligan as sure as I'm sitting here, and buried his body in the sand. You find me Mike Broiles and I'll find Tuffy Malone. They stand in together, the rascals."

"Heh! You find me Tuffy Malone and I'll find you Broiles," Curly retorted. "And another thing, Mister Slave Driver, you crowd me much farther and I'll quit and hand in my star. What's my girl going to say if I go right through town and never even stop to say howdy? A man would think, by grab, you were unhappily married and were. . . ."

"I am," the colonel broke in. "My poor wife is about crazy. And I'll swear I haven't spent a happy moment in months, since I took over this accursed job. But they shoved it off onto me and I'm not the man to quit. . . . I'll get Tuffy Malone or know why."

"Here, too, Jack," Curly agreed. "I'll stay with you till hell freezes over. But have a little mercy on a man. There's such a thing in this country as competition, when you've got a girl as pretty as mine. And I've got something important to tell her."

"Well, all right," growled the sheriff. "Although with Tuffy Malone at large your life isn't worth a dollar. If he's around here, as you say, the thing to do is go after him, instead of idling away your time down at that wagon."

"Yes, but I won't be idle, though," Curly answered gleefully. "Wait till I whisper a few sweet nothings into her shell-like ear. I just can't hardly wait till I see her."

The colonel sighed and brushed back the mane of wiry hair that bristled out over his eyes, then straightened up. "Well, go on and get your sleep," he said. "And then go down and see your girl. I'm getting old, Curly, and I've botched this whole business. Those guards should never have been killed. But I've got to see it through. Good night."

"Good night, Colonel," responded Curly. "Better get some sleep yourself. And cheer up . . . we'll get Tuffy."

Curly groped his way down the dark stairway and out across the yard to the adobe that served him for a home. But before he turned in, he rubbed down Paint and Tige and threw some hay close by his door. Then with the sound of their contented chomping in his ears he drifted off into dreamland. Life had been rough and dangerous since he had left his little ranch to follow Tige to this lawless land. "No law west of the Pecos" had been the saying back in Texas, but now there was the beginning of law. In one big roundup of thieves and killers the colonel had swept the country clean. And Judge Milligan, before his death, had sent to the penitentiary every man whose guilt could be proved. But with Tuffy Malone's escape the backwash had set in and once more there was no law but the gun.

Mike Broiles, who had fled so quickly when he saw the tide turn, had slipped back when he sensed its ebb. And now, secretly as always, he was building up resistance—breaking down the force of the law. Under outlawry the town of Lincoln had been thronging with people. Money was free, and no questions asked. But now the pay of warriors on both sides of the rustler war had eaten up the profits of the game.

In one year—while Curly Wells, drawn into the maëlstrom, had been riding and fighting with the rest—Lincoln County had gone down until its citizens, driven desperate, were willing to listen to anything. And then Mike Broiles came, whispering. To be sure the county was bankrupt while Jack Moore, as sheriff, used its deputies to guard his own cattle. To be sure trade was dull when all the boys who had brought in money were driven across the line into Mexico. Moore was ten times the king that Henry Johnson had ever been—or Mike Broiles, either, for that matter. What the country needed was a change.

It was a battle of giants in which Curly, buffeted about, had almost lost track of the issue. All he knew was that desperate men were intent on his life, and to survive he was fighting back as desperately. Yet, though the year had brought nothing but endless conflict or futile pursuit, he counted the time well spent. For at Deep Springs, beneath the cottonwoods, he had found Melissa McCoy—and now she had come to Lincoln.

Curly was up at daylight to feed and care for his horses and prepare himself for his call. His bearded cheeks were clean shaven, his boots polished, his clothes clean, and to make himself more welcome he rode down on Tige, the friend and *compadre* of Croppy. Only a year before, in the horse herd at Ganado Crossing, Tige had forgotten his love for Paint to take up with this scrubby pony, which in turn had quit its love for him. They were partners still, though their ways had been separated, and as Curly neared the cottonwood grove where the bee wagons were parked, Croppy threw up his head and neighed.

"There's your friend," Curly observed, waving his hand at Honey McCoy. But Melissa was nowhere to be seen.

"Good morning, Mister McCoy," Curly greeted cheerily as he rode up to the fire. "Kind of early up here, ain't it, for bees?"

"Yes, it's early," admitted Honey. "But the maples are out . . . and, of course, there's always the honeydew. The bees ain't active now, and they might as well be up here as down in that windy valley. That's one thing a bee don't like . . . wind. But git down, Mister Wells, git down. Where have you been this long time?"

"Oh, rambling around," Curly answered vaguely. "Say, what's the matter? Where's Melissa?" he demanded, as he sensed something wrong in the camp. "And I don't see Julius Caesar."

"No-o," Honey replied with maddening deliberation, "poor Caesar has had an accident. A big dog took after him, about a month ago, and broke his front leg at the shoulder."

"My Lord," Curly responded. "You don't mean to say you killed him."

"No-o, he's up in the wagon," Honey said. "His leg knit all right, but it's short."

"Well, what about Melissa?" faltered Curly. "She ain't gone or nothing, is she, Honey?"

"No-o, she's here," Honey responded. "But she can't sleep good lately.

> "O sleep, O gentle sleep,
> Nature's soft nurse, how have I frighted thee,
> That thou no more wilt weight my eyelids down,
> And steep my senses in forgetfulness?"

He ran on in a long discourse of jumbled quotations, and Curly glanced anxiously at the wagon. Its covers were drawn but from time to time the flap heaved gently until a cat's paw appeared. Then from the narrow opening Julius Caesar peered out, but all his kittenish beauty had vanished. His pinched face was long and drawn, his coat rough and rumpled, and, as Curly walked toward him, he mewed plaintively.

"Well, poor little Caesar," Curly soothed, lifting him out. But when the cat touched the ground, his eyes turned suddenly wild. He crouched and glared up the road.

"It was a big, Mexican mastiff," Honey explained apologetically. "And Caesar refused to run. Reckon we spoiled him, mebbe, teaching him not to be afraid. Here, kitty!"

But Caesar had fled. With his crippled leg dangling he sprang upon the wagon tongue. Then with a quick leap he cleared the jockey box and crept down inside the wagon cover, whence a sleepy voice was calling his name. Curly glanced at the old man, who regarded him fixedly, then beckoned him mysteriously aside.

"My daughter ain't well," he said. "You'll have to excuse her."

Curly stepped away softly. "All right," he replied, "just tell her I called."

But at his voice the canvas was thrown up. "Oh, is that you?" exclaimed Melissa, thrusting out a tousled head.

Curly gazed in wonder. For Melissa had changed, too. The old, undaunted smile had gone out of her eyes. And on the other hand her little-girl prettiness had given way to a grown-up beauty. She was a woman—but she, too, had learned fear.

"What's the matter?" he demanded. "Say, I'll come back later. Didn't know you'd be asleep."

"No . . . wait!" she cried. "Oh, please, don't go away." And with an impatient gesture she struck the cover aside and leaped out, fully dressed, to the ground. "There's nothing the matter with me," she declared, rubbing her eyes, "only I can't seem to

sleep at night. Then I sit around all day, like an owl in a bush
. . . you wait till I wash my face."

She ran down to the creek and dashed cold water on her
cheeks while Honey stood mumbling to himself.

"Mister Wells," he said at last as Curly stirred uneasily, "have
you heard any news of Tuffy Malone?"

"No," spoke up Curly. "What do you know about him? Has
he been around, bothering Melissa?"

"No-o," responded Honey. "Only I just thought I'd ask. He
hasn't been around here at all."

"What's the matter with her, then?" Curly demanded insis-
tently.

And Honey began to quote:

> **"Methought I heard a voice cry: 'Sleep no**
>   **more!**
> *Macbeth* **does murder sleep!'—The innocent**
>   **sleep.**
> **Sleep, that knits up the raveled sleeve of**
>   **care,**
> **The death of each day's life. . . . "—**

"Say, what's biting you?" Curly broke in roughly. "There's
something wrong here, I know."

"No-o, I'm just sleepy," Honey replied evenly. "No trouble
. . . just the need of tired nature's sweet restorer. If you don't
mind, I'll turn in myself now."

He eased himself up into the wagon, but, as he threw aside
the flap, Curly glimpsed Melissa's shotgun, standing bolt
upright beside the bed.

"Something's wrong, here," he muttered. And from his hiding place inside the cover Caesar peered out with wild, startled
eyes.

CHAPTER TWENTY-SEVEN

The same still fear that had laid hold of Honey McCoy, making his bold eyes soddenly furtive, reached out and took possession of Curly. It was something communicable, akin in its way to Caesar's new fear of dogs. Perhaps—and Curly paused—perhaps Honey and Melissa had learned fear as Caesar had learned. He sat down moodily by the ashes of the fire and Melissa came back to him, smiling.

"Let's take a little walk along the creek," she invited, "so Father can go to sleep."

"You ought to be asleep yourself," he said. "Too bad about Caesar, eh?"

"Yes, and he was so brave, too," she answered, leading the way down the bank. "But that big dog never stopped . . . he just rushed in and grabbed him. And now Caesar is scared all the time."

"Has any big dog been rushing at you?" Curly inquired, taking her hand and drawing her down on a log. "You know me, Melissa. Just say the word and I'll run him clean out of the country."

"No . . . I'm all right," Melissa faltered, without taking her hand away. "Only sometimes . . . well, sometimes I wonder if Caesar wasn't brought up wrong. It's all right to be brave, but when a big dog comes along. . . ."

"Better run . . . you bet." Curly nodded. "It's mighty pretty down under these trees."

"Yes, but I'm . . . I'm scared," she confessed, and buried her face against his breast.

"I knew it," he said, "as soon as I saw you. I knew you were scared about something. But I'm back now, Melissa, and you tell me all about it. I'll take care of you. Is it Tuffy Malone?"

"Oh, no, no," she protested. "I'm not afraid of him. Are you going to be in Lincoln long?"

"As long as you need me," he answered steadfastly. "Haven't you seen Tuffy Malone, at all?"

"No, I haven't," she declared. "I'm not afraid of him, anyhow. It's . . . it's Harry Vail." And she shuddered.

"Harry Vail?" he repeated incredulously. "What has he got to do with you? I thought he'd skipped the country."

"No, he's here," she responded miserably. "And, oh, I'm so glad you came home. I can't tell you how scared I am."

"What of?" Curly demanded. "Has Handsome Harry been trying to get pushy with you?"

"He came down and talked to me," Melissa stated indignantly. "Right here, while I was fixing Caesar's foot. And Uncle Jack, and Father, and you, and everybody . . . what made you go away?"

"I had to," defended Curly. "But now that I'm back, I'll attend to Handsome Harry personally."

"You can't find him," she asserted. "Oh, he's the slyest, cruelest thing . . . he wears moccasins now, like an Indian. And all the time, when you were out hunting for him, he would come here and talk to me. But nobody saw him . . . nobody."

"My Lord," returned Curly. "You don't mean to say . . . ?"

"Yes. He came right here . . . to this spot."

"Then I'll lay for him," Curly said vindictively.

"No. It's no use," she insisted. "I never see him coming. And then, like an Indian, he'll step out of the bushes, and grab me, before I can run."

"Grab you?" Curly repeated fiercely. "That dirty dog needs killing. What does he want of you?"

"He wants me to run away with him," Melissa sobbed. "And he says if I don't, he'll make me. He says he loves me, and all that, and he's got lots of money . . . but he won't have any woman but me. And I never even saw him, except when Tuffy Malone came down to our camp at Deep Springs."

"Those Heel Flies seem to specialize in scaring women," Curly observed. "But this thing has got to stop. You come along with me, and Uncle Jack will send you back to the ranch. Then we'll chase this Handsome Harry like a rabbit."

"No. He said if I ever leave here, he'll follow me and kill me. Or steal me, while I'm asleep. Oh, Curly, that's the reason I can't shut my eyes . . . he's threatened to come and get me. He says he'll carry me off some night and no one will even know it. . . ."

"He won't do it," Curly cut in quietly.

"Yes, he will!" she insisted. "You don't know how still he is. I never see him, even when I'm awake. He glides like a snake, or one of these Apaches that can hide in an inch of grass."

"I'll see him," Curly promised. "Which way does he generally come in?"

"He comes from up the creek," she said, drying her eyes. "And the last time he was here, he told me where to go, to be within sight from his camp."

"He did," Curly said. "Where was it?"

"He said to go up the creek to that big, wooded cañon that comes down from the Capitáns and. . . ."

"Yes, and what else?" Curly prompted eagerly.

"He said if I didn't come . . . two days ago . . . he'd carry me off when I was asleep."

"Well, he won't do anything of the kind," Curly comforted. "Come over here." He held out his hands. "You feel safe, now?"

he asked as she slipped into his arms. "All right, then. I'll take care of you, savvy? And don't let this cheap sport run any blazer on you, either. Because Curly Wells will get him, sure."

"But you might be away," she quavered. "And he'd come down while you're gone. I never was so scared as the last time he came . . . he rose right up out of the ground. And always before he tried to talk nice, but this time. . . ."

"He got rough, eh?" Curly supplied.

"Yes, and he scared me," she whispered. "He threatened to kill me, if I told."

"I see." Curly nodded. "That's only talk, of course, but I tell you what you do. You go back and get some sleep and I'll watch for Handsome Harry. I'll lay for him, down here by this creek. And just to make you sleep better I'll give you one of my six-shooters, although I don't reckon you know what that means. Well, when a man thinks enough of a girl to give her one of his guns, it's . . . well, it's kinda like a ring, you understand."

"Why, Curly," Melissa said, her tired eyes brightening, and then she glanced shyly away. "I didn't know," she said, "that you liked me that much. But all right . . . and thank you, Curly dear."

She leaned against him confidingly and Curly turned red as he met her smiling, blue eyes. But his shyness overcame him and he took his arm away, fumbling awkwardly with the pistol in his gun belt.

"I . . . I think a lot of you, Melissa," he stammered. "Only . . . only somehow. . . . Well, here's your gun." He whipped it out of the worn holster and spun the cylinder experimentally, but Melissa pushed it away.

"No," she said. "Maybe I'd better not take it. You know, Curly, I've got my shotgun, and. . . ."

"No. Take it," urged Curly. "I'll get another one."

But Melissa shook her head. "You might need it," she

objected, beginning to wink back the tears. "And if you don't think enough of me to give me a kiss, I . . . you said it was like a ring."

"Well, it is," Curly assured her. "Only . . . say, listen, Melissa. What's the matter if you give me the kiss?"

"No," Melissa said, standing off and showing her dimples. "Somebody might see us and make fun of me, afterward. But if *you* did it, Curly . . . oh, it would make me so happy. And. . . ." She paused, and looked up at him, her smiling lips parted, and Curly stooped and kissed her quickly.

"Good bye," she whispered as she clung to him desperately. Then, snatching away his pistol after all, she turned and fled to the wagon, leaving Curly with his head in a daze.

CHAPTER TWENTY-EIGHT

Long and patiently, while his goddess slept, Curly Wells watched over the wagons. But when Melissa's tousled head appeared at last from the canvas door, he waved his hand and fled. He had not thought that a child like her could grow so quickly to woman's estate, and to a command of woman's wiles. But before he knew it Melissa had lured him on until, recklessly, he had claimed his first kiss.

He grinned foolishly and talked to Tige as he made his way up the creekbed, scouting the bottoms for Handsome Harry's tracks, but his eyes saw only the beauty of flaunting green cottonwoods and maple trees humming with bees. There was a wine in the clean air that went to his head like metheglin, the nectar of the ancient gods, and through his brain, in a jumble of pictures, he saw Melissa, and Melissa again—always smiling, always dancing, always gay. Yet the Melissa who had kissed him was sleepy-eyed and frightened, and she had clung to his neck when they parted.

There was a duty to be done before the old, carefree Melissa could dance her way through the cottonwoods again. Now, for her, every willow concealed the stealthy form of Vail. Until Handsome Harry was captured or given his just deserts, his smug, leering face would haunt her dreams like a nightmare. Melissa could never sleep.

"I'll get him," Curly muttered. "I'll get him myself." But as he rode down the empty street, he felt the old fear come back, and instinctively he felt for his gun. The holster was empty and Curly grabbed in a panic for the gun on his other hip. Then he laughed, for his right gun had been given to Melissa in lieu of a diamond ring. Rings were scarce in old Lincoln, with its half-empty stores. Guns had taken their places, and cartridges passed for money—but someday he would buy her a ring. And if in the meanwhile, like many another promised bride, who slept with her ring beneath the pillow—if Melissa sought sweet dreams to remind her of her lover, she could use the old .45.

Curly threw open the gate and rode into the wide jail yard, where high adobe walls fenced in prisoners and horses alike, cutting off all view of the street. It was a yard so big that a pole corral had been fenced off in it, to facilitate the roping of horses, but now it was empty, except for drowsing ponies and one man behind the broad jail bars. That was Hard Winter Johnson, still expiating an offense that had been forgotten by all but himself, and he beckoned to Curly imperiously.

"Say, young man," he called, "I've got something to tell you." And Curly regarded him curiously. Peering out through the unlocked door, he looked more the scarecrow than ever, and his eyes had a wilder gleam.

"All right, uncle," Curly responded, riding over. "What you got on your chest this evening?"

"I seen a track," Johnson confided, with a wink, "right over by that gate, this morning. Remember the time when you showed me a small boot mark, in the horse pen down at Deep Springs? It's the same danged track, or I'm crazy."

"Well, maybe you are crazy," Curly replied. "What the devil are you doing in this old jail? Why don't you walk out and go home?"

"The Crossing ain't home for me no more," Johnson answered evasively. "I'd rather stay here, with nothing to worry about, than go down and face my wife. Everybody here is my friend . . . but she sold me out, Curly. She done opened that safe for Harry."

"Think so?" Curly replied. "Where's that track you were talking about? Come on out." And he threw open the door.

"No. Not me," returned Hard Winter, nodding sagely. "When I seen that little track, I felt safer inside this jail. And the horses have stomped it out, anyway."

"Say, what's biting you?" Curly demanded, stepping down from his horse. "Do you think Tuffy Malone is around here?"

"I seen his track," Hard Winter repeated resolutely. "Say, Curly . . . lend me a gun."

"Done loaned one, already," Curly said, and laughed. "And what for would Tuffy kill you?"

"Didn't you hear him threaten me?" cried the old man fiercely. "Over yonder when I took away his herd? And don't you ever forget . . . Mike Broiles is in these hills. Ain't they both made their threats against my life?"

"I reckon so," Curly admitted. "But it's kinda unusual, staking a prisoner in jail to a gun."

"You gimme one," Hard Winter wheedled, "and I'll keep watch tonight. And if I see one of them rascals tiptoeing around inside, I'll pot him and save you the trouble."

"You get one," Curly said. "And say, keep an eye on Paint, will you? That's what's bringing Tuffy back."

"No, it ain't," denied Hard Winter. "He's out for revenge. He and Mike are out to kill their enemies. There's something in the air that I don't like, at all. Something breeding, like bad weather . . . I can feel it in my bones. You sneak me out a gun. Understand?"

"Yes, sir," Curly answered, grinning.

Later he laid the case before Jack Moore.

"Why, Curly," the sheriff remarked, "you must be mistaken. It can't be possible that both Tuffy and Handsome Harry are coming right up to our gates."

"Why not?" Curly demanded. "They haven't left the country . . . that is, as far as we know. And when a man can't be found, he's liable to be anywhere. I believe Tuffy's trying to steal Paint."

"Yes, and you believe Harry's trying to steal Melissa," retorted Moore. "But I'll tell you, right now, I don't believe he's in the country. It isn't reasonable . . . putting his neck into a noose."

"All the same," Curly declared, "I'm going to watch that wagon. And if I ever get Handsome Harry skylined, I'm all set to put his light out. A man like that is dangerous."

"All right," agreed the colonel. "But I'll wager it's Tuffy Malone. Melissa is trying to conceal something."

"Well, I'll wager she isn't," Curly answered hotly. "She told me it was Harry and that's enough, ain't it? I loaned her one of my pistols."

"Seems to me," Moore grumbled, "you're lending guns to everybody. But all right, all right . . . here's the key to the armory. Only . . . warn Henry Johnson to be careful. He's an A-One trailer and never forgets tracks, or I wouldn't pay any attention to him. But if Uncle Henry says that Tuffy Malone has been here, you give him a gun . . . and look out."

"I'm looking," Curly stated. "But what about my horses? Who's going to guard them tonight?"

"Well, I will," offered the sheriff. "That is, within reason. But I'll tell you frankly, Curly, I don't believe a word of this. It isn't as easy as you think. Men that are being hunted for their lives all over the country, with a big reward on their heads, are not going to come back here to steal your horse and your girl, no matter how important they seem."

"Didn't I find Tuffy before," Curly flared back, "not thirty miles from town? Well, gimme a chance, then, and try and help a little. I can't be in two places at once."

"Yes, yes," the colonel assented impatiently. "Here's the key . . . take what guns you want. There isn't a deputy in town, but I'll do the best I can. That's all, Curly . . . I'm busy with these books." He turned back to the bookkeeping that was the *bête noire* of his office and Curly stalked away sulkily.

"Huh," he muttered. "Have to do this myself, I reckon. Crabbed as hell when he's working on them books."

He selected two good pistols, and a belt of cartridges to give Hard Winter, and went on about his duties.

That evening at dusk he slipped down into the creekbed, to lie in ambush for Harry Vail.

It seemed preposterous on the face of it that Handsome Harry, an errant coward, would venture back within reach of their guns. And why should he steal Melissa when Tula had fled with him and was probably still hidden in his camp? Yet Melissa had so informed him and never since he had known her had she lowered herself to lie.

Curly crept down through the willows to the narrow trail that led from Honey's wagons to the creek, and there, against the cutbank, he took up his stand, watching Honey as he paced to and fro. At intervals Curly could see him as he crawled under the wagon to search out the darkness with his night glasses. Jack Moore had planted him purposely at the bend of the long road, where he could sweep the country both ways. But Honey was getting old and what he saw did not hold him. He crept into his bed of robes, spread out under the trail wagon, and his campfire died down to coals.

In the shadow of the willows Curly nodded, and dozed again, resting his head on his elbow as he had when a boy, out guarding the horse herd at night. For five minutes, or ten, he would lean on his hand, and then, slipping off, he would come to his senses and gaze at the bee gums and wagons. Sniffing warily, Julius Caesar had padded down the path to cuddle up against him and purr, but the baying of a hound had sent him racing for the wagon and now only the stars seemed to move.

From behind the eastern mountains a quarter moon rose up, and Curly knew it was almost day. But the sounds of the night were silenced except where, down in the willows, old Croppy jumped around in his hobbles. Then from far down the valley the patter of hoofs came up the road, and Curly listened intently. It was a good horse—a rode horse, for he kept to a lope—but down below town he stopped. Then another horse came trotting along up the road—a big horse, pounding hard—and Curly roused up as it stopped. There was some one abroad, some mischief afoot—but this was not Handsome Harry. What deviltry were they up to, these mysterious night riders who had met on the outskirts of town?

For an hour, beneath the willows, Curly watched the white-topped wagons, but no one approached the camp. Then, from far up in town, a dog began yapping. Another joined, and the tumult died away. The silence that comes before the first streak of dawn settled down over the sleeping valley, and Curly trembled inside his coat from the cold. His long watch had been for nothing. Only Harry's braggart words had prompted him to come there, at all. Yet he had promised, and Curly kept his word.

A dim light appeared in the rosy east and the sickle-shaped moon turned pale. Day had come—or was coming, after the false dawn had waxed and waned—and for that night Melissa was safe. Curly glanced at the wagons and turned his face toward town, where the dogs had set up a yell. And then suddenly it came over him—who would be guarding Tige and Paint in case some marauder was abroad? Not Jack Moore, he knew, for he had laughed at Curly's fears. And old Hard Winter would be sleeping like the dead. Curly started up the road on the run.

The dogs that had barked before assailed him furiously as he passed, filling the night with their yapping and clamor. But Curly did not stop until, at the jail-yard gate, he found Paint awaiting his coming. Something had told the Appaloosa that those footfalls were his master's, for he stood there, whickering softly, but when Curly rubbed Paint's nose and started on toward his room, the horse followed after him anxiously.

"What's the matter?" Curly inquired as Paint bunted him with his head. And at the note of alarm in his low, warning snort, Curly stopped and looked around warily. Something was wrong, and Paint was telling him, but the yard was empty of enemies. By the entrance to the corral Tige stood as if staked, the other horses bunched in one corner. But as Curly once more directed his steps toward the door, Paint flew back and snorted violently.

"What's biting you?" Curly demanded impatiently. Then he whipped out a pistol, for he had spied a fresh track in the dust. It was the boot mark of Tuffy Malone, and the toe was turned toward his house.

"Come here," he ordered, dragging Paint into the corral. And by the gate he found Tige with a rope around his neck—a strange rope, deftly looped into a hackamore.

"Aha," breathed Curly. "Trying to steal my horses, eh?" And with nervous haste he tied Paint out of range and crept back to study the footprint. It was Tuffy Malone's, for a certainty, and it led on toward his door. Curly circled around the adobe, his pistol balanced to shoot. Then, standing by the door, he listened intently, but the place was silent as death. He reached out and rattled the knob.

As if touched off by his hand, two guns exploded at once from within the darkened house, and from the cheap, white-pine door two big splinters were flung aside as the assassins' bullets passed through. Then with a curse Curly kicked the door in upon them and shot at the first thing that moved. It was a man with a pistol, but at the blaze of light from his own gun Curly saw a form behind—a huge man, who loomed up mountainously.

Curly ducked, and the flash of a gun almost blinded him. But the bullet sped over his head. He shot back, leaping aside to gain the protection of the wall. A man went plunging past him, shooting wild. Both shot, and with both hands, ducking, dodging and running—but not a bullet found its mark. Curly realized that he was fighting Mike Broiles.

Who else could be the tenant of this huge, sinister bulk, this tub of spiteful venom that even as it fled smashed bullets with both hands all about him? Curly felt his coat sleeve rip, and the wind of a ball that seemed to lift the hair by his ear. But though he went down from the wind of it, he leaped up the next instant, only to be too late. As quick as a scuttling spider, and running as close to the ground, Broiles whipped around the corner of the jail.

From there he could turn and shoot, but Curly dashed after him, then changed his mind and circled to the right. He was peering around the last corner when he heard a gun go off and, almost at his feet, Broiles fell. Curly jumped back and looked around, but the jail yard was empty. Yet somebody else had shot Broiles.

"Who is that?" he challenged nervously, sticking his head around the corner.

"It's me," responded a voice from the interior of the jail. And from the barred door Hard Winter Johnson stepped out. "I got him!" he exulted, giving the body a contemptuous kick. "And I reckon," he added, throwing his gun down beside him, "that Mike Broiles's judgment is satisfied. Who was that you were shooting at, Curly?"

"Don't know," Curly answered, running back toward the house. But down in his heart he knew. Inside the darkened doorway Tuffy Malone lay dead, his teeth bared, his gun out to shoot.

CHAPTER TWENTY-NINE

There was a rush to the jail yard where in less than a minute two outlaws had met their death. Curly Wells stood silently over the body of Tuffy Malone, where he lay grinning vengefully, his pistol thrust out, just as he had fallen in the act of firing. But for Paint and his warning—and the boot print in the dust— Curly would be lying in his place, and Tuffy and big Mike Broiles would be riding off on his mounts.

From his cot in the office Jack Moore came on the run, his bare feet kicking up the dust, but the battle was already ended and Hard Winter Johnson was standing over the body of Broiles.

"I prayed the Lawd," he declaimed, "to judge between us, and He delivered my enemy into my hands. 'Vengeance is mine,' saith the Lawd, 'and I will repay!' He sent Mike Broiles to me, and I killed him."

"You did," the sheriff said. "I thought Curly was shooting. What the devil has happened here, anyway?"

"Here's your gun back," Hard Winter went on, "and I'll never touch another one. But the Lawd judged between us and sent Mike to my door . . . and then you bet I killed him, damned quick."

"Good enough. I'm glad to hear it," the colonel responded heartily, and ran over to where Curly was standing. "What is it?" he demanded. "What's happened?"

"I've killed Tuffy Malone," answered Curly. And he pointed inside the door.

"Well, Curly, my boy," began the sheriff after a silence, "you have certainly made good your brag. But how did you get him? Tell me."

"He came to *my* door," Curly replied soberly. "Only I didn't say any prayers, like old Hard Winter. He and Mike slipped in here while I was down watching the wagons and tried to steal my horses. They got a hackamore on Tige but Paint broke loose . . . and then I reckon they heard me running. When I came in the gate, Paint was down there, scared-like. He told me in the horse language that something was up, and then I spotted Tuffy Malone's track. Right then I knew he had come to kill me . . . his tracks led right to my door."

"Yes, yes," the colonel prodded. "Go on."

"Well, nothing much," continued Curly. "That's an old trick, back in Texas . . . laying in wait inside a man's own house. I kicked the door in on 'em and got Tuffy the first shot. But Mike Broiles came out a-shooting, and damned if I could hit him . . . he was coming too close to me. He ran over in front of the jail and Hard Winter nailed him. Don't it make you feel kinda religious?"

"It certainly does," Moore agreed, "and that's good Scripture, too. 'Vengeance is mine,' said the Lord. The way of the transgressor is hard. Leave 'em lay right where they are and let these hard characters look at 'em. It will put the fear of heaven into their hearts."

He turned toward the gate where the saloon bums from across the street were hurrying to witness the scene, and, as one by one they glanced in at Tuffy Malone, they stepped back and slipped away. For the bullet hole in his breast was exactly over his heart, though he held his pistol ready to shoot. He had been killed in a fair fight, and Mike Broiles had been killed with him, yet neither Curly nor Johnson was hurt.

"I just want you to see, boys," the colonel observed to the

crowd, "what comes from all this thieving and murdering. Times have changed in Lincoln County. Be careful who you associate with. Because the clean-up has just begun."

"Yes, and be careful," Curly added, "whose horses you monkey with." And he went over to feed Paint and Tige.

It had all passed so quickly, he hardly realized yet that his two worst enemies were slain. They had gone out like flaring lamps before his shooting, while he had escaped, unscratched. There was a hole in his coat, another part in his curly locks where they bulged out beneath his hat, but the treacherous Mike Broiles and quick-shooting Tuffy had both been shot straight through the heart.

"Curly," the colonel said, beaming and hurrying over to join him, "this has been wonderful . . . miraculous. And something tells me the tide has turned. These outlaws are cowed . . . and there's a lot of reward money to pay you for the chances you took. Outside of the governor's offer and the federal rewards, the cattlemen's associations will pay you handsomely. How'd you like to ride the tide and be sheriff?"

"What, and keep all them books?" Curly demanded incredulously. "Uhn-uh, Mister Sheriff, you've done got yourself elected. Go ahead now, and hold the wild bunch down."

"But think of the prestige it would give you," argued Moore. "I've got my cattle to attend to, and all my other business. And besides, you know what I promised Julia. I haven't had a moment's peace since I accepted the accursed job."

"No, and neither have I," Curly answered. "I could stand a little peace myself. In fact, I was just waiting to shoot it out with Tuffy before I turned in my star."

"But, my Lord, boy," protested the sheriff, "you oughtn't to quit me now. Just when we've got them licked and plumb scared of your shooting. No, no . . . you're just kinda excited."

"No, I'm not," denied Curly. "But I'll give you to understand

I've got a few plans of my own. Melissa and me are liable to go into pardnership . . . and, besides, she won't want me to get killed."

"Well, what of *my* wife?" the colonel demanded wrathfully. "Do you think she wants me to be killed?"

"I reckon not." Curly shrugged. "But that's different. You've done married her and she can't very well quit you. But me, I've got to be good or Melissa won't have me. And besides, I'm a man of peace. Why should I be swelling around as the sheriff of the county for all these danged renegades to take a crack at? Some *hombre* is liable to pot me."

"Yes, yes," the sheriff snapped irascibly. "But, all joking aside, I think it's your duty. And I'll see that you're amply repaid. This is a wonderful country, if we just had law and order . . . the finest cattle country in the world. We've got to drive these rascals out and. . . ."

"Not me," Curly said firmly. "I tell you I've got a girl. And by grab, Jack, I've got to be going down there. Melissa might think I was killed."

"There comes Honey McCoy, right now," Moore observed uneasily as the old man pushed through the gate. "I hope there's nothing wrong."

Curly, as he spied Honey's haggard countenance, started down toward him on the run.

"Where's Melissa?" Honey quavered, staring about through the crowd. "Didn't she come up here? She's gone."

"Where to?" demanded Curly. "Didn't you find any tracks? She hasn't been up here."

"Well, she's gone," Honey repeated helplessly.

Curly ran back for a horse. "Keep this quiet," he whispered to Moore. "She's probably been taken by Handsome Harry." And, leaping up on Paint, he was gone.

Chapter Thirty

As he dropped off of Paint and ran to Honey's wagons, Curly knew at a glance that Melissa was gone. He even knew that Handsome Harry had taken her. For there, deep in the trampled sand, was the imprint of a moccasin—and no Indian would dare steal Melissa. Yet Harry Vail had dared, and his telltale tracks led straight to the edge of the creek.

Its waters were muddy now from the run-off from the peaks, but one footprint showed where he had stepped in. Then the waters had been splashed out again—a struggle had taken place—and in the shallows Curly spied a gun butt. He snatched it up eagerly—it was his own pet six-shooter, given to Melissa instead of a ring.

"Lord," he gasped. "She dropped it . . . they were fighting."

But hunt as he would, he could not find another track to show where they had crossed the creek. First on one side and then on the other, he pushed his way through the willows, searching the mud along the bank for some trace of Harry's moccasins or the imprint of Melissa's bare feet. Harry had waded up the river—or perhaps he had waded down—and now he was carrying her off.

A horseman came galloping up and shouted from the wagons, and Curly ran back to meet Moore.

"No use, Jack!" he called. "He's far away by this time. Covered his tracks by wading in the creek."

"Yes, but which way?" demanded the sheriff. "Can't you find

a track, anywhere? Here's Honey . . . perhaps he knows."

"I don't know nothing," wailed McCoy, "except just what I told you. I never heard a sound . . . but she was gone. I was asleep, under the trail wagon, when that shooting broke loose, and, when I looked into the wagon, she was gone."

"She wasn't gone till daylight . . . I know it," Curly asserted. "I watched that wagon till dawn. Then I heard two fellers riding their horses around below, and the dogs up in town began to bark. I had a hunch right then they were trying to steal my horses. I wish now I'd stayed."

"No, you did right," answered Jack Moore consolingly. "And we'll get her, give us time. But it's necessary, first of all, to know which way they went. Have to search that creek by daylight."

"But I've searched it," Curly insisted. "A hundred yards, both ways, and there isn't a track on the bank. He's outfoxed us, Jack . . . but I know which way he's gone. Upstream. That's where Melissa said he always came from."

"What's this mark?" the colonel inquired, pointing down at a track. "Are any of your buffalo robes gone, Honey?"

"Yes, that light one," Honey answered from the wagon. "Must've used it to muffle her cries."

"That's what he did," Moore agreed, following the drag mark toward the creek. "Poor child, he slipped up and seized her in her sleep. But there's a hereafter coming for Handsome Harry."

"Up the creek, then," Curly said, swinging up on Paint. And side-by-side they went pelting through town. The street was crowded now and in front of the jail-yard gate men looked up astonished as they passed.

Curly had had a hunch and he never drew rein until they came to a certain wide cañon. Melissa had mentioned it—a big, open cañon that headed in the Capitán Mountains. Handsome Harry had commanded her to go to the mouth of it. But she had refused—and he had made good his threat. It had not been mere bravado. He had come as he had promised and snatched her out of her wagon. But if, from his camp, he could see her in this cañon mouth, then from the cañon mouth his camp must be in sight. It was somewhere on the slope of Capitán.

"Let's cut for sign," Curly suggested, splashing across to the other side. "If they're afoot, it hasn't been long. Here's two shod horse tracks, the first rattle out of the box . . . I'll bet you that was Tuffy and Mike Broiles. Here's where they've been hiding, Jack, and they all came down together. There's a moccasin track right here."

He pointed to a slim footprint in the dusty trail, but Jack Moore regarded it dubiously.

"That's Harry," he assented, "coming down. But show me a track going back."

Curly stepped down from his horse and began his search among the boulders that rose up like polished skulls through the sand. They had found the fox's lair, but had Harry come back? Perhaps he had ridden down the valley.

"No," grumbled Curly, "he'd come back and hide. I know the damned whelp and he wouldn't take a chance. He couldn't . . . and carry off Melissa."

He circled back and forth desperately, walking the boulders himself to avoid marring a single track, and then from down the stream Jack Moore whistled and beckoned and Curly came on the run.

"Look at that," gloated the colonel, holding up a strip of buffalo skin. "They stopped here to cut up her robe and make moccasins to protect her feet."

"Nope, he's wrapping up their feet to kill the trail," Curly contended. "They're not far ahead of us, Jack."

"Up this cañon, for a certainty," agreed the sheriff. "Shall we ride for it, or follow the trail?"

"Let's ride," Curly said, vaulting up on his horse.

While Moore loped ahead with his eye out for tracks, Curly searched the wooded slopes on both sides.

It was by far the biggest cañon leading up into the Capitáns, but the bottom had been gutted out by cloudbursts and storms until only polished boulders remained—boulders and sand and bits of soil, made damp by the seeping stream.

At a crossing Moore reined in to point. In the shade of a bare rock a sopping footprint had been stamped, the marks of the buffalo wool showing plain.

"We're close, Curly," he said. "That track isn't dry yet."

"Half an hour, maybe," Curly ventured, and spurred on.

To his excited imagination there appeared a picture of Melissa, trudging wearily up the cañon, and Handsome Harry close behind. Harry had covered his tracks well; he would no longer fear pursuit. The hillside on both sides was densely covered with scrub oaks, where at the first sound of hoof beats he could hide. Yet to hesitate was to lose even the chance of coming up on him, and they hammered recklessly on. Then suddenly before them the narrow cañon opened out and three forks led up to the heights.

Here at last were pines and aspens, and fir trees on the peaks. Every hillside was evenly wooded, with open spaces between the trees. Where was Handsome Harry's hidden camp? They reined in on the rocky flat and looked out over the country in silence, each seeking some winding trail, some distant, moving form, to guide them on their last desperate dash. For Harry Vail had taken a step that would bring swift retribution, and from his camp he would flee fast and far. There was no mercy for him now, once the men who followed after him got the woman stealer within range of their guns.

But though they had gained on him from the start, in spite of his Indian tricks, the trail had now ended in a jumbled boulder patch from which three great cañons forked. Using all their trailers' art, they cut back and forth, trying to pick up a single footprint. But the trail had run out and after half an hour of frantic search they stopped and looked each other in the eye.

"It's no use," said Curly, "we'll have to go it blind."

But Jack Moore shook his head. "No, Curly," he answered. "We're in sight of their camp . . . it's up one of these three cañons. Now the Rangers had a sign that was seldom known to fail in looking for a hidden camp. These men have been here some time, and they must have killed a beef. Anyway, they've thrown out some scraps. Now you watch those cañons and you'll probably see a turkey buzzard, circling around."

He stepped down off his horse and fetched out his glasses, and, though every nerve tingled for action, Curly searched the empty sky. There was not a buzzard in sight.

"There's an eagle," Moore announced at last, "flying out of that left-hand cañon. No, there's two of them . . . they've been frightened."

"Well, if we go it blind," responded Curly, "that's the cañon we'll take. What's that, now . . . a hawk or a buzzard?" He snatched away the glasses and scanned the pine-clad ridge, and as he marked down the first bird, another appeared, flopping up from some hidden bait.

"It's a buzzard," he spoke up tensely, "from that same left-hand cañon. There's two of them . . . one rose from the ground."

"Then spot that place," directed the colonel, "and locate it by several landmarks. That's their camp, and they've just got in."

Curly gazed long and intently, noting every point and rock, searching out the lower ground for a trail. Then he closed up the glasses and struck out at a fast trot, while Jack Moore followed, smiling. Not for nothing had he spent four long years in the service, pitting his wits against Indians and whites. His resourcefulness had found a clue.

As they spurred up the cañon, they cut into a well-used trail. It came in from the west, around the shoulder of a hill, and the marks of shod horses were plain. These were the same two horses that Tuffy and Broiles had ridden when they had come out in the lower cañon.

"We've got him," the sheriff exulted, and Curly nodded grimly, craning his neck as he rounded each turn. "There's the camp," he signaled as they topped a side ridge, and jerked his horse back out of sight.

In a small valley, shut in by rimrock, they could see the bare stumps where trees had been cut for a corral. There was a pole shack, set into the hillside, a bucket by the spring, but the camp itself was deserted.

"Maybe he's seen us," Curly whispered, handing back the glasses. "I can't see Melissa, anywhere."

"Probably shut up in the house," answered Jack Moore hoarsely. "Is that a dog, down under that tree?" He snatched at the glasses and rose up, his eyes blazing. "It's a buffalo robe," he said. "Follow me." And he darted off afoot, down the trail.

Curly trampled on his heels, ran around him, and leaped ahead. But at the edge of the low rimrock he stopped. The shack was just below them, not two hundred yards away, and beneath a tree in front of the house, half covered by the buffalo robe, there appeared a head of tangled yellow hair.

"It's Melissa," he hissed, dropping down out of sight. And from the top of the trail they gazed down, fascinated, as her white face came in sight to them. "Let's go get her," Curly whispered, rising up to a crouch, but Jack Moore pulled him down.

"I want Harry," he rasped. "If you show your head, he'll shoot you. Keep down . . . this is only a blind." He whipped out his glasses and searched the hillside, section by section, then turned them back to the house. "She's tied," he said, "and that's a rawhide reata. No chance of working it loose."

Curly reached for the field glasses, and Melissa appeared before him, so close it seemed that almost he could touch her. But an open slope lay between them, and somewhere, skulking Indian fashion, Handsome Harry stood guard with his gun. He had bound her hands behind her and tied her fast to a big pine, but Melissa had kicked away the enveloping buffalo robe and was struggling against her bonds. With bared teeth and straining muscles she put her weight against the rope, regardless of its cruel bite. Every ounce of her strength was exerted, but in vain, and she fell back, panting for breath.

"I can cut that rope," Curly said, suddenly thrusting out his rifle.

But the colonel held him back. "Wait!" he commanded. "Harry's gone, but she expects him back. That's why she's fighting that rope."

"Then flag her," Curly urged. "Let her know that we're up here. My Lord, she's killing herself."

"I'll fix it," Moore promised, and, reaching down into his pocket, he brought out a small, round looking-glass. "We'll flash her," he said. "That's a favorite Indian trick. Then nobody will see us but her."

He glanced up at the sun and caught its light in the mirror. Then, creeping down the trail like a living thing, the messenger of light sought her eyes. Melissa was struggling madly when it played across her face, and was gone. She leaned back, staring, and as the flicker came again she traced it quickly back to its source. Moore held up one hand, beckoning the captive to be quiet, and Curly could see her smile.

"Where is he?" Moore signaled, pointing his finger different ways, and Melissa thrust out her chin.

"He's gone up that mountain," Curly said. "I can see her . . . she's pointing up that trail."

"Good girl," praised the colonel. "She knows what we're up to. Now keep quiet, while I watch that hill." He took back the glasses, and for a long time, silently, he scrutinized the rugged trail. Then he laid them down quietly and pushed out his rifle, like a hunter watching a salt lick for deer.

Handsome Harry was coming down slowly, his rifle in one hand, dragging a reluctant horse behind him, and Moore followed his course through the brush. Sometimes for a moment his trigger finger would tighten, but always some limb was in the way. The trail was steep, and at each cat's step the horse held back, while Harry turned and jerked at it angrily.

Jack Moore waited on him doggedly, ever ready for the shot that would send his soul to hell, until at last Vail stepped into the open. But as Moore's finger pressed the trigger Vail lurched violently downhill and the horse came stumbling after him. There was a whang from the big buffalo gun, and horse and man went down together in a smother of leaves and dust. Then an agonizing scream cut the air like a knife and Curly leaped to his feet.

"*Oooh!* Help!" shrieked Handsome Harry. "He's crushing the life out of me! Drag him off! He fell on me! *Oooh!*"

"I'll go," Curly offered, his voice hushed by the note of anguish, and he darted off along the side of the mountain. But as he turned sidewise between two trees the front of his shirt was ripped away, as if a sharp snag had torn it loose. Then bang! to his ears there came the sound of Vail's rifle, and Curly dropped down, clutching his gun. He had been lured into a trap on his errand of mercy, but as he rose up Jack Moore shot from the trail.

"Look out!" he yelled as Curly came in sight. "I missed him . . . he's heading for the house!"

Curly jumped to the rim, his rifle ready to shoot, but Handsome Harry was gone. With the strange Indian cunning that he showed at every turn, he was making his escape, running low along some ravine that cut down through the rim.

"Oh, help! Help!" screamed a voice. And from her place against the pine Melissa suddenly struggled up, shrieking: "He's coming down that gulch . . . to kill me!" she cried.

Curly saw the rope stretch taut. Then his rifle leaped to his shoulder, he set himself like granite, and at the shot the tough reata parted.

"Run up here!" he shouted, starting down over a steep jump-off. And Melissa fled toward him frantically. But as he bounded out into the open, Curly spied a skulking form, running low to cut her off. It was Vail, his rifle in his hand. Instantly Curly's gun came up and he shot through the brush, three times like three cracks of a whip. For Handsome Harry had seen him and dropped on one knee—with his rifle trained on Melissa.

The third shot found its mark, for Vail dropped his gun and whirled. But as he headed down the cañon Jack Moore's big rifle roared out, and Handsome Harry fell forward, flat on his face.

"I got him!" whooped the colonel, rising up on the rim.

But Curly had seen a movement in the sprawling form—the gleam of a pistol barrel, wavering. "Run!" he yelled, making a dash down the trail. And as Melissa came toiling toward him, her eyes big with fear, he snatched her up like a runaway child. Harry's pistol had begun to bark, there were bullets flying past, but as Curly ran for cover, Moore's big buffalo gun boomed out, and suddenly the valley was still.

"That finished him," he announced from the rimrock above.

Melissa still hugged Curly close.

CHAPTER THIRTY-ONE

With Melissa in his arms Curly crouched behind a boulder, now glancing up at Moore as he came pounding down the trail, now peering down toward Handsome Harry. The latter lay huddled in a heap on the edge of the open, his gun fallen into a pool of blood, but Curly had learned a lesson.

"You look out," he warned as the sheriff dashed past. "He'll strike like a broken-back rattlesnake. Keep down, or he'll plug you, sure."

But Jack Moore pounded on. "I'm betting on my shooting," he answered. And the body did not move. "Dead center!" he called back. "Is Melissa all right? I'm going up to look at that horse!"

"The old man-killer," Curly snorted as he put Melissa down. "He just can't believe he missed. Lemme cut this reata off, Melissa." He whipped out his knife and severed the rawhide bonds, which had cut deeply into the flesh, and Melissa opened her eyes and sighed.

"Where is he?" she demanded. "Is he dead?"

"Good and dead," Curly responded. "Your Uncle Jack finished him. But it looked for a while like he was going to kill all three of us. I never was more surprised in my life."

"Were you scared," she asked, "when you found I was gone? And, oh, Curly dear . . . you aren't hurt, are you? He said . . . he said you were killed."

"When was that?" Curly inquired, sitting down against the

rock and drawing Melissa closer. "They've all taken a shot at me since you saw me last, and Harry sure got my shirt." He indicated the great rent across the slack of his shirt front, and Melissa shuddered fearfully.

"I was asleep," she began as if living over her fright, "when something fell over my face. I was too scared to move, but I knew who it was . . . and when he snatched me out, I grabbed your pistol. But he wrapped me up tight, and, before I could use it, he knocked it out of my hand."

"I found it"—Curly nodded—"right by the creek. And I suppose he threatened to kill you?"

"He said if I uttered a word, he'd kill me like a dog. I can't understand what came over him."

"He was crazy," asserted Curly. "Crazy as hell, and I knew it. Well, we trailed you by that buffalo robe."

"He took it off," she went on, "and made me wade up the creek. And just as we got past town a terrible shooting sprang up. That was when he said you were killed."

"They had it all planned," explained Curly, "to get Jack and me and ride off on Tige and Paint. That way they'd never have been caught. But when it came to the blow-off I killed Tuffy the first shot, and Hard Winter Johnson nailed Broiles. So getting Handsome Harry kind of makes it unanimous. Don't you want a drink of water, or something?"

"No, I don't want anything," she answered, smiling wanly, "but just to sit down behind this rock. I'm so scared, I declare, I can feel my hair on end . . . but I just had to do what he said."

"That's right," Curly agreed. "And you sure did your part well. Your Uncle Jack is awful proud of you. But what did you say when Harry told you I was dead? Did you call him a dad-burned liar?"

"No. I believed it." admitted Melissa. "Because he said they were lying in wait for you. And then . . . oh, Curly, I didn't care what happened. So I just went along, the way he said. He had me put on the buffalo robe the way Indian women do, in case anybody should see us. But when we got to the big canon, my feet were so sore that he stopped to make these moccasins." She thrust out one foot and laughed a quavering laugh, and Curly patted her hand.

"We found the very spot . . . and a piece of the buffalo skin. But I'll bet you he dragged out his tracks."

"Yes, he did," she answered, "with the robe. He'd agreed to meet Tuffy and Mike Broiles there, and, when they didn't come, he got scared. I could see he was excited . . . he was talking to himself. Then he laughed and said, all right, he was glad to get rid of them. There'd be just that much more plunder for him."

Curly nodded. "Go on."

"Well, we came up here as fast as we could. And I'd decided, on the way, that I'd fight him till I died. But he pretended to be so nice . . . until all of a sudden he grabbed my hands and tied me up to that tree. Then he laughed and said all right, to get away if I could. He was going up the mountain to get a horse, and dig up the rest of his money."

"Well, say," Curly stated, rising up, "we'll have to look into this matter. I'll bet you that's the banknotes that he got in Saint Louis, when he sold old Hard Winter's cattle."

"Oh, don't go now," she pleaded, laying hold of his hand. "Can't you see, Curly, dear, that I'm scared?"

"Yes, but you don't need to be," he answered practically, "because Harry and all the rest of them are dead. And besides," he added, "look who's here to protect you." And he led her to the cabin.

"Jack," he called, "did you find any money?"

And from the hillside came the answer exultantly: "A big money belt . . . stuffed full! Right here where I shot his horse. That first bullet broke its neck."

"And did it fall on him?" demanded Curly. "Well, good. I only wish it had killed him. That's the last time I'll ever try to help a danged crook, no matter how bad he's hurt."

"We've got to search that cabin, and get out of here," the colonel sputtered as he came bounding down the trail. "There's more money in this belt than you'll earn in a lifetime, and his confederates may have heard our shots."

"Let's go, then, right now," Curly suggested, "and come back later with a posse. Melissa doesn't like it up here, nohow."

"We'll do it," Moore agreed, throwing the robe over Harry's body and turning back up the trail. "I'm going to return this money to poor old Henry Johnson, so don't say a word about it. It isn't legal, perhaps, but it's justice, anyway. We all know it was stole from him."

"Suits me," Curly said, and put his arm around Melissa. But this time she pushed it away.

"Who'll you ride with?" the colonel inquired as they came to their horses, and Melissa seemed to meditate.

"I'll ride with you, Uncle Jack," she decided at last, "to thank you for coming to save me. And for flashing me with that looking-glass, and everything. I won't be too heavy, will I? And then, when you're tired, I'll ride with Curly a while. That is, if he asks me," she ended.

"Sure, sure," Curly rumbled, swinging up on Paint. "But don't you kiss your Uncle Jack unless you figure on kissing me. Because I helped make this rescue myself."

"I won't kiss anybody," Melissa replied demurely, "until I get home and wash my face. But, oh, Uncle Jack, how ever did you find me? I couldn't believe it was you."

"Well, well, my little girl," the colonel responded modestly, "that's quite a long story to tell. But a man doesn't serve four years in the frontier battalion without learning a few tricks of the trade."

The old terrapin, Curly thought. *He'll never put her down now, until we get plumb back to town. But you wait until I get a chance. She'll know who it was that saved her.*

CHAPTER THIRTY-TWO

There was plenty of work to do when Curly reached town, but before high noon he had invested two month's pay in a wonderful diamond ring. He did not pry into the circumstances that induced its owner to part with it. When love is young, and the loved one is on the wing, it is only right now that counts.

Curly had learned that Honey McCoy was hunting his horses, and that his bee gums were sealed and on the wagons. And though Jack Moore had ordered him to search the cabin for hidden treasure, Curly figured that the cabin could wait. The loot of the Heel Flies would still be there.

Melissa was sitting on the tongue of the trail wagon, glancing negligently up the road while she brushed out her hair and bestowed it in golden ringlets. If her nerves were shaken, it did not keep her from buzzing the song of the worker bee, and when Caesar hopped up and nestled down in her lap, she stooped and kissed him playfully. Then a paint horse flashed down the road, gay with silver and Navajo saddle blankets, and she retired discreetly behind the wagon. But she was out again, smiling, when Curly rode up and stopped short as a bee went humming past.

"What's the matter?" he complained. "What are these bees all buzzing about? Excuse . . . me." And he turned Paint on a dime.

"They won't sting you!" she called as he clattered up the road.

Presently he came back, grinning. "It's just Paint," he explained, looking the bee gums over dubiously. "Wouldn't like him to get stung, of course. If anything like that was to happen, I'd have to visit my girl on foot."

"Oh, they're just mad because Father sealed the hives while some of the workers were out. We're going back to Deep Springs, Curly."

"So I heard, and I'm glad of it," answered Curly. "But hold on, now . . . just let me explain. I mean, after what's happened, I'm glad you're getting away from here. And you won't take the road with you, Melissa. What I mean is . . . I'll be coming down."

"Oh, good." Melissa sighed, smoothing out her new dress and making room for him on the wagon tongue. "Are you going to quit being a deputy?"

"Well . . . maybe," Curly replied importantly. "But just feast your eyes on this." He reached down into his pocket and fetched out the diamond ring, which gleamed like a dewdrop in the sun, and Melissa caught her breath.

"Why, Curly Wells," she said, and burst out laughing. "Well, of all things." And she reached out for it audaciously.

"Uhn-uh," Curly objected, holding it back. "There's a little speechmaking comes first, before the actual presentation takes place. You know, Melissa, when I first saw you, you were only a girl, and I didn't rightly know how to . . . well, to talk to you."

"You refer, I suppose," returned Melissa, "to that time when I called you a horse thief? Well, I take it all back, Curly . . . and that ring is just too beautiful. What was it you wanted to say?"

"Well, I was going to ask you, Melissa . . . when you get moved and everything, and we get through rounding up these Heel Flies. . . ."

"Oh, Curly," objected Melissa, leaning her head against his shoulder, "haven't you had enough of this fighting? You know it's terrible for a woman, if she thinks much of a man, to know that any time he's likely to be killed. I was all a-tremble when I saw that big rent where Handsome Harry shot through your shirt. And, oh, this morning, when I heard all that shooting and he told me that my Curly had been killed. . . ."

"It was pretty tough," Curly admitted huskily. "But we've got 'em all tamed down, now. There'll be nothing but a little work . . . rounding up cow thieves and such. Say, let's try on this ring and see how it fits. By Joe, you've sure got pretty hands."

"No, I don't think I'd better," Melissa said at last. "Although it *is* a beautiful ring. But, Curly, before I take it, you'll have to promise me something. I don't want you to fight any more."

"Sure not," Curly agreed, slipping one brawny arm around her and drawing her very close. "And what do I get, Melissa? You know, when I gave you the pistol. . . ."

"No, but listen," she protested, trying to move his arm away and blushing like a wild peony. "I want you to be serious, Curly. I'd like to take your ring . . . and maybe I'll kiss you, too, only you can't be a deputy any more. Will you promise me . . . cross your heart?"

"You bet," Curly answered promptly. "Now gimme your lily-white hand."

She yielded it reluctantly and he slipped on the diamond ring. But as he stooped down to claim his kiss, there was a clatter up the road and Colonel Jack Moore came galloping.

"Come back here and take charge of this posse!" he yelled to Curly. "I knew I'd find you down here, but that cabin has got to be searched before some renegade slips in and loots it."

"Well, all right," responded Curly, "only. . . ."

"I don't want a promise . . . I want you to come," the sheriff insisted, and Curly glanced at Melissa.

"Might as well humor the old walloper," he grumbled, and ran off to get his horse. "I'll see you down at Deep Springs!" he called back as he rode away.

But Melissa did not seem to hear. Her yellow head was bowed, and on the newly given ring a tear fell.

Chapter Thirty-Three

The rustlers' cabin was duly searched and the body of Handsome Harry was brought back to be buried with the Heel Flies. What they had stolen was very little, compared to the joy of being alive, and three of them had passed out in one day. The three leaders, and the last of all—Tuffy Malone, Mike Broiles, and Handsome Harry—and no one shed a tear. But when the crowd had gone, Tula Johnson appeared from nowhere and cast herself on Harry's grave.

Yet the sun still shone, and under the cottonwoods at Deep Springs there was the hum of nectar-laden bees. Honey McCoy, in his shirt sleeves, moved slowly from stand to stand buzzing soothingly as he lifted the comb, and in the shade of the wagon Julius Caesar rolled and purred, blinking up at the smiling sky. Only Melissa sat idle, her eyes on the purple field, where the alfalfa nodded heavy with bloom. Then with a brooding smile she drew a ring from her bosom and slipped it on her lily-white hand.

There was dust on the Lincoln trail, the flash of a painted flank as Paint came into view, and with eyes that grew bigger and brighter every minute Melissa took the measure of Curly. He was a big man, riding warily, a pistol on each hip, his rifle thrust under his knee—and Melissa put the ring away.

"Well, well," he hailed, riding right past the house, where Jack Moore and Aunt Julia were watching, "if here ain't the queen of the honey bees."

"You look out," Melissa warned, "or the honey bees will sting you."

But Curly only leaped from his horse. "You can't bluff me." He grinned. "I came down to get something that's been coming to me for over a month."

"You mean this, I reckon," she said, fetching out the ring.

Curly stopped dead in his tracks. "No," he protested. "Why, what's the matter, Melissa? You ain't going to give back the ring? You know what you promised me, up at Lincoln."

"Yes," retorted Melissa, "and you know what you promised *me*. But sit down . . . I guess we can be friends."

"Well, I should hope so," Curly stated, reaching down to grab at Caesar who snapped into a war-like pose. "What's come over you, Melissa . . . are you mad?"

"Oh, no." She smiled. "I still like you, Curly. But you promised you'd give up this gunfighting. And then, just when I was all ready to kiss you, you went off with . . . Uncle Jack!"

"Oh, that's all right," said Curly. "You can kiss me now. In fact, that's what I came down for." He reached out a tentative hand, but she slapped it sharply.

"No!" she cried. "You can take your old ring. Because, Curly, you broke your word!"

"What word?" he inquired, making another grab at Caesar, who flew at him tooth and claw. "Say, old Caesar is a fighting cat. He's getting brave again." And he wrestled him till Caesar spit.

"Now you quit that!" she ordered. "I don't want my cat spoiled. You'll just make him brave and thinking he can whip anything, and then another big dog will come and kill him."

"Oh, no," Curly defended.

But she snatched the cat away and met his eyes defiantly. "I told you," she said, "I don't want my cat killed. Poor Caesar." And she stroked his bent paw ruefully.

"Well, all right," Curly said at last. "But where do I come in?"

"You come in," she stated, "just exactly where Caesar does. I don't want you to get killed . . . and you know, Curly dear, what you promised me up under the cottonwoods?"

"Well . . . yes," admitted Curly. "And to tell you the truth, I'm thinking about turning in my star. What's the use of having a girl if some slave driver of a sheriff is going to keep you riding? But you know Jack Moore. When he races back and begins to holler. . . . Come on, Melissa, let's try on the ring." He picked it up from the robe where Melissa had set it, then sighed and glanced down the trail where Jack Moore had suddenly appeared. "Well, put it on, anyhow," he said.

Melissa accepted it, pouting. Then she rose up and stood beside him, her hand through his arm, and let the light shine on her diamond. For Aunt Julia was coming up behind.

"Oh, you darling," Mrs. Moore said, rushing forward to kiss her.

And the sheriff pulled a fatherly smile. "Well, Curly, my boy," he said, "you are certainly to be congratulated. If I'd known, of course, I wouldn't have come out quite so quick, but . . . Curly, I'm going to resign."

"Good." Curly nodded. "Kinda thinking about it, myself. We've got most of the bad ones, anyway. Let some other danged fool have the job."

"As to that"—the sheriff smiled—"I've talked with lots of people, including the Cattlemen's Association of Texas. And they've all agreed that there's only one man that is fitted to fill the position. You won't need to give all your time, so you can put your reward money into a nice little bunch of cows. But the point is, Curly, we all want you for sheriff and the people won't take no for an answer."

"No! Now, Curly," spoke up Melissa, gazing up at him fondly, "you remember what you promised me, under the cottonwoods, up at Lincoln. I don't want you to be sheriff, and get shot by some horse thief. You'll have to excuse him, Uncle Jack."

"Huh? What's this?" the colonel demanded, glancing from one to the other and then at his startled wife.

"I promised her," Curly admitted, "I'd quit being a deputy, never thinking I might be sheriff."

"Well, that can be arranged," observed the sheriff brusquely. "Only I thought," he added, "I gave you some good advice. But never mind . . . I'm waiting for your answer."

"Can't do it," Curly stated as Melissa squeezed his arm. "You know how it is, now, Colonel."

"Well, as to that"—Moore winced—"I guess the laugh is on me. Julia, have you been advising Melissa in this matter, or has she just done it herself?"

"She's been listening," accused Aunt Julia. "I never told her anything. But she . . . she just heard me talking, I guess."

"There's a kind of a coincidence, about that cottonwood tree," observed the colonel. "But, Curly, I'll tell you what I'll do. I can't insist, of course, on your taking my place as sheriff. And perhaps, after all, it would be better to keep my hand on it, in case the rustler element should come back. But my cattle here, Curly, have been going to the devil. How'd you like to take the job as my superintendent and range boss, leaving me free to attend to my office?"

"Now you're talking." Curly grinned. "That's a nice home job. I could stay right here at the ranch."

"Yes, and Melissa could keep me company," Aunt Julia said, beaming.

But Melissa rose up, raging. "No!" she cried, stripping off the diamond ring. "You go ahead and plan my life and never even ask me. I don't want Curly to be a range boss. That's another way of saying he'll be out fighting rustlers while Uncle Jack is up at Lincoln."

"Well, what do you want me to do?" Curly demanded sarcastically. "Stay and ride herd on your honey bees . . . or raise some more alfalfa? That would come in pretty handy . . . for bee feed."

"Oh, yes," she responded, turning to hug him ecstatically. "We could buy this piece of land from Uncle Jack. And you remember, Curly dear, you promised to quit your gunfighting. I just don't want you to get killed."

"Well, anything to accommodate," Curly returned indulgently. "But I'll tell you, Melissa, I'm scared to death of those honey bees. Them and a June bug getting down my neck. . . ."

"Oh, I'll protect you," Melissa promised, laughing. "And all you have to do is stand perfectly still and think nothing but kind, loving thoughts. . . ."

"And make a little noise, like a bee, eh?" Curly grinned. He unfastened his badge and looked the sheriff in the eye as Moore regarded him with withering scorn. "Well, Jack, I'll have to turn in this star. She's going to teach me," he continued, "to make that bee noise, Jack. So you take this and go back to the house."

The colonel looked at him again from beneath his bushy eyebrows, wagging his head like an outraged buffalo. Then with a parting glare, he turned his back on them both, and Melissa giggled wickedly.

"Poor Uncle Jack," she said. "When I mentioned those cottonwood trees."

"Oh, say," spoke up Curly, grabbing her swiftly under his arm, "that reminds me, speaking of cottonwoods. Do you remember what you promised me on that wagon tongue up in Lincoln? Come on, now . . . right in here."

He whisked her into the willows that grew along the stream and Melissa kissed him gravely. Then she kissed him again and put her arms about his neck and held him very, very close.

ABOUT THE AUTHOR

Dane Coolidge was born in Natick, Massachusetts. He moved early to northern California with his family and was graduated from Stanford University in 1898. In his summers he worked as a field collector and in 1896 was employed by the British Museum in this capacity in northern Mexico. Coolidge's background as a naturalist is a trademark in his Western fiction along with his personal familiarity with the vast, isolated regions of the American West and its deserts—especially Death Valley. Coolidge married Mary Roberts, a feminist and a professor of sociology at Mills College, in 1906. In the summers, these two ventured among the Indian nations and together they co-authored non-fiction books about the Navajos and the Seris. *Hidden Water* (1910), Coolidge's first Western novel, marked the beginning of a career that saw many of his novels serialized in magazines prior to book publication. There is an extraordinary breadth in these novels from *Wunpost* (1920) set in Death Valley to *Maverick Makers* (1931), a Texas Rangers story. Many of his novels are concerned with prospecting and mining from *Shadow Mountain* (1920) and *Lost Wagons* (1923) based on actual historical episodes in the mining history of Death Valley to a fictional treatment of Colonel Bill Greene's discovery of the fabulous Capote copper mine in Mexico, a central theme in *Wolf's Candle* (1935) and *Rawhide Johnny* (1936). *The New York Times Book Review* commented on *Hell's Hip Pocket* (1939) that "no other man in the field today writes better Western tales than Dane Coolidge." Coolidge, who died in 1940, wrote with a definite grace and leisurely pace all but lost to the Western story after the Second World War. The attention to the land and accurate detail make a Dane Coolidge Western story rewarding to readers of any generation. His next Five Star Western will be *Tully of the Wicked Y.*